I0561321

Slip or Jump

Dustin Brewer

ALTERNATIVE
BOOK PRESS

Slip or Jump
Alternative Book Press
alternativebookpress.com

2025 Second Paperback Edition
Copyright © 2014 Dustin Brewer
All Rights Reserved
First Published in 2014

Cover illustration by CL Smith

Brewer, Dustin / Slip or Jump / Second Edition
Fiction, General
ISBN: 979-8-9924613-1-2

Printed in the United States of America

To my parents, who patiently endured the wanderings of their eldest.

Preface

I wrote this novel when I was a somewhat lonely undergraduate at a large Midwestern university. I was experiencing many things for the first time, including living away from home in a heavily populated area—'heavily populated,' at least, for a country kid. I wrote mostly in the evenings to process the many new experiences I was having. Some of this writing turned into a novel, which still isn't published. And then more experiences—and the heartbreak and dread and hope that came along with them—led to more processing and writing whenever I got a chance. I can still distinctly remember hurrying to computer labs between classes to weave my latest observations or imaginings into the story that became *Slip or Jump,* which I finished by the beginning of my senior year.

There are some parts of my undergraduate life that I'm at least a little bit embarrassed by, looking back now. For example, pictures clearly show that I didn't take good care of my hair. Memories, though less reliable than pictures, tell me I was slow to understand people, which caused avoidable pain. I was idealistic, and quick to leave situations that didn't live up to my probably-too-high moral standards. I'd like to think that I've improved in these regards, similar to how I've improved as a writer.

It would also be fair to say that I should have spent less time writing in my early twenties and more time having fun. Maybe I should clarify: 'normal undergraduate' fun. To be honest, writing this novel was a lot of fun for me. More importantly, though, writing helped me to make sense of many things that otherwise might have been too much to handle. Some of the sentences in this novel I would never write today, and I'll let you guess which those are. However, there are also truths that I could clearly see when I was an undergraduate that I have to squint to make out now. But they're still there, at least so far as I'm concerned, and I'm glad to be reminded of them.

I hope you feel similarly—about some of the truths you saw, that is—when you reflect upon your youth, be it now or sometime in the future. I think we all have a sort of naïve wisdom in the beginning of our life that is often eroded away with time. I'd like to think that *Slip or Jump* will remind you to appreciate your wisdom, and maybe even regain some of it.

—Dustin Brewer, 2.22.25

Chapter 1

"Well, all I know is that I'm here."

"No, you aren't. You live in a dream world. And haven't been *here* in a long time."

The sea gently sighed. And a human being who knew that he didn't know exactly where 'here' was tried to explain why.

"Listen—this world is made for dreaming. To you, we could be on a pleasant, sentimentally soaked beach. Full of lousy grains of sand. Nothing more. And to me we could be on a tiny fraction of some grain of sand nestled in the most beautiful of beaches. Nothing less. It could be said that we are both dreamers, I think."

"It could also be said that you are insane, I think."

There were a few moments of deep, silent thought.

"I know."

They stared at each other. The eyes of the accuser were a mixture of anger and frustrated confusion. The eyes of the accused showed nothing. There was a brief gust of wind which mixed the sand on the beach. And a couple of shooting stars streaked across the night sky.

"You aren't really going to do it, are you—become a master's degree bum?"

Accused spoke. "I'm going to leave while I am still able—am in the business of seeing as much as I can. If you cannot understand why, so be it. Call me what you want, stay on your beach. I'm going to let the wind take me."

For a moment the wind stopped entirely. And the waves, lightly lapping against stone, sounded like someone choking.

"Do you have a place in mind, at least?"

"Mexico, Idaho, San Francisco, Morocco—I just don't know."

The slightly taller, skinnier young man smiled faintly and shook his head, repeating the truth.

"I just don't know."

Some of his thick, dark hair fell over his eyes, the remainder resting on his shirtless shoulders. He was unconventionally handsome. His narrow, clean-shaven face seemed to shine due to the light from the moon that reflected off of the smooth water. There was an entire ocean in his eyes. He kicked a little, dark stone off of the bigger rock from which he and his brother stood, on the wall of boulders jutting into the sea. The moon's light caught the wake that splashed, and there was a flash of white in the dark. It was easy to breathe and be in the cool night, unlike the day. And when he spoke his voice was calm and sure, like the smoothest, softest strum of a guitar.

"How do you do it? I mean, how can you stand all of this?"

He gestured towards the gentle glow of the city, which sprawled from where they stood for miles southward. The beach was silent. And there was no answer to his question.

"Well, I guess that you have her."

The slightly shorter, sturdier man barely nodded his head. He was conventionally handsome, with hair that was cut short, and a face that was covered by a short, healthy-looking beard. He had white streaks on his temples from the sunglasses that he wore at work. He took off his suit jacket, sat down on the rock, and looked at his golden ring—the first that he had ever worn. From the ring, he gazed at the illuminated, tallest tower in the dark city and thought of his new wife. They hadn't even had their 24-hour anniversary yet. She was sleeping in one of the dark rooms. People were just beginning to get up for the day. Every few minutes another room lit up in the dark building. The flight south would be leaving soon. He would be waking her up sooner. A warm feeling came to him, as he thought of Erica, until he looked at his gaunt brother, which twisted the pleasant feeling into a guilty one. And when he spoke his voice was rigid, as if he was fighting with every word that he said.

"Sam, listen. It isn't so bad."

"Nothing is real. Robbie, you must be brave—or something."

The one young man, exasperated, stared at the other slightly less young man, who stared out into the sea.

"You are as hollow as you look, aren't you?" Rob said.

Sam hoped not. The mirror had become uncanny. He alone knew how very *not* hollow he was, though. And that substance was what made everything so hard. Rather than saying this, though, he decided not to answer the question of the guy who never answered his questions.

"Really, isn't it amazing how much more real everything used to seem, how much more frightening, meaningful…or is it just me?"

"We worry about you, Sam."

"Hey, I shaved didn't I?" he said, shaking some of the pillow-sand from his hair.

Sam took off his belt, and the black slacks that he wore began to fall down his waist. He pushed them down to his ankles, took his shoes off, and walked out of them.

"Rob, you and Erica looked beautiful and, um…something not so beautiful at the same exact moment yesterday. I'm very happy for you, really I am. That feeling you two have is one of the best there is. But a part of me feels a little sad too. So I'm going to take a break from it all. I know that you have a lot of Mom in you but try not to worry. You are taking a break too, right?"

"Yeah, but I *plan* on coming back to the States in less than a week. Why are you doing this now, of all times?"

"I don't know. It just seemed right. Sound like a familiar answer? You knew that I was not going to wait any longer than this day. I told you that when I graduated, when you proposed. I hope that you two enjoy Brazil. And, *please*, try to get away from the resort, see the forest. Should be beautiful, I mean really, enjoy it before they cut everything down and turn it into a place like this."

Rob rubbed his beard, which made a scratchy noise that he liked.

"I'm sure that we will."

"Maybe I'll see you when you get back at some point. I hope so. Do you want this belt? It's expensive."

"No."

The belt slithered through the air, and down into the ocean. And then the slacks were kicked in as well, followed by his splashing shoes and silent socks. He stood there, glaringly white in yellow boxers on which had bluebirds flying in every direction. They were his all-time favorite pair. None of the birds which had the ability to peck were pecking, which was an appropriate juxtaposition because his 'pecker,' for mainly philosophical reasons, had taken a considerable break from what it was mainly there to do. .

"If people back home ask, you can say that I drowned. That way if I come back I'll get to know how a ghost feels when looked at. Don't think many people see right through me as it is. Or you can tell them the truth—whatever it is to you."

"Why aren't you wearing clothes?"

"Always been a sucker for symbolism."

"You are too smart for this."

Sam treaded carefully across the sharp rock, and placed a hand on his brother's muscled shoulder, ready to say what he had wanted to—though had not been able to because it was too noisy, just not right—at the reception.

"I love you Rob."

Rob looked off towards the dark ocean. After waiting a few moments for any sort of reply to what he had said, Sam laughed silently to himself, and carefully walked back across the wall of cool rocks and onto the cool beach that looked blue.

Maybe it was true that for every action there is an equal and opposite reaction. The love thrown towards someone must be returned back as hate. Sam hoped that there were exceptions to the rule—but for the most part it seemed to hold true.

He picked up the plastic bag which contained a pair of jeans, a shirt, and a few other things he had brought from his hotel room to the wedding ceremony.

There always had to be a last look, so Sam looked back at his brother who was watching the water, about to start a new life. Sam realized at that moment that he was very proud of a person who seemed to hate him. The guy was, at least ostensibly, strong in this world that saps everyone of life.

With a big toe in the coarse, wet sand, he wrote the first word that came to his mind in large, clumsy letters: 'brothers.' He hoped that the high tide, which was inching in, did not wash it away before it was seen. From the message, he looked up at his brother like he did at soldiers— hoping that Rob realized what it was that he was giving up, risking, and subscribing to. He was still so young. There was nothing sadder than the one who gives away what they have yet to understand or know.

Sam had to look away. The sky had long been a salve for pain which his eyes brought. The morning light was just beginning to arrive, and the stars were faint, but there. It was nice to know that they always were. From his salve, he was soon gazing at the lights of the city, which he couldn't bear looking at for long.

He picked up his bag and walked away from them.

*

Sam slowly turned his head, past his displaying thumb, and watched a BMW on the Florida highway speed by. The driver pretended that he did not notice the hitchhiker—just the same as most other people. Sam estimated that he had walked five miles on the highway while trying to hitch a ride north, looking back with a blank, but hopeful face at every car that passed. It was hot, even though the sun had not yet made it more than half-way over the eastern horizon. And he had already sweated through the white T-shirt that he had chosen to take from his suitcase of abandoned possessions. He had also taken his favorite, broken-in pair of jeans and his hiking shoes. With the exception of his phone, iPod, headphones, and wallet, everything else that he had brought south for the wedding was still in the hotel room. Some cleaning lady was sure to be happy.

He was beginning to wonder if his parents, who would be driving through soon with their rented car en route to the airport, would be the ones to ultimately pick him up. It would be extremely awkward if that happened. He had assumed that he would be picked up by some friendly person within ten minutes of trying to be picked up. It was becoming very obvious how wrong he had been in so thinking.

The night before, at the wedding reception, he'd been sure to hug both his mother and father even though both were extremely mad at him because of a job offer that he had declined. He had an unrelenting feeling that he might never see them again. It is strange to hug a person who does not know what you do, especially when what you know feels so very heavy.

He'd explained that he'd be leaving very early in the morning in order to catch a bus, on a trip 'out west' as a graduation gift to himself. But he had absolutely no idea where he was headed, did not know if a bus would be involved. Indeed, he could end up 'out west,' somewhere, possibly after some time on the Greyhound. There was just no telling. He had said nothing to his parents of hitchhiking, nor of his plan to travel extremely light, nor of his lack of plan for anything else.

So, it was getting a bit nerve-wracking, as the next car speeding north could be the neon green Porsche that his dad had insisted on paying extra for. The guy had a thing for flashy cars.

But Sam somehow knew that the Station Wagon would pick him up as soon as he heard it gasping in the distance. He calmly turned and raised his hand, gazing at the windshield—until he could make out the driver— then gazed at her. The car puttered past, as the driver craned her neck to look, and stopped thirty yards past him. He felt extremely relieved, and tried to think of something to say that would calm the girl as he crunched the gravel, jogging with excitement.

He opened the passenger door, after waiting for her reassuring nod, and it screeched terribly. The air conditioner in the car worked, and cool air permeated onto his face.

"Hey stranger, you're not going to kill me, are you?"

He had thought that his innocent-sounding question would make her feel safe—then thought that he probably should not have put the word 'kill' in her head. But it all worked out just fine.

"That's exactly what I'm thinking. You see, I'm just so very reckless this morning."

She smiled, tilting her head which caused her reddish-brown hair to fall over her eyes. Her teeth were very straight, and very white, face nicely narrow. She was young, a little plump, wearing a white camisole, green sunglasses, and yoga pants—just like the girls at college. He hoped that she was not like the majority of them.

He looked at her and smiled back warmly.

"Reckless…hmm…I've reckoned too much and not enough. Not sure where I'm currently at. Well, sir, I'm sure that you and I will make an exciting pair. Get in, before all of the warm air does."

He screeched the door shut and leaned back on the carnage of strange entrails—foam—and the skin of ripped fabric. It was as if a dog, or another creature, had determinedly ripped into the passenger seat. But that was O.K.

"I was beginning to think that I'd let my hair grow too long and gotten too old for anyone to be willing to pick me up."

"Oh, you just look interesting—which is actually *why* I picked you up. And too old? How old are you, twenty?"

Her half-squeaky voice created an interesting combination with the engine that fought loudly as it accelerated.

"Well, thank you. I try to be interesting. I got my life sentence over twenty-four years ago, by now."

She looked at him strangely, thinking about prison bars—no doubt. Sam felt a need to clarify—imagining how awful it would be to think solely in literal, one-dimensional ways. Thinking that way would be a lot easier, though.

"I'm twenty-four, and without *amor*. If life is not a sentence, then I do not know what is. It is one that you can come to love, though."

They threw pleasantries back and forth for several minutes until silence settled. Her name was Suzy, headed to Tallahassee to commence summer classes at a community college. They sailed across the burning asphalt, well above the speed limit, through the smooth, green, watery Everglades. It was strange for him to think that he could feel so good, so close to feeling so bad.

He watched the dashed yellow lines flying by and couldn't help but let loose a self-pacifying thought to break the silence.

"You know, I've been thinking about bi-polar disease, depression, all that. Everybody feels low. I think that these feelings tell you that a change is needed, that there's a better cure than a pill. Which is kind of why I'm here, I guess. I don't know how I feel about diagnosis, specifically medication, —if it's a good or bad thing. What do you think?"

She looked at him oddly.

"My boyfriend is clinically bi-polar. That boy will be smiling one moment and hit you in the face the next."

She bit her lip, which exposed a cracked incisor, as she thought about her situation. She answered his question.

"I hope you don't mind a little smoke."

She reached her slightly tremulous hand into the glove box, retrieved a lighter and a joint, and began sucking on the latter after lighting it expertly. She held it out to him—assuming, like seemingly everyone did, that he would want a hit.

"No thanks. I've had that out of my system—literally and figuratively—for quite a while now.

She shrugged and continued smoking.

It appeared that the girl truly was reckless, and 'self-medicating.' The bluish smoke gradually filled the car. He tried to roll down the window, but it did not work. There was no escaping.

Sam thought of the second time that he had almost died, which he knew of.

The yellow stripes continued to speed by a bit too slowly. And despite the fact that they were travelling at least ten miles per hour above the speed limit, Sam noticed a neon green blur speed past from the south, and then out of sight. His dad had always been a lead-foot.

For a few more miles, they drove in silence. Sam tried to breathe as little as possible and decided that it was about time to have her let him out. He was overcome by the nostalgic situations that he often found himself in and was eventually able to utter a remonstrance.

"Blatant speeding coupled with an illicit substance, *not* the best combin…"

His eyes stopped his lips, as he saw it before she did. Everything happened as fast as three thoughts. *Puma*. The sleek, small brown cat crouched at the edge of the highway, frightened and about to move either to safety or to danger. The way it moved was beautiful. *No, no.* Sam kept himself from closing his eyes and holding his breath. The graceful creature, as if it were stalking prey, leapt directly in front of the car. *Shit.*

There was a heavy thud when the body hit.

"Shit!" she said.

The cat had veered away from the car at the last second, though it was still squarely hit in the shoulder and flung into the opposite lane where it lay twisted. Only its tail seemed to have full life left in it. The body slightly writhed. The rushes from whence it had emerged gently blew in the wind.

Suzy pulled over to the side of the highway, shaking visibly. The front left side of the car was dented in to the point that it rubbed against the rubber, which was quite loud. Sam opened the passenger door, and with the smoke exited. She did too.

Sam ran his fingers through his hair, getting it out of his eyes, as he thought about what to do. Before he could convince himself otherwise, he found himself walking towards the panther. Darker spots were vaguely perceptible on the tan hide. She was young, and looked up at him with wild, tired eyes. Her tongue was out, and her sides expanded and contracted rapidly. A disc-sized, red spot was on her shoulder where the skin had been rubbed off by the asphalt. There was a foot-long track of blood leading to where she lay. He knelt beside the poor creature in the middle of the road, and after a moment's hesitation gently began stroking the shivering fur.

"You know," he said to Suzy, "we just hit one of the most endangered animals in the United States."

She did not look compassionate, standing beside her 'Protect the Panther' license plate.

"Yeah, it's tragic. The thing is going to bite you. I don't even have insurance, and the car reeks of smoke. Get in. We're leaving, *now*."

"I'm not. Can't leave her like this."

"It will die soon enough. Just leave it."

"You are an awful person."

A car was approaching fast. Sam put up his hand, hoping that the car would slow down. The image of a panther's trembling legs being snapped by tires flashed in his mind. There was no time for further thinking. He gently picked up the kitten. Her body was very warm, shaking, and did not weigh more than fifteen pounds. With the cat in his arms, he moved quickly towards the side of the road opposite of Suzy. The cat's head limply fell as far as her neck would allow. The car sped by within three feet of Sam without moving over at all, and the driver viciously honked his horn as the tires went over the blood on the pavement. Sam placed her gently in the grass, not even mad about the driver's idiocy. He was only thinking about the poor cat.

Suzy was already smoking again, trying to escape from the problem in front of her which needed to be fixed. He walked back across the pavement.

"Can I use your phone before you leave?"

*

The kitten lay shivering in the grass and seemed to be going in and out of shock. Its eyes were glazing, little claws contracting. Sam hoped sincerely that the officer from Miami would arrive soon. The dispatcher had vaguely said that it 'may take a while.'

He smelled the smoke on his shirt which made the memory of death stronger, a memory that he could not shake. Everything that he had known, after that night, had become either less real or more important.

*

Walking back to his motel room at the edge of a little, desert town, he had known that something was wrong—not what he had expected.

"This stuff is strong."

The people with him laughed, which spiraled into the night. Their laughter seemed evil.

His heart beat faster and faster in proportion with single and disconnected images replacing the smooth flow common to vision. He lost awareness, walked fifty yards before being 'awaken' by the 'See ya' later man,' of one of the guys who were a part of the road trip as they walked to their rooms.

Something's not right.

His heart seemed to be doing over two hundred resonating beats per minute. As much panic as is possible for a human being to encounter was experienced, and it seemed as if he had finally been hooked, a whole life simply leading to that instant, and a whole life over with.

People want to kill their time until it's almost dead. Then everything changes.

And to Sam, the last grains in his hourglass were about to fall through to the bottom. But some strike of lightning had turned those grains into a glass mirror. His last moments, he had to watch.

Through this endless canyon of mirrors, he walked towards his room and everything gradually slowed to nothingness, became infinitely distant once his hand reached the shiny knob. From the closed door he stared across the yellow-lighted parking lot towards the neon sign of the bar where some of his friends were still at. From the sign, he looked at his blinking hands and then slowly collapsed, mind circling and certain that it was all over. Unconsciousness. Death accepted. The end.

But it was not over. The awakening was sudden, and the amount of time that was lost was unknown, though could not have been long. The red boards of the deck were in front of his face. He looked at them as the distant sounding beats of his heart went from sounding dampened to crystal clear—like a motor that was slow to restart. Memory of what had led to where he was came back. He stood, shaking. To be found like that by a concerned neighbor would have been to lose everything, he knew. There'd be an attempt at an explanation, confessions, hospital, and shame… pending survival. He entered the motel room to take a shower.

Once beneath the silvery beads, the heartbeats began exploding again, and the image of a dead college student found in the shower by friends filled his mind.

This is how it happens.

He dressed and made it to his bed, dripping wet, muttering words of explanation to his half-drunk friend, Brad, who was on the couch with a girl who he'd met at the bar.

"I'm just so tired."

It was 9:30 P.M. when he fell onto his bed, when the next wave hit.

And everything shattered—like pieces of glass which his time had become, in a weightless container that was reflective on all sides, with prismatic light being shined in. All of the pieces of his life, forgotten thoughts, memories, sensations, childhood dialogue, floated around in a phantasmagoria consisting of all those colors which human eyes can see. He could put none of the pieces together. They even went into the future, somehow, and became tormented atoms rejoining the Earth from which they had originated. Then he was at his own funeral, and felt like sobbing even though he did not know who he was. He felt awful, knowing that he would be missed, though had no idea who would miss him.

Hell, he had seemingly found.

*

Sam took off his shirt. The little creature's breaths were closer together, more shallow, and its eyes were shuttering. He put the shirt over the lolling head, though knew that nothing could truly calm or help the dying. The morning was getting hotter, and for one living being the world's greatest mystery was being solved. To die…

*

In and out of consciousness he had gone at least five times, forgetting and remembering each time who he was. The dreams were tedious, forced committals of actions that the instant before made were foreseen. There were no surprises. Voices said that he was dead. An endless cycle of both ecstasy and horror he was led on, with a message being chanted in his mind by an admonishing, pulling voice which was further revealed after each seemingly eternal cycle of randomness as it turned closer and closer to completion.

From each lapse he would awake, and gradually realize who he was and what he had done. The patterns on a towel were an endless staircase. When he was able to understand what the towel was, it was possible to read the time on his watch. Only three reality minutes had gone by during the dream eternity. He remembered where he was and what he had done, relieved to still have a link with reality, and then closed his eyes again—acquiescing to the dream-world. In and out he went.

The line between the continuing dream and reality were further blurred each time that he awoke until finally the internal message was complete and said that in order to end the tedium he needed to get off of his bed, sprint into the desert night, and leap off of the cliff which was a hundred yards behind the motel. The voices said to do so. And the message seemed divine, a way for him to finally win the game, to be free and fly away—*to go home*. All of the world's senselessness was senseless no more. It all had meaning, had been leading to this one moment of ultimate freedom, flight.

He could almost feel the cool night, and the bright moon, see the silhouettes of the cacti. He was completely convinced, and could not wait to awake. It would be a race to complete the task before the next eternal cycle came. It would be a leap of faith.

*

The little cat's eyelids shuttered. Its eyes were starting to look glossy, and the twitching of the body was becoming less intense. He looked at the wet, muddy prints that were on the highway, at the blood, and then at the motionless paws with mostly dried mud on them. The end looked to be near. It was to the point that Sam, at least, just wanted it to finally be over. There was no hope.

*

When he awoke, he excitedly got off of the bed and nearly ran to the door. Brad was now lying on top of the drunken girl on the couch, and neither paid any attention to Sam while they giggled. He opened the door and entered the cool night, extremely excited. The dream could resume at any moment, so he had to hurry. Remarkably he made it away from the building and across the hard, desiccated ground without stepping on any cacti or snakes. A few more steps and there he was approaching the edge of the cliff. He breathed in the cool, dark-purple air. He was ready and stepped towards the edge.

Clods of dirt and stone clattered to the bottom. It had to be a two-hundred-foot drop—at least. He felt incredible, the thought of the fall was exhilarating, even relieving. It was almost over, just a step away, *supposed* to occur.

But a strange thing happened. With a bright flash, and a sudden, involuntarily deep breath, reality returned—almost providentially. Like the snap of fingers. He felt a light breeze on his face which was wet from perspiration. And there upon the edge he found himself standing, mostly awake, looking down into the deep darkness, just barely able to make out a sheening creek at the bottom of the valley. Rock continued to clatter down the near vertical wall, hit a ledge, and kept falling. He saw the faint splashes, though it wasn't until the sound made its way up to him that he realized where he was and how he had got there.

Fuck. He took a step back and understood how close he had taken himself to death. Suddenly, he became very dizzy. The stars seemed to spin. He turned and walked back towards the motel urgently, trying to put space between him and the abyss, still able to hear the splashes and rattling of rocks falling, for far too long.

This time he did step on a cactus. The pain was terrible but good and shot through his body. Everything became clear again, and what was narrowly avoided became exponentially more terrifying. He walked quickly back to his room, ignoring the sounds that his friend and the girl made, and collapsed on his bed—where he didn't sleep at all the whole night.

Life was maintained and would somehow have to continue.

*

Sam wondered what exactly the little cat was experiencing as it laid there, cars rushing by, sunlight beating down, a faint giant hovering over, casting a shadow. It was surely strange and unexplainable, and different for everything that lived. But it probably wasn't *that* different. It must not matter, he thought, how close one actually is to death. To merely believe that you are dying probably produces the exact same thoughts, mutations of the mind, which occur when truly dying. And dying in either way will always result in a drastic change, for better or for worse—especially for those who live.

He didn't even notice the police car approach until it was within ten feet.

The crunching of gravel beneath the black and white car's wheels broke Sam's intent gaze from the kitten. The engine hissed for several seconds after being turned off. Then, a tall, burly officer in his ranger hat professionally exited the car and walked over to the unquestionably dying, and the somewhere in between living and dying.

"Morning," he said, with an all too familiar and suspicious scowl.

Sam echoed the word.

It did not seem as if the officer had the nose of a bloodhound, which was a relief. He had not been in the smoke for very long.

The officer looked emotionlessly to Sam, and then down at the cat as he placed a hand on his belt of leathery pelvic accessories—which made an important sounding noise as he leaned down and made a wincing face.

"Sir, you may want to look away."

Sam did not.

The pistol shot was startling, and though the kitten stopped shivering instantly, Sam suddenly began to. The officer unceremoniously grabbed the scruff of the corpse's neck and flung the body into the car's trunk, without any hesitation whatsoever, and then turned to Sam.

"They'll take blood samples and perform tests. You know, the Florida Panther is one of the most endangered animals in the nation."

Sam nodded, unable to say anything.

"It's the worst part of the job—putting down suffering animals."

Sam was quiet, staring at the lifeless body. Lifelessness was always near. Eventually he delivered the police officer from the uncomfortable feeling which the silence brought.

"I'm sure that they would appreciate you putting a stop to their suffering. Even if they did by some apparent miracle eventually recover, they could never be the same."

Chapter 2

"First, there's complete acceptance of what's been presented, easy fulfillment and joy. Like a child has. Then you begin to wonder about it all but are still mostly happy. After that, quiet desperation gradually sets in, and you imagine what *could* be. It's tortuous. And if you stay at this point, you usually become a cynic and/or a depressed individual."

Sam looked through the window of the train, which was just reaching top speed.

"But you shouldn't stay there. Awful place to stall. The next stage involves probing for freedom and tremors of hope. There's a timid re-invention of self. Then it happens one day: all-out rebellion, freedom from internal chains, and a feeling unlike any before."

He nodded his head, pleased with his assessment.

"Those are almost surely the steps that he took."

The boy, who Sam could already tell was intelligent after only brief discourse, was quiet. He didn't try hard to amuse and seemed sincerely thoughtful. He had taken the only vacant seat available when he boarded the train, which was a window seat beside Sam—who did not know the kid's name because he had forgotten to listen after he had asked. It was a very bad habit. But the kid had listened when he said his, so Sam felt guilty whenever he was addressed by name.

"Wow, Sam. Seems like you know what you are talking about."

"Maybe a little. You know, they say that that photograph is the most famous in the world."

"Really," the boy said skeptically, "I hope that you realize that you can't always believe what's been said."

"Oh, I realize."

"What do you think it is about the photograph that makes *them* say that this is the most famous photo of all?"

Sam smiled at how much like a professor he felt, like those mostly men who mostly annoyed him, but a few of whom he really admired. He had known some cool ones, and sometimes imagined that he would be one too someday, so answered imagining that he was one. It was nice to have a student again.

"It all has to do with two things: what the man stands for, which may have nothing to do with what he actually was, and where the majority of people are at. To me, it seems like most people will stall in the second stage, if they ever are daring enough to leave the first, and merely admire the rebels from a safe distance. They will do nothing when their idols are burned at the stake. They will do nothing to save themselves, either. But he was not like them, which must be why the idea of him is revered. People marvel at what they are not."

The train rattled violently as it went over tracks that were equivalent to the final stage of consciousness but was soon gliding over wrought steel that completely accepted its sentence like the first stage.

"Man, that's so lucid. You must be a reader too."

The pale kid with reddish hair that was shaved closely to his head looked at the upside-down face, from his perspective, of Che Guevara on his chest.

He laughed scratchily. And Sam actually appreciated the compliment very much. Most of the reviews that he had gotten from his students had been merely comedic commentary in regard to a sex-scandal which he was involved in—and not much about his actual teaching abilities. All of the other comments were positive, though, just like this kid's was. Maybe he *could* be a professor someday, he thought.

The kid continued.

"I thought that he just looked cool, you know. So intense. Never even *knew* to think about his path."

"Ironically, Guevara was seriously anti-capitalism. The capitalists got him in the end by putting his face on that shirt and selling it."

"Huh. Capital. Speaking of it, I made seventy bucks today. Ten hours of work." The kid spoke with a proud voice. "Could've made over a hundred, but it's not worth it to me. Too many hours. How much is a day worth to you?"

"Well, to me a day is priceless," Sam said. "You never know if you are going to have another one."

"Nice. That's true, man. Very true. Working all of those hours really does suck out the life. All of that energy for someone else. Guess I'd better pull a Che and rebel while I still can. Maybe I'll burn the shirt for him—when I'm ready to enter the last stage."

Sam nodded, and looked through the window as pine trees flew by. After a few moments of silence he heard a determined-sounding female voice speak from behind.

"You are wrong. The last stage is acceptance, *not* rebellion."

He turned in his seat beside the young man, who also turned, with the intention of seeing if the eavesdropper looked as he imagined her. She did. A middle-aged woman in a flowery dress with her hair in a tight bun looked at him, leaning slightly forward in her seat. She seemed to want an argument.

"You know," Sam said, "you may be right."

He would not satisfy the woman with an argument, and at the moment he didn't feel that he could stand one. Orienting himself back to the forward position, away from the disappointed woman, he looked at the kid who arched his eyebrows as if to say, 'what in the hell was that?' Sam winked, and placed his earphones on his head, which ached. Talking was done, he made clear. He leaned back in the seat and chose an upbeat song, lightly musing in the groves set by the music which was accompanied by the words: 'Well I *am* the ancient warrior man, and I hail from the ancient warrior clan…'

The warrior's flag is the flower which precedes his fruit—Thoreau.
So many fucking quotes in my head.

He was glad that he had them there, though. They came in handy from time to time. And anyway, if the quotes were somewhere else, like in his stomach, he often found himself thinking, he would probably have cut lips and terrible indigestion. On top of all this, it would be just plain weird to be a paper-eater. The thought was sort of funny, which produced a small smile on his face. However, the serious thoughts just kept on coming and the smile could not remain.

Wonder how others perceive this kid's flag, what fruit he has in store?

He glanced over again at the boy's shirt, the face so intense.

Appreciated life's mystery. Executed for it. It's in all of us, somewhere. From the very beginning. Warriors. Fearless. Battle.

*

"They're coming!" Sam said excitedly, looking through the undergrowth.

He was still one and a half feet shorter than his mother, and his brother was a half-foot shorter than him. They were playing in the green, summer forest behind their home. There was a petite, golden dog that ran beside them. Her name was Daisy. The scent of a rabbit went through her nose and deep into her head, conjuring instinctual images of the creature and spurring on the primal urge to chase it. She ran off through the woods—towards the enemy that Rob and Sam were preparing to fight.

The world was still pure.

Rob threw his little walking stick like a javelin into a creek that flowed into a river, which caused a big splash. Sam repeatedly shot imaginary bullets from the fingers of his right hand as he accompanied each shot with the "ptu, ptu" sound of lips parting followed by his tongue flicking the cherry flavored roof of his mouth. He crunched the spherical cherry top off of the little white stick and pretended that it was the enemy's head. He threw the skeleton into the weeds. His tongue had blood all oSam thought that he saw a flash of grey in the bushes, so said to Rob, "*Quiet.*"

He was very excited because he thought that it might be a wolf. So, he seriously brought his slightly quavering little hands up to his lips and let loose a long howl—which was much higher pitched than he wanted it to be. For a few moments both of them listened intently. But nothing howled back.

Both of them shrugged their little shoulders. And the battle resumed.

Rob screamed and clutched his shoulder, falling into a mess of poison ivy, which in four days would result in the most uncomfortable rash that he'd experience—until he met a girl called Kate. But that was a ways off.

"I'm hit, I'm hit." In a dramatic, dying voice, he was able to utter, "Bring me the…medicine."

Sam sprinted over with his red-stained satchel containing the raspberries, which Rob grasped for and smeared on his lips as he ate them. They had the ability to cure a wounded soldier in a matter of seconds.

"To the fortress!"

Rob leaped up from the ground, and both started sprinting towards the fort of fallen limbs that they had erected. They leapt over the raging river which ran in front of the fort and huddled together inside, guns poking through the vertical bars of iron, which looked like sticks to an untrained eye. A thousand enemy warriors equipped with the scope of technology from atlatls to machine guns charged. One of their ferocious guard dogs let loose a piercing bark not very far away. Sam and Rob were not scared in the least. They fought together.

*

Rob lay on the incredibly soft bed with his legs hanging off of the edge, stroking the shining, tan legs of his wife whose eyes scanned the brochure excitedly as she sat with her back propped against the headrest. They had just settled in at the resort, after a long plane ride which had yielded her drool on his shirt, and a smile on his face. Even her drool was sweet. Erica was happy. Rob was happy.

He had what he wanted, which was to make it so that the majority of other people would envy him—which was what he was supposed to want. He had a group of like-minded friends, a steady job, a house with monthly payments, a car with monthly payments, a wife with monthly payments…what more could he ask for?

"We should go diving tomorrow," Erica said as she ran both of her hands through his hair.

Rob smiled.

"Whatever you'd like, Mrs. Steele."

He bit her leg, and she laughed as he began to tickle her sides. It went on for quite a while. Everything just felt so good. Through her laughter, he eventually heard that his phone on the little table beside the bed had begun its 'happy' tune. He reached over to get it and, seeing who it was, sighed heavily.

"It's Sam."

"Don't answer," she said with disdain. "I can't believe *he's* calling."

The ironic tune continued closer and closer to its end, and Rob was about to put it back on the table unanswered when a small shred of resistance to the act changed his mind.

"Hello?"

"Hey, how's Brazil?"

Rob stood and went over to the window which made up one of the walls of the room. There were curtains for when they would need them later. Looking out, he saw a bright blue, saltwater pool about a hundred yards from a much bigger saltwater pool, swaying palm trees and smiling people preparing drinks in martini glasses. There were people in swimwear, workers in white uniforms, and bamboo covered structures of various sizes. It was a tropical paradise as defined by tourists. He looked back at Erica who was lying on her stomach atop the bed, looking at him, rolling her big, brown eyes.

"It's nice."

"Good. I've been meaning to ask you, because I didn't ever look, was there evidence of Katrina in Miami?"

Sam laughed quietly, and then composed himself after a few seconds.

"Oh, who am I kidding? I am sure that if there was Erica would not have been surprised, you sinners."

Rob wished that Sam was talking about the hurricane, and almost smiled at the joke but remained gruff by force of habit.

"Sam, what do you want? This call is expensive."

"I just called to say that I'm sorry for making you think about me on your special day. My leaving this morning was selfish."

Silence on the line.

"Where are you?"

"Headed north, on a train. Almost in Georgia, I think. I've already hitch-hiked, and then a police officer gave me a ride. Wasn't arrested, though."

"Wow. Do you have money?"

"Yeah, on my card. Enough to last the summer—I hope."

Deeper silence on the line.

"Rob?"

"What?" he said sternly.

"We don't fight together anymore, and that saddens me."

"What the fuck are you talking about?"

Silence on the line.

"Never mind. Enjoy yourself. Bye."

*

Sam slid the phone closed and sighed heavily. The kid beside him was asleep, drooling on Sam's shoulder. It wasn't exactly sweet.

Nonetheless, Sam gently turned his neck so he could see the eavesdropper, knowing that she would be one to commiserate with.

Quietly, he said: "What do you think, should I accept that I don't have a brother anymore, or fight it?"

Compassionately, she shook her head.

"It takes two, you know."

Sam nodded his head, and then turned away from her.

He looked around the train at all of the people. It was a commuter vessel, long and silver on the outside with two-by-two orange, cushion seats on the inside. People who did not know each other had to sit together, because so many used the train. And it seemed by their silence that they did not want to get to know one another—which was in itself very sad and the cause for many problems. There were businessmen, laborers, government employees, the unemployed, and retired people. They all looked so accepting and lifeless as they sat quietly in their seats, slightly jostling as the train hit bumps. Sam watched them and could not for the life of him figure out how they accepted.

Rob has accepted. Mom and Dad have accepted. Why can't I?

He looked out the window at the fields and little houses that flew past, remembering that he looked just like the people who looked like they accepted.

Quiet desperation.

Trying to look through his reflection in the window, he noticed a couple of little kids running around a pink house with a dog, a man mowing his lawn proudly, and a few trucks poking down country roads. It was about the time that people were beginning to come home from work. He remembered how the little kids with their dog felt. They were gone in a flash, even though he craned his neck to try and watch for as long as he could. The sky was light pinkish and bluish, consisting of variegated streaks, the hills dark in the distance.

Soon, the pink was gone and all that was left was dark blue, which gradually darkened until homes where highlighted in the distance by warm, yellow light. The train kept going into the darkness, and Sam took the headphones off of his lap and put them on his head again. The song that he chose was very good, and had appropriate lyrics, as well as the soothing sounds of a talented guitar player. It even had to do with a train, and ended with, 'I wanna' break on down. But I can't stop now.'

Through the young night, all those aboard traveled together.

Eventually, the train stopped at a glowing station somewhere near the edge of a city. Not long before the stop, the young guy beside Sam was awoken by an alarm on his phone. His head jerked off of Sam's shoulder, accompanied by a bashful grin and some mumbles. It seemed that he had his day pretty well timed out. Sam had noticed a Wal-Mart vest in his bag and imagined that the kid probably went through the same routine each day, going to and from work. There was a nametag on the vest, which Sam was glad for.

Yawning, the kid said, "This is my stop."

Sam took off his headphones and stood. The kid stood too, about up to Sam's shoulder.

"I didn't realize that you were six, six," he said as he moved past Sam, into the aisle.

It was always funny that to the exceptionally short man Sam was six foot six or taller, and to the exceptionally tall man, he was five foot ten or shorter. He was in actuality six feet, three inches tall on a good-height day.

"We are all short compared to mountains, Johnny. Never forget that."

The kid seemed to like this answer, and with a smile he extended his hand which was closed in a fist.

"It was nice to meet you, Sam."

It was obvious that the kid was very pleased that a stranger had struck up a conversation with him, unusual on the train that he rode every day. Sam bumped the kid's fist and agreed that it had been nice.

The kid walked away down the aisle, pulling up his baggy pants which sagged down, and Sam sat back down. The woman in the flowery dress put a hand on Sam's shoulder, giving him a weak smile, and got off of the northbound train without saying a word.

He sat there, staring blankly through the window, thinking about just going home. But it was too soon, and he had something to prove to himself.

"There can still be warriors," he whispered.

The train almost completely emptied. Some people got off of the train to walk to a cold apartment where there was nothing but a bed. Some had a dog waiting, or a kid. Some of them had hands to hold there where the train stopped. Most didn't. They all walked away.

Sam suddenly felt very alone, as the train was about to start rolling again. He wondered where the young man and the older woman were headed, what sort of lives they had, and realized that he didn't even know what city they were in, or exactly what route the train was taking.

Tallahassee? Jacksonville?

He had had his headphones on when the city's identity was announced and did not care to look at the black sign with yellow, electronic letters.

Doesn't matter. Not getting off in this state.

Chapter 3

The state that he found himself in was moderately morose/Georgia.

It felt very good to get off the train. He'd spent the night in a cheap hotel room—where he'd slept soundly. When he awoke, he decided that he needed supplies for walking. He'd always wanted to be a wanderer and was going to do it right. So, he walked from the edge of little city to the center of it, wearing his headphones around his neck because he was not in the mood for music. He wanted to feel the place out, did not want to give up a sense.

The city seemed like an old man married to a young woman—not embracing the years but trying to seem young by throwing out the paintings for posters. There was an odd mix of buildings, both old and new. The walk was nice and quiet, with only subtle sounds. People were just beginning to come out for the day.

He stepped towards the 'super store' just outside of downtown and the doors slid open automatically. The store contained many happily, even if they would never admit it, busy people. He saw an old woman in purple sweatpants intently studying and knocking on a watermelon that she had chosen from a large cardboard box of other watermelons. Sam walked past, and when she looked up, he smiled. She smiled faintly in reply.

Riff-raff. Handsome, though. Needs a haircut. Why did he look at me? Wonder what Bill will do if this seedless melon does not turn out to be seedless like the last one…

Sam picked up a peach and ran a finger over the fuzzy skin. Really, a peach was a beautiful thing, like most fruits. And they tasted beautiful too. He wished that the two qualities were commonly found in humans too—external beauty and soul, that is, nothing to do with cannibalism. He looked at a few other peaches, contemplated juggling, but wisely chose not to. After bagging three of them, he walked through the produce section. It was like having Mary in a bag, who was a friend from college. She was a peach enthusiast, which ultimately got her in the end. He hoped that she was doing well. She had been a good friend.

He was seen again.

Hm. Look at this guy. Tall, tan…Achilles. Like Dan, better. So lonely, still. Wonder if he'd go out with a girl like me…

In general, everything is easier if you imagine yourself to be a hero, or some character in Greek mythology, with the freedom of changing the ancient stories however you please. The gods—much more interesting ones than some single, 'benevolent' one—were behind everything. Sometimes they even took the form of a person. So she thought of herself as Helen of Troy. And Paris, A.K.A. Dan, had turned out to be gay.

So now, Helen looked at Achilles.

Her dark hair was lustrous, curling down just over her eyes. She wore a yellow dress, and watched Sam, who watched several bags of potato chips. She walked past him, hoping that he'd look up, but he did not. Rather, he bent and clutched a noisy bag of Doritos without even noticing her. For all he knew, she could have been an old woman—a sunflower enthusiast, wandering aimlessly in search of the seed section.

He looked at the smooth, white tiles which reflected the lights above as he walked to the end of the aisle, and then turned to walk parallel and in the opposite direction relative to where he had just walked, three yards over. The aisle was full of snacks. It was his favorite section. An Indian employee wearing a blue turban stocked shelves in approximately the center of the aisle, and the girl in yellow walked Sam's way from the opposite end of the aisle, tossing a bag of Oreos into her cart.

Sam looked at the girl in the yellow dress for the first time as he walked towards her. She looked like someone that he knew from college, someone who thinking of caused him to feel empty, like he had missed out on something which was right there for him. Her name was Ellen.

So, he walked towards her wistfully, reminding himself to stay in the present.

Remember, gotta' be free.

Helen looked with quiet panic at the man in the turban.

Taliban.

The man in the turban looked at no one.

There are too many fucking Keebler Elves.

Sam's path converged with the girl's where the man was stocking the shelves. Sam looked at her, smiling slightly, and the instant that their eyes met, hers darted down.

Awful reflex!

It happened to him too, from time to time. He couldn't blame her. Walking out of that aisle, he crossed the tiled cart highway and continued disinterestedly through the clothing section as the poor girl in yellow turned down the next aisle, disappointed to see that Achilles had moved on without even haven been given an opportunity for a conquest.

I'm a coward.

Sam picked up a tie-dye shirt, which reminded him of Ellen. He put it up to his nostrils and took a deep breath. The smell was nice. There did not seem to be much better than a nice smell.

When he opened his eyes, Sam saw a little boy wearing an old baseball t-shirt which had Mark McGwire's name on the back. The little Cardinals fan looked up at him, from a few feet away. The child was incredibly cute—long blonde hair and big, dark eyes. It was strange for Sam to look at a young version of himself with his own eyes.

"Go Cubs."

The kid didn't say anything back, and just stared with those dark eyes.

"You're right. Words are most valuable when rare, like anything else."

Scary man. Stranger Danger. Where's Mommy!?!

The little boy ran off, elbows flailing, and Sam tried futilely, though in his mind semi-successfully, to remember clearly the days and sensations of childhood. He tossed the shirt which he was holding into the cart, deciding that there should be at least a short rotation in clothing, and looked around the place that he was in, resignedly.

Walking over towards where he thought backpacks might be, he suddenly began to feel down and tried to run a song through his head in order to rid himself of the sadness. It was to no avail. If it got much worse, he would have to put on his headphones and play the appropriate song.

He found a sixty-liter, water-proof hiking pack, and decided that it would do. He also grabbed a knife, eating utensils all in one tool, a little camp stove, fuel, and bug spray, putting them, along with the Doritos, peaches, and shirt, all into a cart that he found unattended after taking out of it a ski mask and duct tape. He left the rope.

Someone's lucky day.

He tried to think if there was anything else that he needed and finally decided to grab a small tarp—to be used as a poncho, rain-catcher, or tent. It just felt better than buying a generic tent, more authentic. And with all of these things he felt like he could go anywhere.

Because of the peaches, he thought about another one of his college friends who he missed, and so picked out a green bandana and sunglasses—after a surprisingly long search—both of which he put on in the store with their tags still on. He hadn't found the bandana that he was looking for, but the one that he did find would work.

When he was pushing the cart towards the front of the store, he saw a cute girl in a blue vest. She looked as if she worked at the store. He thought up something quick that he could say to her. For Sam, to be able to talk to anyone without fear or hesitation was the best way to ensure not missing who he was afraid that he would never meet, if she crossed his path. It stung to think of missed opportunities.

Walking up to her, he said, "do you know where I might find a bathroom? It's funny, or maybe tragic. I can never find the shit that I actually *want* to find."

She smiled and pointed towards the corner of the store. He went there, even though he didn't have to go, and then walked towards the checkout area after grabbing a notebook, a pack of pencils, a few protein bars, canned goods, and other non-perishables.

Self-checkout. Hopefully it won't come to that.

The middle-aged woman whose job it was to make sure that people checked themselves out properly checked Sam out with her eyes. She was attractive, and had a glow to her, but Sam was too low to really notice. He was contemplating if there would come a point in time where there was a person whose job was to ensure that people kill themselves properly and decided that there would be—that there already was.

Every day we march towards death exactly like we've been told to. But who's in charge?

He also foresaw a time when people simply refused to breed. It would be the last step in the evolution of man. But this was a ways off. And these thoughts were due entirely to a bad mood.

He scanned the backpack, ripped off the tag, and put his groceries and other purchases into it. He rolled the tarp and strapped it to the outside of the pack, slung it over his shoulder, nodding at the woman who looked at him honestly, and walked out of the store, into the small city. Beside a bus stop where several others stood, he took a moment to extract the things from his bag which he wanted to wear. He folded the bandana properly—*not* in doo-rag fashion—and then tied it on. Then, the sunglasses went on his head. He also put on the tie-dye shirt, which was especially colorful, with red, blue, and green all spiraling on a background of white. It was an interesting shirt, though would have been better if he had made it himself. He then re-slung the pack on his shoulder. The pack was heavy, but everything fit in it just about right. He was ready to go. And so he went.

A man who was trying to catch a bus ran past him, heading the way that Sam had come from. In the city, only people who are trying to catch a bus *really* run. Sam looked back. The man just missed the bus. He was standing alone, looking at his watch, when Sam turned away.

Late morning still had the faint smell of freshness, as he walked towards downtown.

There was a person who he could not help but look at, once he noticed her. Men cannot help but look at attractive women—unless they have been castrated in one form or another.

She walked across the newly paved, asphalt street as if it were there just for her. A chrome sports car slowed as she walked with her eyes oriented up and covered by sunglasses, making it perfectly obvious that she did not notice the man in the driver's seat who studied her every move. Her long, gold-blonde hair bounced with each step, and her white, five-inch shorts made her legs look even more tan than they actually were. Onto the sidewalk she made it, and the chrome car passed slowly. She had never been in any of the shops that she passed despite walking by them every day—acknowledging no one. To her, nobody felt anything besides, of course, admiration for her.

As she walked past Sam, he looked at her face until it was gone. She did not look at him. To her, he was just a homeless man—possibly gang-affiliated—wearing a hideous pair of sunglasses.

Sam sat down on a cool bench of stone, relieving the weight from his back. He watched as she walked past the man who was impatiently tapping his foot at the bus stop as if he was speeding up time and making himself less late. She didn't seem to notice that man either. Sam wondered what she saw when looking at a mirror, if she had ever really looked at the stars and understood them. She reminded him of a specific girl from his past.

*

"I feel that you have been using me."

Just like every other girl I've liked.

The pretty girl with a ponytail turned her head like a confused puppy, though her cuteness was not nearly as convincing. If she were as tall as she was blonde—in every sense of the word—she'd be fifteen feet tall.

She put down her yellow pencil and grabbed the boy's hands who had just explained the calculus problem to her. The boy wore hair nicely shaved like all of the other nice boys. He knew nothing of women, yet.

"I'm not using you, Sam."

She smiled a smile which did not betray the worried thought which was running through her head: *Not even halfway through the semester!*

"'Your' being super-silly-ous," she whined.

'The word is supercilious, you dumb bitch, and you obviously have no idea what it means,' Sam almost said.

But, for the moment, he was able to maintain his composure and remained silent.

He looked at her fashionable, dark rimmed glasses, and V-necked, white Hollister t-shirt with a little swirl of orange flowers on it. She had blue bracelets on her wrists that said to fight a disease that she knew or cared nothing about. Her pink phone was in her lap, and he knew that she was thinking about pecking away at it. He took his hands away from hers, and crossed his arms, looking straight into her blue eyes.

"You are using me. I am trying to use you. You are a *fucking tool* that doesn't work."

She seemed shocked—but not in the way that she liked.

A group of Asians suddenly stopped arguing about the correct construction on an algorithm, and they looked like they had just seen Godzilla. Sam stood, closing his book with a gentle clap and walked away, entirely amazed at what he had just said.

*

He only felt partially bad about what he said to her that day. She ended up failing the class because he'd stopped doing her homework. As he thought about it—how angry he had let her make him—Sam began to silently laugh on the bench, and a woman with concerned eyes passed.

Messed up man...

The past gave way to the present.

Through his sunglasses, he looked at the city, at all of the people going in circles, and at cars waiting patiently at lights. He looked at businessmen talking to things in their ears who were thinking that they were better than other men who were the same as them, at a houseless man in his best rags lying against a brick wall across the street. There was a difference between being homeless and houseless, Sam knew, and thought that the poor man probably had the misfortune of being both.

Homeless. Is there a worse label?

The man asked everyone who passed for spare change, stuttering the same sorry phrase each time. Most people didn't even stop to let him finish. But it didn't stop him from slowly starting again.

A mother walked by, pushing a stroller and being followed by a blonde-haired kid. The little boy in the Mark McGwire shirt seemed much more confident now than when he had seen Sam in the store. He babbled on about something as important as what a short, stalky businessman babbled on about to a taller businessman. As the suits walked past, they both looked at Sam and by their expressions he could tell that they were holding back laughter, or ridicule, or both.

Point on Mr. Businessman. You can't dress like me. Jimi.

Music was the key to have something stick in the mind, he knew. It was nice to think in terms of Hendrix—minister of the electric church. The mom listened to the steroid-oblivious kid just as little as the businessman who liked to seem tall and in shape listened to the other guy. They both probably had songs in their head, too.

People just kept walking by, people of all sorts, and at all stages of life. There were so many. All of them were thinking, to some degree. He imagined being able to hear all of their thoughts at once, so as it was impossible to make out anything but an awful conglomerate of noise. He looked at them all, and began to feel a bit overwhelmed, especially so considering the thoughts which he assumed that some of them were probably having.

There was one guy in particular, looked to be of about thirty years old, who got Sam's attention as well as that of everyone else in the area. He was screaming, hysterically, and strutted on the sidewalk in a trench-coat, wearing an orange, frayed scarf. His hair was cut short and neatly. Sam decided to attempt to determine what the man's thoughts were.

He generally knew what people meant despite what they said. But this instance was an exception—to say the least.

The man kept screaming, extremely loudly, "NO THEY DON'T" over and over again. He was by himself. It was alarming, especially when he glaringly looked at Sam and spoke even more loudly, pointing a finger that almost looked purple. The only thing which Sam could think of to explain these words, which the man seemed determined to keep repeating, was that maybe the guy was trying to prove that actions do not actually speak louder than words. But by the way that the pedestrians on the sidewalk parted around him as far as they could without being clipped by passing traffic, their actions were certainly more *clear* than his words were. Duly, possibly, he had a point. Their actions definitely did not speak *louder* than his words. "NO, THEY DON'T…"

Eventually the guy wandered out of sight, which was a relief to Sam.

He put his square chin in his hands and continued to look ahead. Cars and busses rushed past. A little Latino woman walked by, wearing a cross necklace that caught the sun's light. She knew only how to look down, and never made eye contact with anyone who wasn't brown. She walked across the street and up the steps of a nice-looking, old, brick hotel. Only very rarely did she ever say anything but 'sorry' to people in there, and that was only when they forgot to put the 'do not disturb' sign on their door.

Across from the hotel, which some people would call 'historic,' there was a tattoo parlor. Sam found himself studying it—just like everything else. The building was made of brick and had no windows. There was a neon sign which said that the business was open 'from 6:00 PM to midnight.'

That cannot be good for business. Who would go to a tattoo parlor which cannot even spell 'midnight' correctly?

The answer came so immediately that it was almost frightening.

A guy with strange dots, tears, and a few other shapes tattooed on his face walked out of the parlor and past Sam, smiling and looking up with crazy, make-up bordered eyes. His arms were entirely covered with ink, and there was no telling what was on the parts of his body that were actually hidden from the public. A woman, whose hair was blue, hurried out of the parlor until she walked beside him. Her tattoos were much the same as his.

Face tattoos. And I thought I was a non-conformist. Wonder what a die-hard non-conformist would do in a group of other non-conformists?

A tall young man on a longboard and wearing headphones sped by, disconcertingly close to Sam's feet. He had longish, flowing blonde hair and weaved through people on the sidewalk very adeptly, gliding smoothly over the sidewalk cracks. He was still cool. A middle-aged man gave the kid a snarling look as he rolled past. He too had long hair—in a pony-tail—but wasn't cool anymore, and kind of knew it. Mumbling, he walked past Sam, with ridiculously straight posture.

A few minutes later a bent over old man walked past the bench. He had been tall and confident in his day, but no longer was either. He wore a long-sleeved, black and yellow flannel shirt even though it was already at least 80 degrees Fahrenheit outside. His hair was thin, white, and shaved close. His head shined with sweat.

Sam decided that he would never get old.

The man turned his head toward Sam, meeting his gaze for a few seconds. Neither man made any gestures. Just as slowly, the old man turned his head away. Then he kept on walking, getting nowhere fast.

The buildings were tall, crumbling, and there were new ones being built that would be torn down too. The people were just the same. Another woman pushing a stroller—she looked pregnant—passed the old man.

Need to get out of here. Can't forget myself.

After a few moments, Sam got up and walked towards the interstate.

*

Sam was first and foremost a people prober, rather than the more common and stealthy people watcher. He even went so far as to sit with random people who were sitting alone at restaurants, from time to time. Risk-reward analysis always dictated that he should sit with a cute girl, but he liked feeling out anyone if they allowed—especially unusual-seeming people. It was a good way to realize how many people find friendliness to be creepy. But it was also an excellent way to learn how much some people appreciate being approached. Their reactions were almost always the same.

Sam would say:

'Hello, do you mind if I join you?'

They almost never said 'no.' After a stranger acquiesced—seeming almost stunned by the absurdity of being joined by Sam when an open seat was within sight—he or she generally looked away from him, quietly wondering what the long-haired freak wanted from them. It was rare to experience them saying much in the beginning. But after a few soft-toned questions from him they usually began smiling and feeling good, seeming sincere. And then they usually 'have to get going' if the silence sits too long.

Joining a lonely person, having a nice conversation, just might be what gives them the strength to keep on going. Doing so gave Sam the strength to keep on going.

The extroverted, middle-aged black man, driving, who sat to Sam's left, was a people entertainer. Which was why he had picked up the hitchhiker. And so, in a fairly rare occurrence, Sam the prober was entertained.

"Will, what do you use to get through each day?"

The man chuckled and bobbed his head a bit, flicking on the windshield wipers to combat the little droplets of the day which had turned grey. His face was happy-looking and scruffy with a bit of wiry, partially grey beard covering it. He was heavy-set but seemed to be in good shape.

They both had to talk loud, because the engine of the truck was very strong and noisy.

"A philosophizer we have, eh? Well, I use this truck. Takes me wherever I want, each day. So, are you a determinism kind of guy, or the free will sort?"

"I'm determined to practice free will."

Will laughed so loudly that it startled Sam.

"Free will, wow, that's tough. Brave, though. What about you, my man? What do you use to get through each day?"

Sam briefly wondered if his name had been forgotten, but would not be offended if it had been, and then acted like he was thinking for several moments longer than he actually was.

"Knowing that we are all in this together."

"Nah, man. Right letters, wrong words. We are all in this *to get her.* Only takes one eye to see that."

The surprisingly quick-witted man laughed heartily again, holding up his left hand which had a gold band on the ring finger. And after reviewing in his mind a brief history of the world and of his own life experiences, Sam laughed too at how true the statement was.

"So, where are you from?" Will asked.

"The north… I'm actually from Maine. But I went to school in New York."

"Ah, wow. What brings ya' to Podunk Georgia?"

"Well, I'm just passing through. It's nice to be out of the city. Coming from a wedding. My ex-girlfriend is actually from the area, so I'm a little familiar with the lay of the land."

"Ah, I see. 'Her.' What did I tell you?"

He laughed. It was very nice to actually hear someone laugh so sincerely, so often.

The truck went over rough train tracks that cut through the fields, and a picture which Will had taped to the dash of a cute young woman fluttered. Sam assumed that she was his daughter.

"Why do you look both ways at train crossings if you don't even bother to slow down?" Sam asked.

"Well, I guess I want to see death coming if it's my time. Don't want it to come and go without even knowing. Don't want to be cheated."

It was a good answer. Will was very adept at giving good answers, and quickly Sam grew to like him. Driving through the rain was pleasant, and hours gently passed interspersed with pleasing conversation.

There is nothing more encouraging than talking to an intelligent, happy person. It gives hope that you may one day be able to be one, even if the combination of intelligence and happiness is so very rare.

They drove through a small town which did not have much to it. Just a general store, a post office, a factory building where most of the men worked, and some houses where most of the women spent their boredom-filled hours. But there was a little boy in a yellow rain jacket walking across a lawn of grass in front of the awful, brown factory which belched dirty, chemical-ridden smoke into the air. The little boy looked to be whistling despite the rainy, grey day. And the thing was, it was just so goddamn beautiful to Sam. Because the kid was carrying five big, red balloons which sharply contrasted the rain and overall dreariness which others perceived. But this kid's perception was different. And that's all that it takes for hope.

Both Sam and Will saw the little gesture of the boy's right arm, pumping in the air, which wanted the truck's big horn to be honked. After looking to Will, and getting a nod of approval, Sam pulled the string and the horn blared. They both smiled at the little dance they got to see. And as the big truck passed, one of the balloons slipped from the kid's fingers amidst his excitement—or he might have let it go purposely—and it went up through the rain bravely. The kid looked up into the rain falling, smiling as the thing flew up and away.

As that balloon rose out of sight, and the truck drove out of town, Sam knew what he needed to do. He ripped out a piece of paper from his notebook, and for a few moments tried to collect his feelings. Then it just came, like anything true does. It was almost heart-wrenching writing the words. But then they were done, recorded, and he folded the piece of paper in half, fastened it with a rusty paper-clip that he had found, and put the message in his lap.

He was surprised that Will did not ask him what he had written, though wouldn't have been if he knew that the man was completely blind in his right eye, gradually losing vision in his left.

It might not be best for a passenger to not know that the driver is blind—but it is the most pleasant. They kept on traveling through the rain, on a road which Will knew very well, as somewhere far above a red balloon exploded.

The cotton fields were very large. One of the fields had three massive crosses driven into the ground. The crosses were about ten feet tall and were as wide as a large man's wingspan. It was a definite statement that the farmer was making, and probably an admirable one. Sam looked at the wooden, weather-beaten crosses amongst the cotton plants as the truck drove by.

Even though everyone sane person is a slave to a certain degree, Sam could not help but think about how utterly awful it would have been to be forced to work the fields, especially so sitting next to such a thoughtful and kind person of color like Will. He could also not help but think how awful it would feel to be crucified.

Such things as slavery were evidence of the boundless stupidity that humans are capable of, and a reminder to be very sure before trusting what one says, or doing as the rest do. They did, of course, crucify a great man who cared enough to devote his life to the effort of pacifying a bunch of belligerent apes. And then they used his name to fuel their belligerence on global proportions for a couple thousand years after they killed him.

But it wasn't long and they were far past the crosses.

Moments after he saw a sign that said '10' miles to where he wanted to be, Sam got a text message which said, 'I'm here.' He smiled slightly, responding with, 'Almost there, see you at the spot.'

"There's that brown sign you warned me about," Will said approximately eight minutes later.

"Ah, glad *you* are being observant. I routinely find myself lost in my head."

The big-rig soon pulled over to the side of the Georgia highway where a small gravel road intersected it. Will prepared to say good-bye as he turned off the truck.

"Can you take this?" Sam said—a little too loudly—holding out his turned off phone. "It causes too many distractions."

"You sure, boy?"

"Yeah, and could you do me another favor? Call the number that I have programmed in as 'home' if I don't call this phone within a couple months. Don't even turn it on until August. I'll leave a voicemail message. If you make the call, tell whoever answers not to worry, and that I'm where I want to be. Say that I went to France with your beautiful daughter. Ran away with her. You can even act mad if you want to. Remember, only do this if I *don't* call."

Sam was quiet for a while as he thought.

"Our secret word when I was little was 'donkey,' say that. They will know that you didn't abduct me, or any shit like that. Here's a note too, please send it to the address that I have written on it after the two months. You don't even *have* to call if you don't want to, but please send the note if I *don't* call. I just want to make sure that they get something. They'll recognize my handwriting, so you shouldn't worry about them causing trouble for you."

Will took the phone and the piece of paper which was folded in half and paper clipped. He couldn't think of words to say, which was unusual for him.

"Thanks Will. I really appreciate it. And please don't take off that paperclip. It's a message that only my family should ever read. If I do call, burn it."

For some naïve reason, Sam actually thought that Will wouldn't read the note. He put a twenty-dollar bill on the dash and before Will could object was about to hop out of the truck.

"Ever-onward."

"Hey, wait. Are you sure about this plan of yours? Whatever it is…"

Sam smiled and thought of his conversation with Rob on the beach, and at how later he had decided what he should have said rather than being abrasive.

"Man, I don't know much, but I know that to live on a whim is the way to go. Monotony only delivers inadequate contentment at best, for me. Have to take chances to receive thrills, to learn."

Will put his hands on the wheel, and smiled slightly, shaking his head because he could not think of words to voice his concern.

"Thanks again," Sam said.

The door to the truck slammed shut, and the engine steamed, wheezed. Sam walked through the mist, which was almost done falling, down the gravel road to where the brown sign pointed. The gravel and the sweet-smelling rain in the warm air smelled good. Sam just had to smile. But for the first time of the day, Will's smile was not there as he watched Sam go. Being the father that he was, something just didn't seem right.

Nice kid. Parents must be good. Must worry.

The truck roared to life, pulled back onto the highway, and got Will through the haze which his days were becoming.

Chapter 4

Sam walked into the state park and took a deep breath of the damp air. No one was around—as far as he could tell. Memories of happy times began to gently flood his mind. These memories led to less than happy memories, though were not regretted. The freshly cut grass smelled just the same as when he had been there for the first time.

The lawn was still mowed closely, buffering a nicely paved driveway which cut through the forest. He walked on the driveway for a few minutes, thinking about the gravity that somehow held him to the ground, how unlikely everything which allowed him to live seemed.

He slipped into the forest when a shed and truck became visible in the distance—where a ranger surely sat waiting to take money. It was not that he did not have the money, but he did think that people should not have to pay to enjoy nature, and occasionally enjoyed breaking rules. So he walked around the shed, through the forest, in a half-circle that probably ended up having a diameter of about five hundred yards. Then, he walked on the paved road again for a few minutes until he saw the familiar parking lot.

Her blue Volvo was sitting there, with the distinguishing white peace sign on the rear bumper. Sam smiled. The sun was even beginning to come out. He walked across the gravel parking lot and onto the trail which went through the forest.

Everything was dripping. The ravines were covered with thick, dewy moss on bluish rocks. There were a few species of trees, ferns, shrubs and herbs which he couldn't identify. He knew almost all of them in Maine. And the fact that he could not identify them in Georgia really did not bother him. To think of trees and other natural things in terms of names assigned by man is to think of man, which for the moment he was trying not to do.

That tree is… beautiful.

He walked for a while without seeing anyone. But this changed when he came around a bend of the trail. There hadn't been another car in the parking lot, so it was surprising to see people other than Brit. It was a pleasant surprise, actually.

There were two of them standing on the trail, a man and a woman. Both wore floppy hats and khaki-colored shirts and cargo pants. Both had binoculars. The man had them in his hands, in front of his eyes, looking up at what looked to be a very difficult angle. The woman was kneeling down to look at something on the ground.

Sam walked up to them, and looked down at the intricate, purple orchid with white highlights that the woman was observing.

"Morning," he said, which he had decided was an age-old celebration of making it through the night. Beautiful day, and that's a beautiful flower."

She looked up and smiled, standing. Her hair was white, her face friendly.

"Yes, there is beauty this morning."

Her smile remained.

The man was still looking through his binoculars, not seeming to even notice Sam. He looked to be about 55 years old too.

"Jenny, I swear that I saw it this time."

Shaking her head, with that nice smile, she looked to Sam.

"He's been looking since 1978 for this bird, which was the biggest woodpecker in the US…"

The man interrupted her, still looking through the binoculars.

"Is, *is* the biggest woodpecker. The Lord God Bird has a wingspan of over two and a half feet long, a black and white body, a golden eye, and a wicked beak of ivory on a red-crested head that can destroy any tree east of the big river. But the things are pacifists, so they pick on trees that are already dead."

"It's extinct."

"No, it's not," he said as if he had said it a thousand times before. "The Ivory-billed Woodpecker is alive and well in the state of Georgia."

She spoke to Sam again.

"We are hardly even in its historical range. And there hasn't been a confirmed sighting since the 1950s, and that was in Louisiana. Not here. Carl sees one every time he takes a walk in the forest. And that's *a lot*, now that he's retired."

"There is very good evidence that they were seen in 2004, and a few times since."

"Not in Georgia."

"Did ivory hunters drive them to this disputed extinction?" Sam asked, actually interested in this ghost bird.

The binoculars finally came down. The man's face was kind. His eyes were close together, behind glasses with circular frames, and he was very tan.

"Probably not, but the Natives did use their bills for necklaces, and actually…"

In mid-sentence, his right hand bolted from his side and he pointed up. His eyes lit. And he exclaimed:

"Prothonotary Warbler!"

"Excuse him," said his wife. "He just heard a bird."

The man smiled.

"What does it say about a man who understands what birds are saying better than what humans are saying?"

For a while there were only chirps. Sam thought a few moments and replied.

"That he was wise enough to take the time to learn the more beautiful, honest of the two languages."

After listening a little while longer, Sam asked: "What were you saying about that big woodpecker?"

The tone of the man's voice changed from merely informational, professional, to solemn and heart wrenched.

"We cut down their trees. That is always the problem. Everything goes to shit when the trees are cut. But a few birds made it."

To himself, he whispered: "They just have to have."

Watching a species struggle with extinction is especially interesting through the eyes of a species struggling with extinction. Beauty and tragedy are laced in every move of both the watcher and the watched.

"There really is something *to* finding what others say is gone," Sam said after a few formulating moments. "And this bird that you describe, I believe that it is out there. Keep looking, man."

The man finally smiled the smile that his face indicated was there often.

"Thank you," he said emphatically, and then looked to his wife.

They seemed very happy. She smiled too. It seemed so very nice, what they had.

Quietly, the three of them walked down the trail until it forked. The birder and the birder-supporter went right. Sam went left, after wishing them luck.

It was not long before he could hear the steady flow of water nearby. He imagined her, sitting on the rock that looked like the palm of a hand, beside the copper-colored creek.

The trail became rocky and the smell of the place was intensely natural, like wet stone and soil.

Walking alone on a familiar trail where the last time it was walked with another warm hand is cold.

But one must keep on walking.

The trees turned to shrubs, the trail turned too, and there he saw her with her nose in a book. She must have heard him coming, because the pure red cover was replaced by her slightly readable face.

Reserved happiness?

Sam walked towards her with a small grin on his face.

She spoke first, with her slight southern drawl—which at one time he had found to be cute.

"How are you feeling, sir."

"As healthy as a sick horse, madam."

She smiled at their old greeting joke, even though it was not the same as it used to be, and he sat beside her, taking off the backpack and leaning it on the wrist of the rock—the part where a suicide scar might be.

"So," she said, "what's up with the bandana?"

"I liked the way it looked on a friend of mine. It's nice to think of friend-days. Want a peach?"

"No."

He reached into his bag and pulled a peach out. It tasted amazing, but Brit kept looking at him without saying anything, so he spat out something to turn back her eyes.

"How has that nice new job in the city been treating you?"

"Oh," she said, seeming to liven up at bit, "It's amazing. Everything is going how I planned it."

"Good. And at the very least you won't have to deal with the winters up there anymore."

She hesitated a moment, with eyes which seemed to be about to say something that she did not want to say.

"Sam, why are we here?"

"I don't know. I always find myself wondering that."

She looked at him somewhat coldly, and rubbed her temples with her very white fingers, and then pushed her very dark brown hair out of her very blue eyes. She looked good, even though she was wearing old jeans and a plaid shirt that looked to be Tom's. She had been at Rob's wedding, was a very good friend of Erica's. At the wedding, Sam had not spoken to her besides to ask her to meet him where she now sat, without Tom. He looked at the ruby ring on her left hand, which he had not known about.

Probably not invited.

After a few more moments Sam broke the silence.

"It's amazing how much can change in a short amount of time."

"Yeah, Tom and I already have the date set. I'm sure that Erica told you about the engagement."

She had not, surprisingly.

"The ceremony is going to be outside, in his hometown, hopefully as the sun sets, on a beach, probably. Not sure if there are any good beaches around there. Hm. We are *really* excited though. He said—what was it—well, not that long ago we were talking and…"

She was not and never had been anywhere near concise in speaking and would go on for a very long time if allowed to—saying nothing. He couldn't stand it and decided to answer the question that he had evaded earlier.

"I experienced death last summer. I thought that I finally needed to tell you. You know, as an explanation for why it might have fallen apart between us. Honestly, I really don't know why it fell apart. But I did change."

Silence, of course, returned. She knew that he was serious.

"How?" she asked sincerely, and with a tone of panic. "What happened to you?"

"It doesn't matter. All that matters is that it got me thinking, which has led me here. There is just so much that…that if I had died I would have missed. I just can't bring myself to do what you are doing right now. And I'm sorry."

She didn't look cold anymore, and suddenly looked like a sad little girl.

"But what do you even want? Why did you turn down that job after graduation, where are you going to get money?"

He shrugged, and smiled as he thought of what he was about to say.

"Lou Reed said it best, 'money is like us in time, it lies but can't stand up.'"

She gave him a disgusted look.

"Are you afraid that making a little money would corrupt you, or something?"

"No. Money does not corrupt a person. It just magnifies corrupt people—allows them to show what they really are."

"Oh my God, Sam. How do you come up with all these answers?"

"I've asked a lot of questions. And anyways, the job wasn't right. I want to be my own person, I guess. Make my own decisions. Engrained in almost everyone's psyche is self-denial, which I just cannot do anymore. 'Propriety' makes me sick. We've talked about this. I just can't allow myself to become a cold, 'professional' person like I'm expected to."

A person like you.

"Sam, you have to grow up."

He laughed silently, throwing the pit of the peach into the weeds.

She continued: "Seriously, looking at you is like seeing a dead German Shepherd at the side of the road, which is terribly sad, but what's worse is that it has that fucking collar on And I know the owners, sometimes feel like I was the driver. ."

He looked at her and nodded his head.

Clever girl.

"Brit, *I* was the driver. And anyways, I just feel like everything could be so much more beautiful. I feel guilty that everything is so easy for me, and that so many people try so hard, getting nowhere. Actually, I think most people just give up. I just can't stop thinking about how close to the end I was, how close I always am. post-traumatic stress."

"Sam, that's serious."

"I've mostly made it through. What I'm trying to do is experience life without all of my old crutches for a while. Life stripped of diversions is terrifying, but purifying. I want to feel in a way that has not been sculpted by other people before I commit to anything. If I don't do this now, I never will be able to."

For a while her blue eyes looked at his not-blue eyes.

"Oh, Sam. Wouldn't it be nice if we didn't have to die?"

"No. There would be even less urgency to live. Don't think that I could keep on living if I didn't know that I was going to die someday. It'd be frightening—to not be able to die."

After a while of silence, she said: "Do you ever feel like you just couldn't die, even if you wanted to?"

"Yeah, actually I do. Like that tiger that we saw at Central Park Zoo, you know, just lying there on the cement as people outside of the cage laugh at it. There's a feeling of being trapped, knowing that you're being laughed at, but also knowing that you cannot escape—living somewhere that is not your place."

"Sam! I was just thinking about that poor tiger at the zoo too. It was so sad. I guess great minds think alike."

"Maybe they do once in a while. But it's the not so great minds that cannot help but think alike. And that's why the idea of being condemned to live here forever is so damned scary."

She looked at him, nodding her head a little, and smiled like she used to. Then she rested her head on his shoulder, which felt nice. Her hair smelled good.

Thought it'd always be like this.

For a while they just sat there, thinking about how it used to be.

He reached into his pocket.

"Can you take this?"

She lifted her head from his shoulder and looked at the iPod, shaking her head.

"But you don't love anything like you love music."

"I'm trying to find new things."

He took the headphones off of his neck too.

"Are you sure?"

"Yeah, gotta lose the old things. It's funny how music can bring back memories—so clear that you are there again. Every time you listen to a song it's like a plugging into the past. Many a good song has been ruined that way."

"I know, Sam."

"And it's just about out of juice anyway. I forgot the charging cable."

She took the device and headphones. Then, she put her head back on his shoulder, and they continued to sit in their old spot. They stayed there in silence, watching the water going over logs and rocks, ever replacing itself in a smooth flow. They listened to the birds sing, to the insects rattle, and to the frogs makings noises which sounded like the single strum of a banjo. If the frogs ever got it right, then they could really scare people who are afraid of hillbillies. A large duck was followed closely by a line of tiny ducklings, fighting the current and diving to see what was at the gravelly bottom. It didn't take long for them to pop back up. The fragrance of all of the flowering plants was subtly, beautifully present. A breeze blew against the current of the river, and golden grains of pollen drifted from the pine trees. It felt wonderfully natural upon the rock which held the two in its palm.

"I have to get going," she said.

*

Sam firmly closed the passenger door of her car and put up his right hand to signal 'good-bye' as she sped away, giving him a last admonishing look, which seemed to say, 'Be careful, stranger. If a gang member don't cut you, the druggies will. Cannot believe that you convinced me to drop you off here.'

And then he was alone again.

He looked around at the rundown part of the city, in what would have to be considered downtown of 'the hood.' Most of the buildings were made of brick. Almost all of the windows had bars or cages over them. There seemed to be either a church or liquor store on each block.

Red-soled, black shoes tied together by their laces hung from sagging telephone wires, gently swaying in the gray. Other than them, there was little decoration.

Sam walked along the root-havocked, cracked sidewalk imagining being robbed. His imagination was very vivid. After a few minutes of walking, he passed a tall young man. The man was black—like almost all of the other young men in the neighborhood—and had a face which was completely opposite of the open-mouthed, laughing and mohawked caricature of the Native American which was on the Atlanta Braves baseball cap that he wore. His eyes were indifferent, frighteningly so. He walked like he had nowhere to go. Sam looked at him and nodded.

"What tha' fuck ya looking at, ya' no-good, shit…"

His voice trailed off, the obscenities becoming less audible.

Sam kept on walking, as did the man wearing the cap. He could see why the guy was mad but was still a little hurt by it.

Depressing, both cap and man. Cap: a travesty of a poor, suppressed people. The cap's ignorant head: allowed by the society that made that awfully offensive cap.

Soon Sam passed a girl with an extremely short, black and shiny skirt sitting on the steps of a closed business. There was really no point in wearing the skirt if she was going to sit the way that she did. He could almost see the chlamydia. Her eyes looked very glazed, and she moaned/spoke words that he did not answer. He looked at her compassionately. She made a face which seemed to suggest that he had insulted her.

He had always felt sorry for prostitutes, and all of the other people who sold themselves, but could do nothing but keep on walking.

A couple of adolescent boys on the same bike, one standing on the pegs of the back wheel, rode closely past. They both stared at him as if he were an alien, with the big pack on his back full of probes and laser-guns. Suddenly wondering if his bandana meant anything other than a way to keep his hair out of his eyes, he nodded at them, and the one on pegs laughed.

Sam took off his bandana.

He left the business sector, went under a dark bridge on which ran a rail-line, passed shredded sleeping bags up near the top of the embankment, and then found himself in a small park with some grass, but more exposed dirt. There was a bench, and a basketball court. Some young men were in an intense game, cussing at each other. They were very good and seemed exceptionally lively, flaunting their skills which were demonstrated primarily in an effort to humiliate their peers. A tall, shirtless guy with a doo rag stood under the basket, hacking at people who got too close. He seemed especially arrogant.

I'd dunk over him. He'd never expect it.

Sam briefly considered getting in on the game, to see if he could do what he imagined, but thought better of it, deciding that it would probably only end in injury which would be very difficult to deal with. He walked to the other side of the park so that he would not be tempted to play.

A dozen or so pigeons were crowded around an old man with a grisly grey beard who looked genuinely happy in the rags that he wore, on the bench that he sat. He had only a duffel bag of belongings, and a tarp. The pigeons fought fiercely over every crumb that he tossed. The man made himself a king by making peasants of the pigeons. He laughed and laughed as they fought. Sam passed and dropped three quarters into the man's hat. The pigeons scattered in a frantic moment and the king was dead. Sam felt bad, looking at the guy who slowly nodded his head until it was oriented down—and wished that he had not given the coins.

He continued walking on a beaten, dirt path beside the straight road that he had been dropped off on until his surroundings turned into a residential area. It took only about five more minutes of walking before the path turned into another cracked sidewalk.

A car with resounding music and shiny, showy rims passed slowly, but did not cause any trouble. The top of the car was down, and all of the men in it were wearing red bandanas.

Sam kept on walking.

A happy family made up of a man, a woman, a boy, and a girl were in their front yard together, laughing at a little puppy that confidently trotted around. The dog reminded him of poor Daisy. The father and son played catch with a baseball, the father no doubt having fond memories brought back by the smell of the mitt, by the feel of the ball in his hand. The mother and daughter sat on lawn chairs—watching with love in their eyes. There is something incredibly beautiful about happy, devoted parents and their little reflections that do not yet know what the world is or how much the mirror gives, sacrifices.

Sam smiled inside, thinking of family, but looked like a creepy loner on the outside. He kept on walking. The little island of warmth was replaced by empty-seeming houses as the ship that was his body sailed on. All of the houses looked the same—greyish, with peeling paint and a tiny, un-mowed lawn.

In the driveway of a house, that was a few blocks down the way, a little girl of about four or five years old played with a bright pink truck about the size of herself. There was no one else around, but the place was kept very well. Purple and gold crocus—delicate-looking flowers which are tough enough to be the first ones to peek up through the frost—were planted in a neat row along the dirt path to the house, and the lawn was mowed nicely. The home stuck out like a sore thumb—*does a sore thumb really stick out?*—on the sad-looking block, which was being attacked by the angry screams of a woman and the sounds of a man throwing things. Glass shattered.

The little girl looked up to Sam and smiled with the warmth and purity that only children can get away with. He smiled and stopped walking.

"What's your name?" he asked.

"Wendy," she said quietly.

"Where's mommy, Wendy?"

"Workin.'"

"Where's daddy?"

She shrugged as if the question made no sense.

"Who's watching you?"

"Gammy."

He knelt beside her and looked at a pizza-sized oil stain on the cement, thinking how awful it was that approaching a child usually seemed suspicious.

"Can I see your toy?"

She smiled, pushing it noisily towards him. He took out a twenty-dollar bill from his wallet and tucked it securely into the underside of the truck.

"Ask your mom to play with you when she gets home. And if she does, you become a big wind that tips the car over. And your mother will put it right-side up. Can you remember that, Wendy? It's just like your name."

She nodded.

"Alright. Go on inside by your gammy. Go on."

She ran towards the open garage door, dragging her pink truck.

He continued walking through the largely abandoned neighborhood until he reached the pedestrian bridge that gracefully over-arched the slate-grey Chattahoochee River. Yellowish-orange lights from the buildings and from cars were just beginning to be obvious in contrast with the darkening sky. He marveled at the glittering towers, and at the bright sun which would soon be setting behind them. It was very impressive what humans had done despite it all—the manicured society and more or less uniform thought in a place born of and therefore trying to deny chaos.

But it was disconcerting to think—as a result of this—how easily people are controlled. And it was utterly terrifying to imagine the kind of people who were almost certainly in charge.

A sculptor of minds is the most secret artist.

Everyone has a brush. They can paint anything. But there are a few people who are in control despite never being seen. They draw the lines through television or computer screens which they want to be painted in. And a nation, a world, goes about spending their lives painting someone else's picture. Anyone who is brave enough to point out the glaring blemishes in this 'painting of man' is usually executed. The default human reaction is to destroy anything contrary to their system. But the thing is, it's not *their* system to begin with. They are subscribing to the convenient, accepted, system of another, usually flawed, mind.

"All of these people with brushes in their hands refuse to acknowledge their mistakes," Sam whispered to himself, to get the words out of his head. "And entire civilizations are built based on lies so as not to think about 'it all.'"

Every year the buildings grew taller, as every year people grew more desperate. Buildings, though, can only grow so tall before they fall. The same might be true for the attainment of knowledge and a mind. *What are the first signs of a crumbling mind?*

It seemed, to Sam, that scientific thinking had the ability to drive everyone insane, end the human species, or save the human species.

For a certain type of person, the advancement of science allows for the hope of understanding and wonder amongst all people—a universal quasi-religion supported by evidence that yields results. Mitotic cellular division, electron orbits around the atoms in everyone, physics, evolution, astronomy… To understand the common constituents of oneself, and everything else, to know that the stone, the star, the tree, and the person, along with the air that we breathe, are all made of and came from the same explosion of atoms, might be the best way to find compassion for and fraternity with everything—knowing that it all will likely be united again. Everything is one.

But for a different type of person, science might be seen as the death blow for a species which cannot tolerate knowing what they are. A world of genetically engineered clones, atheists, and nuclear weapons.

Sam was not yet sure which type of person he was—though it seemed better to aspire for a moment of understanding than an 'eternity' of methodical deception.

One thing was certain: human beings must think about scientific implications, from an ethical standpoint. Scientific ability has far surpassed the qualifications of those using it. And if we are not careful, the few who can see and understand the value of molecules, genetics, pharmaceuticals, etc. could be just as dangerous and immoral as the few who could 'see' witches only a few hundred years in the past. The opportunity for an abuse of power is much the same if the majority of people are not educated. Otherwise, the next Salem Witch Trials will involve multitudes of people smoldering on the stake who do not realize it—subservient genes manipulated to serve the few again. Education must be the key to equality.

Many say that they do not think in an effort to combat insanity.

An interesting thought is that maybe humans are a 'lab mouse' of another species which is watching from afar, studying our behavior. They've been watching us from the beginning, long before we began experimenting on other species. And after watching us develop to the point where we put mice in mazes, it made them wonder, 'what if we are just an experiment too, controlled and without a purpose? Does it ever end?' And down the ladder, the scientists went insane…

Four pistil shots rang out in rapid succession from the direction that he had just come from. A number of images and situations were placed into Sam's mind. He thought of the happy family with the trotting dog, and hoped that no bullets went their way.

The little girl.

It was sad to think of the situations that people are put in through no fault of their own, that they don't know enough to fight.

One step nearer, evil world. I dare you.

He thought of universal feelings, common to every human being, maybe even every animal, which all variables combine to create—love, hate, frustration—pure emotions that everyone and even 'things' experience. But the feeling that Sam was thinking about specifically was helplessness, the most common of them all, the one that all of the others are just islands in. It's the same for the guy who dropped out of high school, a slum-steader pushing drugs on the streets, as it is for the college graduate pushing pills across the pharmacy counter. Both realize a little more every day that they are stuck in a life that they cannot really escape.

It was too sad to think about for long. And another gunshot kept him from being tempted to keep at it. It sounded very close. Sam heard someone screaming hysterically and someone laughing, which was an all too common combination.

He desultorily walked across the bridge towards the nice buildings, towards downtown. The reflective water reminded him of the desert and cliff that he had stood on. Looking at cold, dark water used to remind him of when he fell in as a child not long after Daisy fell in. He still remembered the panic, being beneath the icy water of the river, and the numbing cold, the whimpering of that poor dog, and then the look in her eyes as he grabbed onto a root and the current took her away. They told him that his heart had stopped then, too. But now he mainly thought of the time that he almost fell in. The time he almost jumped in. He imagined falling down into the water, and wondered if it would break his legs—as it was supposedly like falling on concrete after a certain elevation. His legs would snap like a couple of frozen sticks. It would be numb at first, almost no pain, just shock, and then it would hurt very, very bad. Broken bones are not nice to think about—especially if you have broken one so badly before that a new angle was formed by it. Those awful throbs… He shook away such thoughts and made it to the other side of town—the side where tourists visited. He hoped that the little girl had stayed inside by her 'gamma' and that her mother would take the time to play with her when she got home from work, that Wendy would be 'windy.'

Into the towers he walked, feeling like a stranger. The city swallowed him, and he looked through its guts for a cheap place to rest.

Nothing in the world sounded better than sleep—the great eraser.

Chapter 5

The epitome of being away from home: alone in a hotel room in a strange town. A colon sure seems like a shitty indication. Never use colons—or at least never use their half-siblings.

Sam sat on the bed and looked at the red-numbered digital clock. It was 9:48 PM. One of those awful waves had come over him where everything seemed either pointless to pursue or beyond his ability to acquire.

Every sixth girl out there his age would be glad to sort of deliver him from his awful melancholy and loneliness for a few hours. There was a possibly biased independent study to prove this. In some way, most girls were unquestionably experiencing many of the feelings that he was. But he couldn't will himself to go out in search of a friend and thought that it would probably be a monster that he would end up meeting anyways. So, he stayed on the bed looking at the walls.

The art work was banal abstract, and not particularly stimulating. The ceiling and walls shared the same khaki color and stippled texture. There was a big, flat screen TV that he'd rather not watch.

It had come to the point that he hated watching most television shows—even if doing so could be relaxing, mindless. There was very little worth watching. And the idea of billions of people spending so much of their time sitting back and watching other people—very foolish people, at that—was terribly depressing. Those who have nothing to eat and live in plastic huts—all over the world—are systematically forgotten by those who from a recliner in an air-conditioned home watch television sets which broadcast every aspect of 'celebrity' life, mainly who they are fucking or what clothes they are wearing. Inaction is the definition of most people's days, most people's minds. If people realized the change that could be had mentally, and then eventually on a global scale, if they worked out their minds like certain gym-rats do their bodies, they might turn off the television set or close the computer screen until the hijackers of the media finally provide that which stimulates rather than distracts Or so thought the guy who had long ago unplugged his television.

It didn't seem right that so much frustration could be had from looking at a turned-off flat-screen television. So, Sam closed his eyes. The image of a plastic village where starving children ran about without shoes amidst gun-bearing militants—and many other injustices which he knew of though rarely heard about through media outlets—was still in his mind, however. Though in the next room, the image in the person's mind being transferred via the same brand of TV was of a big-boobed bimbo who had her own reality TV show. She snobbily told the waiter that the food was a too cold to eat and said, seriously, "This is unacceptable."

How can anything change if people are too cowardly to think, and are constantly barraged with media trash?

He would have gone swimming, but the pool was closed after some freak accident which involved a lunatic, a bottle of scotch, and a dead pigeon—or so he had heard.

There were too many pillows on the bed, which was very soft. He was still wet from the shower that he had taken, and was wonderfully clean of that awful, grimy feeling. Grime is O.K. in the forest, but not in the city. The value of a shower increases proportionately with the length of one's hair, he'd learned. The water pressure in the shower had not been quite right, and the shampoo bottles were too small, but it had felt nice nonetheless. The only notable thing which occurred in there was that his masturbation fast continued.

Day 142, how do you do?

The streak was just another cum-pletely pointless form of entertainment.

It was very easy to just stare at the wall. There was no one around to deter it. The room was clean and tidy other than a little mess of his possessions in the corner but smelled faintly of cigarette smoke. There was a sign on the door with a cigarette and a cross through it.

Someone felt rebellious. Fresh air.

He slid open the sliding glass door, which was surprisingly hard to do. There were no chairs out there on the cement, so he brought one from inside to the narrow balcony which was enclosed by black bars. There was the constant sound of cars driving by. Occasionally he heard someone laugh or yell. There were many unheard. Most remain in that category. The parking lot was directly below, seven floors down. He thought that it would probably kill him if he jumped, but that the fall might not be long enough—a recipe for broken legs and awful questions to answer.

A frightening thought was that maybe death is not possible, like Brit had mentioned in the park, but only an illusion—an illusion just like time is and everything else that people use to comfort themselves. Die in one place, but your life just keeps on going in another. Forever chained to this world, the only power that you seem to have not even there. But this probably was not the case. It would be a good way to scare people, though. So, the option was always there—which was probably one of the most relieving thoughts of all.

Though the thought of a high enough jump was in a way comforting, he did not ever intend to do so—even if he did somehow manage to get old. It really would be a bad example which he would not set for nieces, nephews, and children especially. Having a kid is probably the best insurance policy against doing what you fear that you someday might do.

If anything, one day when he was old he thought that he might walk into the woods and keep walking into the wilderness until he couldn't walk anymore—like he believed his grandfather had done. And in that exhaustion there would be an extreme peace. He'd feel nature taking him. It wouldn't be a suicide, but rather an offering. Old men are never hungry, anyways, so it wouldn't be so bad.

Sam hoped that that was how the man who had taught him to fish had died. The dementia made it hard to believe, though.

The night sky consisted of an orange-ish haze above the city. No stars were visible. But he knew that they were there. It was very sad that so many city dwellers did not know the brilliance of a dark, star-filled night.

He hoped that they knew that the stars were there, and that they went out to see them. Because stars were the best reminder of endless possibility, and a blaring rebuttal to those who claim to know, who sneer and have an air of superiority. After dealing with the awful arrogance that some people seem to exude, one should just walk out and look at the night sky. But it was just not possible in the city, and every day, Sam knew, humanity is moving closer to a sad world cocooned from the stars. Light pollution might be the most deadly variety as far as the human soul goes.

So Sam just sat there on the chair, without stars to look at, waiting until he was tired enough to fall asleep, a little afraid that something in him would make him jump over the railing. He didn't even have so much as a book to read for comfort. Not even The Bible—which he was not against reading and had read in its entirety—had been in the bedside drawer. But the call to 'subdue' the Earth was all too evident and depressing when looking across the cut up horizon. Thinking of that book, with its restrictive pervasiveness and finality in regard to possibility, which influences even those who claim to be free of it, one of Sam's favorite quotes floated through his head.

In wildness is the preservation of the world.

There needs to be ways to distract from all of the fakeness and travesty which people are surrounded by on a daily basis. And really, if one cannot be in the wilderness, it didn't seem as though there were a simpler, more soothing companion for such reprieves than a well-written, open book. Maybe being in the presence of a crazy, bone-hiding, and loving dog. But dogs are not as simple as most people think, and usually do not like being put in a backpack. They also like to shit at the most inopportune places and times.

He decided that in the morning he would do one of the few things which almost always brought joy or at least comfort. He would find a book to read.

*

"I wonder if I should continue to stay in the cheapest hotels that I can find on this trip, or if I should sleep on the streets when I'm in the city. I mean, it might be good for me to know what it feels like to do so, and the streets are probably just as clean. Maybe shoot some heroin too, rob a gas-station."

He smiled, and wondered if she realized that with his last sentence he was joking when she blushed. Nothing is really obvious, he remembered.

"Just kidding, Mrs. Brown. I have to take showers, for my hair. So living on the streets is probably out. And drugs aren't for me—especially that awful one. I'm not here to borrow a Burroughs. Not interested in self-destruction yet."

Sam always tried to be especially colloquial with older people because he imagined that it would not be very nice to be one. This one did not seem to be very talkative, however. Sam thought that she probably thought him to be a suspicious-looking whippersnapper who was probably up to no good.

It was also amusing, to Sam, to have a usually older person look at him who was certain that they were far more intelligent than the long-haired, scruffy-looking young man before them. Especially because they were almost always wrong in so thinking.

He smiled at judging eyes.

The little old woman behind the front desk shook her head like a mother would as she finished putting the information that Sam had given for his library card into the computer. She typed very deliberately, and enjoyed the sound that the keys made when they were pressed. Her fingers hurt, though, because she had been typing for forty years.

"Well, sir, you're little adventure seems noble, but you must draw a line somewhere. Your card should be done printing in a moment."

He stood in front of the desk, looking down as he waited, and feeling a little perturbed at how cold people can become. He thought that it would be fun to stare at Mrs. Brown without saying anything. But he decided against it, on account of her age.

"Here you are," she said, holding the orange card in her yellow hand.

"Thanks. I'll be back in a moment, with some bound pieces of paper."

He turned away from her and walked through long, strangely eerie aisles of books.

Each one full of other people's heads. Scary. So many. Can't ignore.

*

"Excuse me, it's time to begin."

The man who stood in front of the class was called a professor, though was choosing to really profess his thoughts for the first time. His trepidation was obvious. He played with his short, wiry red beard with one hand and, after putting it down by his side, used his other hand to rub the bald part of his head. Forty 20 to 23-year-olds, and a 38-year-old alone in the front row, sat quietly watching him with "Principles of Accounting" books and calculators on their desks.

He moved behind the shield of his lectern and looked down.

"I need to tell you guys something," he said with an unusually shaky and emotive voice. "It has nothing to do with accounting."

This time his hand was trembling as he touched his shiny head. He was about to say something which wasn't cloaked with formality, and it was therefore terrifying to him because he was exposing himself. But it was necessary. He had to look at his notecard to start, even though he had thought about what he was going to say entirely through at least twenty times.

"From your complacency you may one day emerge..."

He had done it, with that line which he had thought much about—wondering if he could actually bring himself to say it. But he had. There was no going back now. Everyone, for the first time ever during one of his lectures, was paying attention.

"....and it will likely turn your world upside down. It will be frightening to realize other peoples' thoughts. It will be frightening when a new awful one strikes you, and you realize that others have been thinking it all the while, how different their perception has been all the while, how many possibilities there are."

He wiped the sweat from his brow.

"What I'm trying to say is that the world can be an entirely different place from one day to the next. We forget how life could end at any moment, and at how small we are, how incredibly amazing everything is. *Everything*, even this cup…"

He held up his coffee, looked at it, and shook his head as if to break himself from a trance that he didn't enjoy.

"…and it is utterly terrifying to suddenly *feel*, to suddenly be alive, to suddenly realize what you are, all on account of complacency being crushed. I mean, think about it: we are just tiny creatures who can somehow think, stranded on an island of rock, which orbits a ball of fire, which orbits whatever the center of our galaxy is—probably a black hole—which orbits God knows what."

No longer was he looking at his card. His voice became louder.

"Most of you will never experience this, never really be shaken, but at least one of you, I'm sure, will, or maybe already has. You'll realize what the phrase 'get your act together' really means, because it's all an act in the end, most people's lives. I mean, isn't it tragically appropriate that people aspire to be, and even worship, big-screen actors?"

He pet his beard for a few moments as his students looked at him in awe, a few of them with their phones out to record the event.

"Really, we are all lost. There is no question about this. And it's nice *not* to know it, but some of you will understand the facts, profoundly. And when this happens you will have to realize that you are not alone in the feeling of utter loneliness. It may not seem like it, but you will have the rare opportunity to really be free. One day you must finally admit that, yes, you are alive, somehow. And you'll have to be brave, but you must live."

He took a deep breath, closing his eyes, and then looked to be about to say something else but stopped. He shook his head as if he was satisfied with what he had said, and not feeling a need to say anymore.

He took a long drink from his cup of coffee. When he spoke again, the life from his voice was suddenly gone—back to normal.

"As I'm sure that you all know from the reading assign…"

Class eventually ended in awkward silence. There was another reading assignment. Sam thought about talking to Dr. Roberts after everyone left, but did not. He felt compelled to follow his friends out the door, and felt like a coward for it. The students immediately began talking about Dr. Roberts when they left the classroom. Down the stairs and out the door, buzzing, they walked amongst the people pouring steadily from the old buildings into the bright summer day. Sam felt a bit stunned at all that was going on around him. It just kept going and going.

The talkers did their deed.

"So what's up with Dr. Roberts?" asked Tom.

Sam and all of the others were beginning their last year of school. He was finishing up his Master's and they were all taking a victory lap—had failed to graduate as scheduled with their Bachelor's. They had been friends since freshman year. All of the guys had gone on the road trip during the summer with Sam. None of them knew how much he had changed as a result of that trip. Really, they didn't know him very well. None of them really wanted to know much about the others.

"The guy's crazy," said Brad (*the blind*) as he laughed, the sun glinting off of his short and gelled, carefully situated, pointy hair.

Mockingly, Jared—the last guy other than Sam who hadn't spoken and felt a competitive, insecure urge to change that—mockingly crooned, "From your complacency you may one day emerge…"

Everyone, besides Sam, laughed as if at the foolish babblings of an old man or child.

"Probably a schizophrenic, or something," Tom laughed.

Sam shook his head as he walked beside them.

Schizophrenia, diagnosis for anyone who admits to seeing the world differently—the tool people use to convince themselves that they are sane.

He looked around at all of the people. They were from all over the world: Asians, Africans, Europeans, who were harder to pick out—and all trying to make a go of it in the same place. Really, it had the potential to be a most beautiful setting. And sometimes it did seem like the most beautiful place on Earth.

The college campus was an amazing fusion of people with different perspectives who quietly went about their way, for the most part, being careful not to mix. They all just flowed past each other, without interacting. And, to Sam at least, the lack of interest that people had in one another was a stark symbol of what humans are becoming. It seemed like everyone was on the path to depersonalization, a world of robots where no one did anything that they were not programmed to do. Very few people seemed to want to admit that they were different, didn't celebrate it.

It seemed that given an excuse to do so, people would gladly interact. But the status quo was to remain anonymous and alone. And so obviously it did not have to be that way.

As the group walked towards their usual hangout place, Sam watched how very careful everyone was not to interact with the different—or the same. He thought that it was such a wasted opportunity. He was guilty too, and knew it, but just kept watching, and walking.

A kid who had an arm in a sling walked with headphones on and his head down, all alone, a few paces behind a guy who walked tall beside a pretty girl. Walking the other way was a girl in green capris pants with a sullen and certain look on her face. She rolled her eyes at some girls who showed as much skin as they dared—which was more than she dared.

As Sam and the group came to the corner of a long, brick building, he dreaded what he was about to see. And he saw it. Brit sat there on a bench with her legs crossed, as she always did that semester on Mondays,

Wednesdays, and Fridays from 11:22 to 11:25 AM. She stood and, walking past Sam without so much as a glance, went to stand on the opposite side of the group.

"Hello Tommy, boys."

Soon, she was laughing about something that Tom had said, grabbing his big arm with her little hand. She made a face at him—squinty eyes and a fake frown—that she used to make for Sam.

When it is realized that a gesture given to you was not exclusive, it makes you wish that you had never received it in the first place—at least in Sam's case.

Tom was a quiet, tall and strong-looking guy who liked to hunt and so wore a camouflage ball cap to prove it. He went fishing about once a year, had a shiny fishing hook on the bill of his cap. Really, he was a nice guy, and for a while had been a good friend of Sam's. He did not know what Brit had in store for him, but had an idea of a by-product of her plans—which he wanted. And that's all that it ever takes to be on the path to marriage.

Sam tried not to listen to them, and quietly took in his surroundings. They were walking behind a tall guy with grey hair in business attire who walked beside a short girl in hole-covered pants, who looked to be his daughter. They both carried Subway bags, so Sam assumed that the dad was visiting his daughter for lunch. She looked like a freshman. They stopped at a bench, where they hugged, and as Sam passed he heard the concerned father say, "Oh, and stay away from guys who like to use the word vagile."

It was kind of funny to hear.

Sam kept looking around. They walked past a handsome lad in plaid, lying on a stone bench beside a fountain. Only the bold girls snuck a look. He just lay there, as everyone passed by, looking at the buildings, wishing that they didn't follow the rules that he had learned in a high school drafting class.

There were people who had tattoos—which were in most seasons hidden—and proudly showed them off to people who looked at the tattoos judgingly, or enviously. Almost all of the lookers wore cargo shorts and name brand collared shirts. They looked like Sam's friends. Sam wondered which ones were feeling like him, and apparently Dr. Roberts, because really it was impossible to tell. It did not matter what they looked like. They could be tattooed or not, collared or not, head-phoned or not, a United States citizen or not. But almost all of them, he knew, would probably think that Dr. Roberts was crazy—which was too bad.

Tom began explaining to Brit, exaggeratingly and in a very animated way, all about the strange lecture. She seemed very interested, and shook her head as if in terror. Sam watched her, and felt bad.

Almost seems best to be considered crazy by most people. But most different people wish only to be diagnosed.

"Yeah, man. The guy is just weird," Brad echoed.

"What do you think, silent Sam?

All of them, besides Brit, who looked straight ahead, were looking at him, waiting for an answer. As he often did, Sam took a moment to think and then responded succinctly.

"I think that he died too."

Everyone, even Brit, looked oddly at Sam. Brad relieved them all by starting to talk about football after a few moments of awkward silence. They did not really want to know him, Sam remembered, and so did not even ask what he was alluding to despite the fact that he had uttered the words for the sole purpose of having someone to discuss the ordeal with. But no one was brave enough to talk to him.

None of them ever saw Dr. Roberts again.

*

Sam sat in the circle of mostly bright young students. Almost all of them looked normal with the exception of one guy, who was sitting directly across the circle from Sam. The deviant wore a tiger-print bandana and sunglasses—which was somewhat exciting. Most people did not wear bandanas in conjunction with sunglasses. And none of them wore tiger-print bandanas. Sam would become friends with him. His name was Steve.

The sign that Sam had seen earlier had read 'Candid Club, meet tonight at 7:00 PM in the basement of Earl and talk about life, *uncensored*!' That, he had convinced himself, was exactly what he needed. He had heard good things about the club, too.

As others talked, Sam thought about what he was going to say. Vaguely, he listened to Steve, who had a hawk-like nose, complain about how much he disliked people, how they were always complaining. They really ruffled his feathers.

There was a nice-looking girl—some people's eye's just made Sam think that they were nice—sitting next to Steve. She was a little overweight and had her dark hair in a ponytail. When Sam looked at her for the first time, she was looking at him. He nodded, and she looked away. They would end up being friends too. Her name was Mary.

Someone asked Steve if he was stressed, because as he spoke he was squeezing a blue stress ball in his right hand.

"Hell, yeah. I'm stressed. But no more than anyone else."

He smiled broadly—as if he had just found something.

"I've grown accustomed to carrying blue balls around since my bone, er, uh, broke."

Everyone laughed. Even Sam, and even the people who did not know what a 'boner' was or 'blue balls' were in the context often used by adolescent boys or unimaginative comedians.

Mary put her hands over her reddening face for a moment, and for some reason felt a need to clarify why her friend actually carried blue balls.

"He broke his arm. He is rehabilitating it."

She then went on to tell her own story of the day.

"I was just impeached from my position as President of the Produce club. Ironic as it may seem, it was due to allegations that I was stealing peaches. Which, I'll admit, were not unfounded. But I artichoke them all anyway."

Sam alone laughed.

Next up, there was a small black girl who stood up excitedly. Her hair was frizzy, and she wore brightly colored clothes.

"Oh boy," she said, "I'm feeling good. This must be the manic part of my manic depression…"

Sam liked her intro, and could relate. It was funny how thoughts just thought or words just learned, or anything else, have a way of resurfacing soon thereafter. They were always missed before.

But he stopped listening so closely when she started talking about her boyfriend who one day had not wanted her to give him a blow job because he was afraid that she would have a mood swing and bite it off. The club really was candid, it seemed. No one even batted the proverbial, or literal, eye.

When she had finished, a guy who looked almost exactly like an aardvark stood up and said: "On that note, I'll go. My girlfriend is from Brazil. Attractive girl and all…she's great. But you'd think that she would have a Brazilian style wax, you know, down there. But *no*. It's more like a Scandinavian nightmare!"

Several other people talked, but Sam only actually listened to a girl who he was surprised to see—a girl who he had once known. She did not try to be pretty, like so many do, but simply was—to Sam, at least. Most guys probably would not have classified her as attractive. No tight clothes, no holes in the jeans, no piercings—not even of the ears. Her short frame was often adorned in tie-dye. Her dark hair and bangs that curled down just above her green eyes, she looked a lot like a girl who would wear a yellow dress, who Sam would walk past in a Georgia supermarket.

Her name was Ellen, and she had been in the same Communications class as Sam during his sophomore year and her freshman year, fall semester. She was one of the friendliest people that he had ever known. After an in-class conversation about how to best fashion tie-dye shirts, they had begun to be friends. They even saw a variety of shows together, as well as sharing other valuable time outside of the classroom. Just walking around campus mostly. It was a nice semester for the two shy kids getting to know one another.

But then, one night, Sam had decided to go to a party, where he met Brit. She was outgoing, and seemed smart—which really she was not—and there was no mistaking what her eyes said that night, wherein the eyes of Ellen there was question. So it began fast, Sam convincing himself that Ellen wanted nothing in the way of a 'relationship.' Before long, he and Brit held hands, and all of that.

Ellen saw the two together for the first time before their final speech for the Communications class, outside of the building that it was held in. Ellen came up and said 'hi' to Sam, and they proceeded to talk about

'Civil Disobedience' by Henry David Thoreau as Brit stood aside, unable to contribute to the conversation.

When it was time for the class to start, Brit showily kissed Sam and smiled just as showily at Ellen.

For Sam, after seeing Ellen's reaction, the pallor on her face, the tremble of her lip, it was like being on a river and realizing that you cannot make it back upstream to where you started. There is no choice but to keep on going.

During the speech, Ellen did not do well, stuttering a little and forgetting what she was going to say. Sam could only watch from the crowd, feeling rather bad. She'd left without saying anything to him afterwards. And Sam hadn't seen poor Ellen since the end of that Communications class—she never wanted to hang out anymore, which, he thought then, was probably for the best because Brit would not like it.

He was ashamed of himself, looking at Ellen now.

She talked about her father dying of a heart attack—the same father who Sam remembered her telling him about adoringly, and about how she was feeling awful. She gave a few very descriptive, thoughtful metaphors. It was very sad. All of the others said nice things.

It was Sam's turn to talk. Everyone looked at him expectantly. It did not feel good to be going after Ellen, who had a better reason to feel bad, who he knew was watching him. But he went ahead, anyway.

"I think that ultimately my problem is that I'm having difficulty dealing with my own consciousness….everything is just so endless. I feel like I'm wasting my time."

He looked down, reminding himself to be honest, and to speak in terms that the club would understand. His voice half-cracked when he spoke again.

"My girlfriend just broke up with me, wants nothing to do with me now. Being suddenly ignored is an awful feeling. I can't stand to be around her, but unfortunately I have no choice. I know that she's not, but she seems so wicked. And my friends aren't real friends. I just feel so…lonely."

Ellen looked at him with sad, compassionate eyes. People said some nice things.

*

Ellen's eyes looked a little less sad as Sam sat across from them in a booth at The Diner. After the meeting, she had quietly suggested that they have dinner together—much to his surprise. He had figured that she would scurry out so as to avoid him. Sam had gladly accepted the suggestion, and felt bad that she should feel sorry for him after what he had done to her. She must still be very kind, he thought.

"I really am very sorry for your loss, not that that helps you at all," he said awkwardly as they waited for their food.

She looked down and nodded her head. He realized that he shouldn't have said that.

"It seems so long since my sophomore year. I'm surprised that you even recognized me."

"The eyes look just the same, even if the hair has grown. Weren't you supposed to have graduated by now?"

"I actually was able to graduate a semester early—because of all of the credits that I got in high school—have taken on a Master's in Creative Writing that I'm about to finish up. It just made sense to stay. I showed Dr. Sanderson my journal of poetry. She got me into grad. school for free—other than the little bit of teaching that I do."

Ellen was an English major herself. She had heard stories about Dr. Sanderson. The woman was a vivacious, sharp-nosed, short-haired woman who always wore thick-rimmed glasses. Purportedly, she was a 'cougar' who routinely slept with her male students, then wrote poems about the experience. And now Ellen believed those stories. There didn't seem to be any other way to explain how Sam had gotten into the creative writing program at Columbia University.

She blushed a little bit.

"Wow, quite the change from environmental engineering."

"Yeah, I mean, I spend all of my time reading, anyways—and realized that I couldn't retire to the office, knowing that no matter how much I wanted to do so, by the end of my life, I would probably have made no difference. I wasn't ready to join the drones."

Sam remembered that her dad had worked in an office.

She seemed very sad—which was especially incongruous with the bright colors that she wore—and Sam felt even worse about how he had made her feel three years earlier. There was not much worse than making someone feel bad specifically because of you.

"You're probably a whole new person now—I know that I am. What makes you, you?"

She thought for a while.

"Well, I still like to read, obviously, and I have a pet parrot now. Which you might say is kind of distinctive."

"Yeah, I'd say so," Sam said with a laugh. "You know that having a parrot is a life-long commitment, right?"

"I know. He'll be my friend to the end."

"Nice. Who's your favorite author, I mean, if there was a writer's words which you would want your parrot to repeat, who would it be?"

"Virginia Woolf."

He smiled, nodding his head.

"She was very good."

Pockets full of stone, went for a swim. Too bad. Too common.

"I actually have started writing short stories. For kids—mostly," she said.

"Very cool. I read too much to write anything good. Maybe someday I'll write a beautiful book about anti-materialism so that I will have enough money to buy all of the brand new things that I want."

"You hypocrite."

He did not deny the statement—even though the only thing that he actually painstakingly tried to do was to stay true to his own moral constitution.

"What can I say? Hypocrisy is the human way. And I'm human. But I'd love to read some of your stories. And that's no lie."

"You'd be the first," she said with a smile, which was nice to see again.

"I look forward to it. Have you ever read Kerouac?"

"Nope."

"He wrote a book called *On the Road* that I've been meaning to read—inspired some of my idols, apparently. Well, they used to be my idols. I don't really know anymore. And he went to school here, for a while. Ginsberg did too."

She nodded her head with interest but looked sad again.

There was an Asian girl sitting in the booth behind them, all alone. A young guy who was dressed nicely, and seemed very together, walked briskly past Sam and Ellen towards her.

"May I have the pleasure of joining you?" he said confidently.

She must have nodded, because he sat down by her and before long was talking away. He apparently did not know her.

"I wish that I was brave enough to do what that guy just did," Sam said, "sit with a cute girl who's alone. Because you just never know if the boyfriend will be joining, then he might pull out a Samurai sword. And that would just be awkward. "

Ellen smiled only slightly, and they sat silently—listening to the other two talk. The guy cut right to the chase:

"The wages of sin are death. And that's—you see—why we've all earned death."

He spoke in an urgent, almost orgiastic tone to the poor girl who responded something in broken English.

"God-dammit," Sam said quietly. "He's not brave, I take it back."

Once again Sam realized that he should not have said what he had and thought about telling her that some of his best friends, and that some of the best people that he knew, were Christians. But Ellen did not seem to mind. She knew what he meant. That was the thing about her—she had always been able to understand him.

"Sam," she said quietly, "I think that you know that the bravest person might be the one who believes that religion is the only way for people to be happy in this cruel world, and so commits to it fully. Devoting yourself to alleviating other people's pain actually seems noble—no matter the means. But death is *not* earned, like the disciple over here says. It's the only gift which we can count on from the moment that we are born."

Sam nodded, and for a while they quietly listened to talk of God. Ellen looked extremely sad, and he could not help but imagine her at her father's funeral. It was very difficult listening to talk of God for both of them.

The black table had several white grains of salt spread conspicuously across it. Sam noticed them and made a show of closely inspecting them.

"Does this particle matter particularly matter?"

She laughed a little, which made both of them feel better.

"Seriously. Questions like that. That's why I'm messed up. The Sodium atoms in salt have eleven electrons revolving around their nucleus. Not that much unlike the planets orbiting the sun. Think of it: life on each electron. I don't care if the orbits of electrons are different than the orbits of planets. The structure of life might not be universal at all levels. Ultimately, we can only magnify, extrapolate so much. There just might be Earths, inside of Earths, inside of Earths, endlessly. Like those Russian dolls."

Ellen nodded her head slowly, reverently, like some people do when a preacher is speaking of their religion.

"If the doors of perception were cleansed, everything would appear to man as it is: infinite," she said, quoting a man who had been way ahead of his time.

"Exactly. Closed off, looking through chinks in the cavern—we lock ourselves in."

Pleased at the connection that she had made, Sam put his fingernail on a single grain of salt and crushed it. And then he felt tremendously bad about it—at the notion of how everything in our Universe could probably just *stop,* that he may have stopped something beautiful.

"Did I just destroy the Sodium-Chloride galaxy, maybe even a civilization or two, or a thousand? You know, Twinkle Twinkle Little Star is a deep little song. Because to wonder what they are is to wonder what you are, too. Only recently have I really been able to understand this. I understand a lot of things now—that I didn't before. We are all just the remnants of dead stars, you know? Everyone has a little twinkle in them."

She smiled a little, though remained silent.

"If everyone realized this, they might treat everything—seemingly inanimate objects, plants, animals, strangers, friends, and family—with a little more care and delicacy. There might be hope, then."

Sam was feeling good about having someone to talk to. When he spoke of such things, people usually just gave a 'this guy is weird, stay away from him' look. And then they almost always fled at the first opportunity.

He felt as though he could speak a little more before Ellen fled.

"There are so many possibilities. You can see that I've thought a lot about this. I took an astronomy class where I saw a theoretical image of the Universe, which is apparently made up of almost an infinite amount of galaxies like our own. Basically, it seems that all of them together look just like an up close image of a brain, with the nerve connections and all. Our Universe is apparently one of those rare brains which grow all of the time—not one of the common ones which willingly close itself off. Two things that we know almost nothing about—the brain and the Universe.

Makes sense that they'd be connected. And I shouldn't say 'the' Universe. Because there are probably many."

He used his fingers to bring all of the grains of salt together on the table—and for a while watched them, lost in thought. But the stars in his mind aligned, maybe as some little creature watched them with awe, and his train of thought came back.

"I even talked to the professor about it after class one day, and he agreed that the similarity is striking. Really, look it up. Makes you feel so small, like your whole life might just be a part of a thought in something bigger."

"Wow," she said. "That makes my head hurt."

"Well, I hope that it's nothing serious in there, the hurting. Wouldn't want the end of the Ellen-Universe. Seems like a nice place."

She laughed quietly, and it ended in a lasting smile.

"So, what's your deal?"

"Actually, I've just recently had a mini mental breakdown. Surprise, surprise. Or it might have been an existential crisis, or something. I don't know. Didn't feel like being totally candid earlier. Don't tell the club, please."

She looked shocked, and a bit incredulous.

"How did it happen?"

"Well, it was a combination a lot of things. All of them had to do with worrying and ridiculous, hypothetical questions. It's not a good thing when you don't have much to do but dwell. And when it doesn't seem like anyone else is seeing what you are, you will feel like you are crazy."

"Believe me, I know."

"Do you remember my favorite quote, the one by Camus?"

She nodded slowly, sadly. The night that he had told her it was the night that she decided that she would let him kiss her if he tried. And she'd been thinking about it a lot of late.

"Something like, 'there's always an hour in a day where a person's courage is at its lowest ebb, and that alone is my most feared hour.'"

She sighed, and he replied.

"Ellen, you're one of the few people who ever really listened to me. I won't make it through my lowest hours unless something changes."

Just then the food arrived and the conversation was broken.

Not long afterwards, the Asian girl scurried away from the guy who wanted her to think like he did. When the guy initially approached, Sam imagined that she had probably thought something to the effect of, 'finally, someone in this foreign land wants to get to know me.' But this was not true. The guy just wanted her to know him.

With her gone, he sat there for a while at the booth, smiling while shaking his head, then sprung up and went out through the door, looking for other poor souls to 'enlighten.'

As Sam bit into his egg sandwich, Ellen tentatively asked, "How are you feeling now?"

"OK. What I'm going through is called metanoia, I think. A rebirth….or rebuilding of sorts. Really, it can be a beautiful thing. There's really no reason to be afraid anymore."

Sam felt very glad that he was getting a second chance with Ellen. She was an amazing person, and he now realized how rare it was to find someone who appreciated the same things, how rare it was to be understood. He felt good with her.

He took a drink of his water, and continued.

"I heard, and immediately downloaded, a song with the same name the other day. 'Metanoia.' Pretty cool. I've come to really love music during the last two years—don't know how I lived without it before. Music is one of the few man-made creations that I don't think that I could live without. You really should check out that song."

She nodded her head, chewing, and about to speak.

"I will. It's funny, my boyfriend loves music too," she said, cutting through a sausage.

Sam was too stunned to make any comment, feeling as if he had taken a punch. After a few moments she felt compelled to replace the silence.

"And anyways, what doesn't kill you makes you stronger, right?

Sam shook his head as he wiped the corners of his lips with a napkin.

"The guy who said that spent the last years of his life in an insane asylum after a mental breakdown, which didn't kill him."

*

Ah, poor Nietzsche.

Sam pulled *Twilight of the Idols* out of the dusty bookcase and flipped through the pages, deciding that it was worth another read. He walked out of one creepy aisle of heads and into another, towards a strange-looking man with a fedora on his head. The guy had someone's head-puke in his leather-gloved hand and was chuckling as he read it.

Just about as Sam passed, the guy said with a dramatic, deep voice: "A tragedy is just a comedy dressed in black. We actors don't know. Cannot understand the joke!"

For a few seconds he laughed, then suddenly stopped, and started weeping theatrically. Sam felt a bit of a relief to get out of the aisle, even though he openly claimed that weird people were his favorite kind. The guy probably had an interesting story, if anyone was brave enough to ask him about it.

As Sam walked through the last aisle, which was aimed at the front desk, he looked down at the books which were by his feet. He could not help but think of how his life was a lot like walking through a library or bookstore.

Don't very well notice much not at eye level. Wonder what I've missed, am missing? The question was constant, one the he could not escape.

He was glad to make it through the last aisle. The old woman still sat where he had left her, and when she saw him she smiled in a disappointingly insincere way. There was almost nothing worse than an insincere smile.

"Told you I wouldn't be long."

She did not remember him—though masked the all too common lapse in memory with a stern, casual look. He handed her the book and she scanned it like a pro.

"Have a nice day," she said, as if it were that easy.

He nodded and left.

Chapter 6

The house smelled like fresh paint. Newspaper was everywhere, covered in paint drips. Traditional paint brushes and rolling brushes were wrapped in plastic bags, and there were five cans of paint which had different colored drips down the sides. Most of the walls were scraped clean of wallpaper, and there was new wallpaper to put up in a few areas that would not be painted. There were rolls of new carpet heaped in the living room, and brooms in the corners. Everything was coming together nicely, almost seemed worth the debt.

They'd jumped right into working on the house when they got back from Brazil—which had been an amazing trip, although they didn't get away from the resort much. There hadn't seemed to be any good reason to. Why go to where there are snakes, bugs, and dirty people?

The kitchen table was covered with loot from the wedding. They hadn't realized that they had so many friends. But all of the things were evidence. Rob looked like a hairy lobster, sitting on a lawn-chair beside the table, which was also a gift. Erica was tanned nicely, sitting at the opposite end.

"Can you believe that he gave me this?" Rob said, holding up a book which had on the cover a young soldier who was wearing a Revolutionary War era hat. "Only Sam would give a wedding gift from Cheap Books," he said, pointing to a sticker on the back, petulantly.

"What's it called?" said Erica, who was exultantly holding a t-shirt up to her body.

"It's *My Brother Sam is Dead*, a children's book that he read when he was in grade school and always joked with me about."

"Doesn't he know that you don't read?" she said with a laugh.

"Never stopped the bastard from giving me books."

Erica shrugged her shoulders and looked through the stuff on the table for shiny things. Rob then held up a yellow sticky note that had been attached to the book, not ready to abandon the indignant feeling which he enjoyed.

"And what do you make of this?"

She took the sticky note from him and read the words aloud.

"'Enjoy. Love, Sam.'"

"*Well*, what do you make of that?"

"I don't know. Maybe he just wants you to read the book, bring back those childhood jokes."

"No, he's being a dick."

He threw the book across the room, the pages fluttering violently as they flew, until it hit the wall.

He's always trying to put me down.

The book lay on the ground, print-side down, opened for what Erica figured would be the first and last time. The cover was bent, along with the first fourteen pages to a progressively less degree. It would never be the same. The creases would always be there.

"Don't you miss Rio?" she said, enjoying her role of defusing the bomb who was now her husband.

"Yeah, it was nice there. I was ready to be getting back to work, though—by the end. You ready to go eat?"

She nodded, hungrily.

*

"And what will you be having, sir?" said the young waitress who was a little older than Sam.

She had mid-length hair that was dyed black and to Sam, at least, looked intriguing—tall, with a slender body and a narrow, pale face accented by a sharp nose. She wore a short red skirt, beneath which were dark yoga pants. To her shirt she had a nametag pinned, which said 'Mercedes.'

Cool name.

She seemed friendly, in a genuine, non-professional way. But something about her looked out of place, maybe even out of time. He couldn't decide what it was. It might have been her eyes, which were the first thing that he looked at when talking to a person. Not just the colorful iris, but whether or not they seemed open. Eyes were one of the best windows into the mind, he thought.

"Um, why don't you sit down while I think about it," he said in his own ingenuous manner that often frightened people, was corrupted by them. "Your legs must be aching by now."

"You've got that right."

She sat down across from him in the booth after only a moment's hesitation. She looked back towards the kitchen, probably to see if the manager was looking. Sam looked at her and, as he often did, forgot that people are almost never in reality as imagined. Even the slightest unknown can be morphed into what it is that a person wants to know.

"Would you suggest anything from this quaint menu?"

"Don't let it fool you. This is just another corrupt corporation in disguise. And everything here is shit," she said in a friendly, resigned voice as she put the weight of her head in her left hand.

"Ah, well in that case I'll just have diarrhea. The soup of the day, that is. Black bean, I think. And also some of the piss-lemonade."

She half-smiled, wryly, and began to write down his order on her pad. As she wrote in the pink ink, all five of the hemp bracelets that she wore below her right wrist fell down towards her elbow. He could not help but notice that there were about ten parallel cuts through the flesh of her inner arm, all about two inches long, all as straight as the razor that put them there. They were still fairly bright red, just beginning to scab over, and it looked, at least, as if they were not very deep—though it is generally hard to tell how far in a cut has really gone.

It was awful to think about, hard not to imagine the scene. He felt that it had happened shortly after looking at herself in the mirror, the blade kept in the cabinet beside the pills which she abused. The cutting had to have been cold.

Her story was suddenly different than it had been before. It wasn't blank anymore. She was suddenly real, and the imaginary version of her vanished. That old version can never return—which is a fairly good reason to refrain from getting to know someone who you admire.

After finishing writing up his order, she quickly pushed the bracelets back up, covering the cuts. Her lightish-brown eyes, which were striking in their unique hue and purity, met his for a moment and looked away. She knew that he knew.

Cutters, living on the sharp edge. Must prefer physical pain to psychological pain. A momentary replacement, and then a reminder.

"Thanks," he said, trying to think of something nice to say, something that might make her feel good.

He always tried especially hard to communicate with the super-sentient, just as he did with the old. But, in this case, he could not think of what to say.

She didn't say a word as she scooted out of the booth. Then she walked over to a young man who had just sat down in the corner, and Sam listened.

"What do you want?" she said brusquely.

The man replied politely, but Sam could not quite make the words out.

"Alright, soup or salad?"

Super salad!

Sam watched her walk back into the kitchen where a man in a suit stood with his arms crossed, and dense eyebrows frowning. Animatedly, he began to speak to the waitress.

She watched him blankly until he was done, nodded her head, and walked out of sight, further into the kitchen. A reason for the blade Sam began to understand as he watched the angry, suit-wearing man bustle around. It is very difficult to deal with people like that manager. And some people are simply too fragile to do so.

He had seen the self-inflicted marks on people's bodies more and more since he had first been exposed to them in college. Once he started looking, he started to see them quite commonly—the same as when one opens their eyes to anything. He often wondered how many had flesh covered with self-inflicted cuts beneath their clothes, or how many had psychological equivalents.

No telling what people hide.

He looked at the people in the restaurant.

An old couple sat in a booth across the room, quietly eating. A walker with tennis balls on the bottoms stood closest to the woman, and a cane was propped on the table too, but they looked to be cheery. Either, or both, could be wearing a cross necklace, could have a tattoo of a tree, or could have a swastika cut into them.

The young guy in the corner, eating a salad which had just been brought to him, had a tattoo snaking around his arm and ear buds blocking out the world as he stared at the brick wall in front of him. The fingers of his left hand took their turn rising and falling from the table, like a wave of ennui. But then again, he could have been thinking contentedly of his happy, meaningful life.

A mother, who seemed to be somewhere else, ate quietly as both of her children messily tossed food into their mouths while babbling happily. The father chewed quickly as he read a newspaper which blocked his family out. The little boy and girl thought that something was very funny. They were the only ones in the restaurant who it was possible for Sam to tell the emotions of—where they were really at. The two laughed loudly. Food fell out of their mouths. Their little feet stomped, and the excited voices were just beginning to reach the point that Sam could make them out, seemed to be talking about what powers they would have if they were super heroes.

"Quiet down!" said the mother in an angry, almost shrill voice which caused the newspapers to flinch before dropping and revealing dazed, disinterested eyes.

"But why?" the little boy and girl said in unison.

"Because I said so," she growled.

The children began to duly hide themselves, with heads down and the sounds of silverware tinking on plates audible again.

I'd be Word-man—weaving the way to world peace!

Sam considered screaming the phrase across the room towards the kids—but was sure that it would do no good. They would be whisked away and a he'd receive a dirty look. There was so little reason in the way that most parents dealt with their children—just a sharp voice and a 'because I said so.' And because of the lack of logical instruction, the child becomes a whipped individual just like their parents who cower and behave due to a loud voice, or a government, which tells them what to do through the equivalent of a sharp voice and a 'because I said so.'

Reading seemed like a good avenue for escape to Word-man. Sam opened his library book and read for a few moments, trudging through a few pages until his eyes locked onto the term 'superman' and 'will to power.' He closed the book in frustration—thinking about all of the children who were told, and believed, that they could not be heroes.

Why did I check this out? Who am I trying to impress?

Lighter reading would have been much more tolerable. Because he didn't want to read anymore, Sam had to look at the little boy, who was blankly staring just as his father did. The little girl was practicing the stupid frown which her mother had taught her.

Without any words, only brooding silence, the family got up and left.

Sam was glad to see his soup put on the marble ledge from the kitchen, followed closely by the lemonade. He watched a fly buzz over the soup and land on his bread. He felt sure that it was rubbing its little hands as if it had a sinister plan. The planning was interrupted when the waitress frightened the fly terribly, thwarting its deposition of future maggots, and began walking towards Sam with the food and drink.

She placed the soup in front of him, the tip of her painted black thumbnail in it—which made him think that her rule of thumb might be different that most people's—and then placed the bread and lemonade before him too. He noticed a pack of cigarettes in her waist pouch—which made her story clearer yet. It seemed that she must take comfort in the thought, whether it was true or not, that she was causing her life to expire more quickly than it otherwise would. Just another person content with destroying themselves.

Funny—the fuck-ups that I'm drawn to. The smart, nice girls that I should get with are too much like me.

"Enjoy," she said in the same perfunctory tone that she used with everyone else, even though she felt different about Sam. The voice, too, was a shield.

Would mess the kid up.

"Thank you," said Sam, still drawing a blank.

She walked away, fleeing into the back of the kitchen.

He began to shovel the soup into his head. The maggot-larvae bread tasted very good dipped into the shit-soup. The taste of food, the act of eating, only momentarily stopped his thoughts.

"'Emo.' Those who openly grapple with what most hide or have been hidden from. And are laughed at for it."

He was done with his food in six minutes. The girl came back with his bill and took away his bowl and cup like an owl that had been eying a mouse from the shadows. As she bent down, the white ear-buds from her iPod dangled and were dragged across the table. He heard an abrasive sound coupled with screaming coming from the ear-buds, and then she was gone. He did, though, endeavor to catch a moment's glimpse of her light brown eyes looking at his darker ones. They reminded him of a pair of eyes that he had misjudged in the past.

Looking into the kind eyes of the thief, the fool naively said, 'will you watch my things? I'll be right back.'

There had been a cute girl sitting alone in a café near campus. Sam had seen her sitting alone many times and had decided that he would join her the next time that he saw her. When he did see her again was not long after he'd watched the disciple try to enlighten the Asian girl.

Somehow, he raised the courage to say, "do you mind if I join you? I'm in the business of meeting new people."

She'd said: "Um. Ok."

Her eyes were very striking, very much like the waitress's—weren't timid.

After a few minutes of nice conversation, Sam asked, "If an alien came up to you and asked, 'what are you?' and 'why are you here?' what would you say?"

He thought that this would be a good way to really feel someone out.

"I'd say that I'm one of the cancerous cells destroying the body called Earth. That I'm here to get my kicks and to not be fooled, to take advantage of fools. And then I'd bash the alien on the head, charge people fifty dollars a minute for a look at the space freak."

She had smiled sweetly, and said: "You're not an alien, are you?"

For some reason, Sam felt very happy to have met her during the following moments of their conversation. Her slight abrasiveness was endearing. She was one of the fuck-ups that he had been drawn to. The girl was witty—and actually a quicker thinker than Sam. Her eyes were kind, mischievous.

They talked so long that he had to use the restroom and left his things with her. As he washed his hands, looking at himself in the mirror, he felt good, proud of himself.

When he returned to where they had been sitting, his backpack and computer were gone, along with the girl who had told him that she takes advantage of fools. For a while he thought that it was a joke. But after fifteen minutes of waiting for her, he realized that it was not. He paid both of their bills, and left alone.

It was a disappointment—to say the least. But he didn't let that first failure plague his mind with fear of failure in the future. The 'random sits'- even though they weren't really random- would continue. They could only get better from where they had started.

The lesson was valuable: do not be fooled by seemingly kind eyes.

With another meal to pay for, he placed ten dollars on top of the bill, stood up, and went to the other side of the booth to put away the book and put on his pack. He then began walking towards the door, but stopped just as he was about to it and went back to the booth where his money lay. He took his partially filled notebook and ripped out a page. It was awful to think of her cutting herself again. He wrote something which he thought might help.

'You aren't the only one who feels the way that you do. Remember: every moment is a gift—even the difficult ones. Most people who think have a hard time. But after a certain amount of thinking, everything can become beautiful, and tyrants lose all power. There's no reason to let another fool get you down. We are all so small. Try to treat life as the amazing mystery that it is—isn't it incredible that with all of the mystery which surrounds us that people can be bored, sullen?

That manager-man is scared. He covers it up with meanness. He talks fast because he thinks slow, he is quick to jab because he has been beaten into a role which deep down he despises. If he is going to feel bad, he wants you to as well. That man is small. That man is afraid. We are all the prior. But we do not have to be the latter. All that it takes is to realize this and you can be happy almost anywhere.

And as for the cigarettes, whatever gets you through, I guess, but remember: you're just helping 'another corrupt corporation' by smoking. You should not help the world in the destruction of yourself. It needs none.

Be a good human being. And pass on the message when you get the chance. It really means something.

S.S.'

Content with himself, Sam put away his journal and walked out of the door, putting on his sunglasses.

The highlight of some days, he'd found, is only something like a meal, a commonplace occurrence that happens every day. Always, though, learning is possible if one is willing, and helping someone else is always just as possible. You just have to make it happen.

Through the window, as he walked past, he noticed her coming out of the shadows again, swooping towards her tip(s).

*

Rob and Erica walked into the steak-house, holding hands.

The floor was checkered—green and white—and there were cushioned seats, which spun, beside a bar. There was a colorful jukebox at which stood a small, young woman with all of her dark hair pushed to one side where it was hair-sprayed to stay. She clinked a quarter into the machine, and then rummaged through her bag in an effort to find the other one needed for a song to be played. The back of the restaurant was open, so you could see the hairy Armenian chef in the back wearing a hair net over his balding head—space which he refused to surrender until the bitter end. He was tossing sizzling meat onto a large stove. The place was about half-full, mostly with old people.

A blonde, middle-aged woman with a half-way wrinkled face greeted them at a little sign which had halted them, and led them quickly to a booth by a dirty window. She placed yellow, finger-printed menus in front of them, and after a little deliberation they both ordered steaks—one medium-rare and one well-done.

They sat across from each other, still holding paint-dotted hands. Two glasses of water were placed on the table, but they chose to put their straws in the same one.

Both of them were cognizant of and enjoyed the way that the older couples looked at them.

A white, middle-aged man wearing a tank top and tanned, hairy arms cleaned the windows immediately outside. He wore a blue bandana to keep the sweat out of his eyes, which looked in at Rob and Erica. From outside, in the humid air, he saw her, in her nice clothes, laughing and taking quick looks at him. All that he could do was hurriedly run the soap side of the cleaner over the glass and then flip it to the seal-tight, drying side and wipe up the dripping suds. He did this quickly, missing a few spots that Erica did not miss pointing out to Rob, and felt better when he got to the next window outside of an empty booth.

A song played in the restaurant.

"Dammit," Rob said, "she found the quarter."

Both Sam and Erica heard the tune, but did not, and never had, notice the desperate voice of the singer who said, 'You never turned around to see the frowns on the jugglers and the clowns when they all did… tricks for you.'

Erica took a quick glance behind Rob, through the window, and looked at the window-cleaner.

"I think that he's still looking at me," she said with a sick laugh.

He wasn't, and was actually trying very hard not to.

Rob smiled.

"Disgusting creature. That age, cleaning windows for a living. They should shoot people like that."

Their waitress arrived with ovular, flowery plates of meat for them to eat.

With a smile, she said, "Here you are, hons'" as she placed the plates on the table. "Let me know if there's anything that I can do for ya'."

She walked away towards the kitchen. Erica cut a piece of her steak and put it into her mouth. After masticating like a master, she spoke.

"Such a happy woman. I hope that I can be like her when I'm that old."

She nodded her head at their waitress who cried for no less than thirty minutes before finally falling asleep each night.

Rob swished blood around in his mouth, nodding.

"She certainly is cheerful. When you get a chance, look at the guy behind you...not now, I just looked."

Erica, after a few more bites, turned and looked at a young person who was wearing skinny jeans and a plaid shirt, a ring in his nose, and long hair. The girl with hair pushed all to one side sat across from him.

"Don't let me ever become like that guy," Rob said with a shudder.

He was reading a book on top of it all.

Erica laughed again, and when she composed herself spoke.

"And don't let my head ever be like hers."

Chapter 7

The music was slowly rising. It was wavy, psychedelic, like a spark from a fire twirling freely through the black night. No one knew where it would go. Not even the drummer or the electric guitarist, who were waiting for the guy who had responded to their want ad to start singing again. The first of their two songs had been delivered perfectly, and the crowd was still buzzing from it.

The guitarist was a wild-haired communications major with a black "Cream" shirt on. The drummer was a cute Indian girl with half-green and half-jet black hair. She had in earnest uncovered herself from the veil that her parents thought she wore when she got to the States. The guitarist desperately wanted to impress her. But, ever since she had met him—four weeks prior—the girl thought only of Sam, 'the poet.'

They were waiting for Sam to release what seemed to be building, and played their instruments accordingly as he collected his thoughts and courage. They were only scheduled to play two songs before the next band started. Sam had refused to sing the second song that they had planned on—the one that he had matter-of-factly said, 'had no hope of causing a revolution.' The guitarist had written the song that would not be sung. It was about the drummer, and she pretended not to know it. So, they were beginning the only other song that they had—Sam's song. One looked at him with admiration, the other with blooming hate.

The crowd was mostly silent. They were surprisingly well hypnotized, in anticipation. And on the stage the front-man stood, looking down with his sweat-wetted hair over his eyes. His face shined under the lights that were directed on the stage. He wore his favorite dark jeans which nicely fit his sleek body. His right foot slowly rose and fell with the beats of the drum. The microphone was in his right hand, at his side.

He felt his heart beating quite fast, and was surprised at how nervous he was, all due to thinking about doing something that was not expected of him. The first song had just been pop, feel-good, essentially screwing music. Almost anyone can do that. It's what people are taught from the moment that they are born. Duly, the crowd had really seemed to like it. But he had written the second song, came up with the concept. It would either be a smashing success or complete failure. One must not let a complete failure smash them, he knew. So he would give it everything that he had.

Sam was not used to being at the center of attention, having grown accustomed to the powerless edge. The band had done a few small performances, and had earned a good reputation, but had never played in front of more than twenty people. Slowly, he looked up, wondering if Brit and her brand new boyfriend Tom were out there, even though he had not told her or any of the others about the show. He knew that Ellen sometimes went to the Friday night shows with her boyfriend who 'loved' music, but quickly forgot about her—because he had to. He could not be self-conscious, had never before done anything like he was about to do.

He saw a hill spotted mostly with drunken college students who had mercilessly booed the last band off stage, as if they were not even worth the three-dollar admission.

If Dr. Roberts could do it, so can I.

He raised a hand and the music dropped to a very soft, unordered sound.

"This next one's my very own retarded brainchild. Seems normal for a while, then it bites you. But I love it just the same. I hope that you will too."

Sam blew gently into the microphone which made an eerie sound in the near silence. He had all of their attention and tried to take them. The guitar started into quiet riffs, and the beats of the drum were slow.

He whispered/sang clearly: "We're almost there, we're almost there... pack as light as you can, there's no telling what we'll encounter, if we'll have to run."

Sam had been excited when those words had popped into his head, and had immediately written them down a few days before, but was not sure why. They felt right. But in that moment there on the stage he felt that he needed to say more, so he just said what came to mind in addition to what he had memorized.

"There's a temple out there somewhere,

or at least one that we can build.

Stone by stone.

It won't matter that we're in a senseless desert.

We'll feel at home."

His voice had assumed a mesmerizing, louder quality as if he were waking up. His heart wasn't beating so fast anymore.

"We'll be humble and beautiful creatures there.

No one will pretend to know anything.

Self-righteousness dismissed.

There'll be no fear, no awful inhibitions.

No repression, no depression.

No one alone.

We'll finally be at home".

For a while, he just stood there on the stage without any words, nodding his head as a thought came. He spoke again to the audience, who were listening to the near-magic that is a human voice coupled with music.

"But we gotta' get there first.

And it all starts with you. Yeah, *you*.

Just say to the prim man with the awful grin,

the guy who seems to have so much wealth,

who tells you to sit down, be an adult,

'why should I be afraid of *you*,

 when it's so obvious that you are afraid of yourself?'"

He turned around and nodded at his band-mates, and the flaming sparks began to go every which way, faster and faster. The adrenaline-filled fingers caressed the strings and beat on the drums. They weren't very good musicians, but the three of them were prepared to set the night on fire. Sam took a deep breath and at the appropriate moment released urgently, but in a controlled, smooth and slow voice which had careful pronunciation.

"It's all a strange fusion of clarity and delusion here.

Where one stops and the other starts, nobody knows.

Can you see that our beautiful rose is sick?

Do you know that *we* are the worms?

Things could be much better.

But we worms have no eyes,

happily blind, wasting our precious time."

A few red solo cups began to pelt the little stage. Many of them did not like to be told what they already knew. Others were simply infuriated at such outrageous effrontery—*a worm*? About a quarter of them had absolutely no idea what he was talking about. A small percentage of people, though, were truly enthralled by the words. The music was still rising and seemed about ready to explode. But suddenly, as rehearsed, it dropped again to a delicate level, so Sam could speak and have the crowd's full attention.

Gently, he spoke in a mocking tone that had an almost seductive clarity: "I *want* to do this, it sounds so nice, but I can't, because…"

The instruments stopped. There were two seconds of complete silence. Then Sam screamed the best that he could.

"Stop!"

He saw many of them jump, startled, in the crowd—which pleased him. The music started again like a heart that tries frantically to beat after being stopped. He spoke in a strong, loud voice.

"Every reason is a lie that you contrive."

As rehearsed, the music quieted again. And Sam spoke urgently.

"Do you know what the dancing flame said to the wet match?

That flame said to the forever unlit, 'you've only yourself to blame.'

And people, I want you to know that it's going to rain.

The time is now,

Let's burn it down!"

The music exploded into controlled, nice-sounding chaos. Sam threw the microphone into the crowd, and closed his eyes, looking up at the stars. It was a spectacle. Even the person who got hit on the chin with the microphone didn't seem to mind. Everyone was looking at Sam, whose hair went down to its shoulders as he looked up to the heavens. The moment could easily have been made into a statue, he thought.

The guitarist did his best Jimi Hendrix impression—though everyone pales in comparison—and briefly considered smashing his guitar on the stage. But he remembered that he was a college student with no money and only a guitar for comfort. Resignedly, he continued the smooth riff as Sam walked off of the stage, down the steps and into the night. The song ended in sputtering, heart-like drum solo.

The people were chanting, and in an amazing frenzy. There was the sound of glass shattering. Kids were running all over the place. They were lit.

"You're awesome. Here, man, take a hit," said an awful-looking student who was pale and thin with semi-long, straight hair.

"No thanks man, I like where I'm at," Sam said as he walked through and away from the teeming crowd.

The girl with green hair abandoned her drums and ran after Sam. The poor guitarist could only watch as people began rushing the stage.

Sam felt alive for the first time in a long time as he walked across the dark lawn. It was much better than sitting on the couch. He had not given the charity organizers the 'good, Christian' fun for the students that they had expected, been promised. There would be Hell to pay, but it was worth it.

"Sam!" he heard from behind him just as he was about to cross the deserted, yellow-lighted street.

He looked back and smiled, seeing the soft features of the cute drummer.

"Brilliant," she said, walking close beside him, "just brilliant."

He looked down at her and she smiled. Her eyes were different than he'd seen them before. The look was nice—there is something incredibly alleviating and almost sacred in another pair of eyes and a true smile. He put his arm around her, and she put hers around him. He looked down to her. She was tall enough to be at his chest. And she seemed to be trying to get on her tip-toes, to get closer. It was chilly out, but she was very warm beneath the very bright stars. So they got as close and warm as they could.

As soon as she could, the girl made sure that Sam felt like a rock-star. The night was truly amazing.

Bluebirds flew through the night.

*

It was still early enough for the temperature to be pleasant. Sam had checked out of the hotel very early in the morning—two nights had been more than enough. The man at the front desk had delivered a wake-up call at 6:00 AM. When Sam groggily picked up the receiver, a gruff voice had said 'rise and shine, sleepyhead' as requested. It was not nearly as nice as when his mother had used to say it, but it reminded him of when she had—which was nice to think of during those waking moments. After the continental, 'free' breakfast that he had more than paid for with the price of his room, Sam decided to walk out of the city, towards some green—a park, presumably—which he'd seen on a map by a trolley line, which itself went nowhere near the green. All that he had to do was follow a single road. Getting lost would be very hard to do.

It was nice to walk the streets before most people were out and about. Everything seemed so much more fresh and calm in the morning. One could almost forget about everyone else.

The most interesting part of the walk was seeing a little white car, with a Velvet Underground banana on the bumper, parked in a two hour zone. Its back tires were covered in white splashes of chalk, at least twenty pairs—the first of the pair marking the beginning of two hours, the second the end. There was also a brand new ticket beneath the windshield wiper. Parking violations seemed to be the driver's badge of recklessness. Sam did not wait around to see who drove the car, but thought that it might be interesting to see what they looked like. He imagined the driver to be a five foot five Rastafarian man, who always carried around an oboe, and enjoyed listening to the VU. This could not have been further from the truth—but that did not matter. The truth is rarely in play, and rarely matters.

After that, it was just walking—which was nice.

The green on the map turned out to be a nice little patch of forest, despite people who had left soda cans and wrappers beside the trail. And once he got into it he could almost forget that he was still surrounded by city. Almost.

He sat on a green bench with a backrest that had an odd, uncomfortable angle. There was no one else around. Habitually, he reached his hand in his pocket for his phone to check what time it was. But the phone wasn't there, he remembered. There were only five quarters and a dime. It was nice not knowing what time it was—especially so because he saw no reason to believe in 'time.'

'It's nice to be a way from time for a while.' If that's not ironic, I don't know what is.

It was also nice, in absence of the phone, to not know who had no desire to contact him. It was, however, not very nice to be without music.

He was still getting used to not having the crutch that had almost grown into his side during the lonely years.

Music, my anti-depressant.

But, he had convinced himself, it was necessary to be without it for a while, because he was using other people's pain to distract him from his own. And anything avoided, but there, owns a person. So, Sam went directly into 'there.'

He sat up as straight as his curved back allowed and closed his eyes, turning them towards the 'third eye' position between his eye-brows. He took ten deep breaths.

We're all in this together. This is your journey. Just as it is that singin' Robin's journey, just as it is that playful fox's journey, just as it is that crawlin' worm's journey, just as…

It always began the same, but could end up anywhere.

The breaths went in and out, in and out, and he listened. They merged with the gentle sound of water going over the rocks and the sound of a slightly less gentle wind in the leaves. His breaths became soft and far apart, and everything kind of went away. He was with just himself—aware of what he was, where he was. His mind was clear and memories were like a room of curtains where he could go from one to the next with just the wave of a hand. He used them to decide where he would go and where he would not go.

I am alive. And know it.

Like something free and unaffected by gravity, he let his mind go all of the way out into black, starry space, further and further away from the world. It felt so wonderful out there, free from all old perspectives. And he just kept going and going, knowing that there was no end. The Earth looked so small and insignificant in his head—like a speck of dust in a sunny window. This used to terrify him, when the vision came involuntarily, though it did not anymore. He actually cherished the knowledge. There was a certain soothing feeling in knowing that something, maybe even terrifying, has always been but simply remained unnoticed.

That dark, lonely abyss has always been there. It did not kill you before and probably will not kill you now. Just try not to stare.

'To know what's out there and still walk tall—difference between the brave and the ignorant.' It is always exciting to discover a mantra from within. He knew that he would remember it forever, and probably relay it.

After a certain point, he came back to Earth—the little speck which we must call home, that we should realize is just a speck. He went to a warm garden in a far off place, dotted with smooth ponds and full of so many colors and aromas. There was the sound of gentle bees buzzing and water slowly flowing, with colorful fish rippling the surface. He saw a woman sitting beside him, her warmth on his shoulder. She looked up at him and smiled, one that was pure and didn't want anything to change.

"Sam, I'll sleep 'on your wings'—and you'll sleep on mine."

He then saw a young boy with big, dark eyes and a soft little hand holding his own. The kid took it all in, and was not scared of most of the little things that Sam had been taught to be afraid of. He knew that there was no reason to be, and just looked at it all, imagination unharnessed. And that image in an exotic garden with a woman who he had yet to meet, and Clay that was yet to be in his hand, was the one that Sam chose to move towards during this day.

He slowly opened his eyes and looked at the little stream that ran through the small, forested park on the edge of the city where people left soda cans and other trash. It was always surprising how much time had passed after such a venture in his mind. Thinking was more effective after such exercises, and it was always easier to figure out past situations— calmly and rationally. Before long, his mind went back to college.

Dangerous, stimulating place to realize that you're alive.

"Do you know that inciting a riot is a criminal offense?" a reporter for the school newspaper had asked the day after the concert with an edgy tone which suggested that she took her work very, very seriously.

"Yeah, but even if I wanted to do so, the kids just didn't have enough heart, which I guess is the definition of being an adult. It's what college, life does to people. People forget who, what they are. Some never know."

The reporter had had a field day with Sam and his interesting quotes, embellishing whenever possible the 'epic-ness' of the band's performance and of his intriguing, ambiguous nature.

"What is your philosophy behind the lyrics that you write? Is there a reason that they are mysterious/cryptic?"

"In general, all that it takes is to say something that doesn't make total sense to a person and they will think that you're deep, or an idiot, or both. To be both of these things is to please everyone."

With a surprised smile, presumably in regard to his unexpected cogency, she'd then said: "Tell me something about your mind."

"Well, I set my mind free one day and have been searching for it ever since. And from what I can tell, it seems as if most minds like mine get blown out of their heads before they produce anything. I guess the jury is still out on me."

He even made her form questions productive.

"Do you consider yourself a rebel?"

"Not really. Just an honest human being. To do anything but rebel is to accept lies. But if you rebel too much—if you are too 'free'—than you won't be able to relate with anyone. Sometimes being free is just not worth the pain. It all comes down to where your ethics lie, I guess.

He spoke as if he were bored and just saying something that everyone knew. She loved it, and finished the article with the incendiary quote: "Listen—we have an amazing opportunity here in the college setting. Like we'll never have again. So much young energy is here. But it's channeled through insanely inane avenues such as basketball games, where the pulsating excitement is ashamedly amazing, through the effort of getting into fraternities or sororities, through trying to look a certain way, and through things like drunken parties. Yeah, it can be very fun. And I love it as much as the next person. But eventually you'll have to ask yourself, 'what is it that I am celebrating?' Yeah, we should all celebrate life—though to be blinded by the celebration is foolish. Because, to me, it seems like an old, evil master is running the young pups until they are too old and tired to break the chain."

No one really listened. And I just seemed like a madman. Poor Jim.

He thought of the rock star from the 60's, Morrison, who wanted to break every rule to prove that they had no power. It seemed that men or women who openly renounce God or authority so completely often times come to be seen as something that resembles God or authority by their followers. And, eventually, they can stand it no more.

That crackling sound that a young person brazenly generates on the thin ice, which they knowingly walk upon, is intoxicating to those watching from the shore—especially when the ice suddenly gives way. It might be the key to being remembered.

Sam, though, knew how it felt to fall through the ice. Somehow he had survived. He did not plan on falling through again anytime soon. To live to be remembered puts too much faith upon a forgetful species.

The reporter had made a point of explaining in the article how Sam had acted the way that he did without being intoxicated, how it was almost noble. It seemed obvious by the way that she wrote that she had attended the concert and was one of the many people who are secretly, very much so, discontent with the way that things are, an admirer of those who try to do something about it. His picture—a very dashing one, actually—was printed on the third page of the paper, along with a column and a half article about him and the show.

He had suddenly become a minor celebrity on campus. Most people still did not recognize him after the article was ran—but many did. They often looked at him as if he were a face they knew, whispering if they had someone to whisper to. And others just came right out and said 'hey,' followed by something about the show. Even more girls looked at him steadily, whereas before they might not have given him a second look.

"Unchain my pup," an attractive girl had almost commanded on the sidewalk. He'd kept walking, in a daze, until she was gone and he realized that he had missed what might have been an interesting experience. And that was the worst realization.

His roommate, Al, had given him a funny look the day after the article was printed, but that was all.

Secretive Sam.

The drummer and guitarist had gotten a sentence to share between them in the article. Sam felt a little bad about their lack of recognition.

The band had never done another show after the big concert. The guitarist saw to that, in Sam's opinion. The drummer had suddenly stopped talking to him almost immediately after the night of the concert. She pretended that what had happened never had, and was suddenly another person—one who avoided Sam at all costs. Really, it was very disappointing. Sam insisted that they all get together in the guitarist's garage for a rehearsal, jam-session two days after the concert. They did, but neither the guitarist or drummer really spoke to him. The drummer would not look at him. And the guitarist could hardly hold back his smile. None of it made any sense, but that's how it goes. It was just too bad.

The loss of the band meant less to Sam than the loss of a friend—especially so considering that he could not understand why the friend was lost. He and the drummer had had some good conversations—which is rare.

There were particular Dylan lyrics which comforted him in this regard, back when he still was allowing himself to listen to music. He had listened to the song so often that the words easily came to his mind. And there in the park for no one to listen to, the ex-rock star sang softly.

'Though we kissed through the wild blazing nighttime,

she said she would never forget,

but now morning is clear,

 it's like I ain't here

she acts like we never met...'

Sam loved 1960s Bob Dylan as much as anything. Because he had had something to say, said it with a poet's voice, was listened to, and survived. To do all four is a very rare achievement.

All that Sam had really wanted with the drummer was someone to talk to who had a different perspective than him. Not a different perspective in that she was a lot shorter than him, but because she was not like those he had known before—being from the other side of the world and all. Her green hair too had made him think that she might be interesting, made him think that she might not be afraid. But hair lies as much as any group of words or anything else does. It ended badly, between she and him, and he thought that the guitarist had something to do with it. In the absence of the cool, honest night there are often such problems, he had decided. So that was the end of that. Rehearsals had stopped. And he didn't see either of them again besides for awkward encounters on the sidewalk.

There always seemed to be an undesired guitarist who wanted to keep him away from a desired drummer, in one form or another. Then again, he knew, there always seemed to be a need to blame someone for what could not be understood. He tried to do the hardest thing to do when dealing with people—think from another perspective. The guitarist may have had nothing to do with the drummer's sudden disinterest in and avoidance of him. There may have been something deeper in her psyche, her Universe, which he could simply not understand because he had only been granted superficial admittance. Regardless, one can never fully know another.

The whole situation reminded him too much of Brit, the subtle but pointed avoidance which stemmed from changes that neither fully understood. There was no use in begging for a relationship with an uninterested person.

Gotta' find a girl who is willing to be free with me. Wasn't either of them. Feel alone now, in every way. Worth it?

And yet, there was something appealing about being alone. To interact with someone who you really like on a regular basis is a dangerous thing. You will become more and more tied to them. And with each knot, possibilities lessen.

To not have a 'relationship' to focus on preserving may be lonely. But it allows a person to have the time to think and realize what they are, whereas otherwise all effort and brain energy may go to trying to impress some stupid girl. And so a person might be married before they've realized that the job and life they've chosen, revolving around the effort to support their wife and children, is completely unsuited for them. All life leaves them until the day that they die.

Sam found himself with no one to answer to, and no safety net. There were no friends to lean on, to be made to think the same as without knowing it. He no longer had to think in terms of pleasing someone else. The warm assurance of being told what to do was gone. And there was a new, more profound type of satisfaction as well as fear. It was all on him, every success or failure.

The feeling that he had was just the opposite of how it used to be. He thought of when he was a child. He thought of home.

There had been warmth then, and a comfort in being small. Less was known, so there was less doubt. It was easy to have faith. There was a wonderful family. There was always someone to fight with. Pets were still alive, friends were still real, and if Daddy was around and awake there was no fear of 'bad guys' when sleeping. The point had yet to be reached where dying didn't sound so bad. There was only opportunity and no regret. There was untarnished emotion. The world and human feelings weren't evil yet. There was warmth like being under the covers on a cold day when a storm was going through, when Daisy wanted someone to comfort her. Everything—the walls, the creaks, the smells—was familiar. Mommy could do anything.

It was a wonderful illusion—which is all that anyone can ask for.

There was not the feeling of being used every step of the way. There was not the, 'wow, this is what I'm going to be,' disappointment. There was not the feeling of wasting time. There was no reason to ask, 'why the fuck can I think, how does that voice even work, how does time exist—does it exist at all, what *am* I….?" There was not the very real possibility of insanity.

To dwell on what cannot be understood, Sam had found, is Hell.

But wait, even as a child there was reason to ask.

Sam suddenly remembered as a child being in the kitchen of his childhood home, looking down at the stone-tiled floor. It was as if a wave of wonder had suddenly, out of nowhere, enveloped him. This had happened not long after he fell into the river—maybe even only a day or two afterward. In this memory, he was still cold. He remembered looking at his hands, moving them, and thinking about each movement, thinking about how amazing his existence was. Slowly, he had looked from left to right as his mother prepared his food. He was somewhere else, somewhere sacred. In an almost trance-like state he had walked into the living-room, holding his little plate of chicken nuggets, as if he were seeing the world for the first time. The memory there ended. But, of course, uncommon pain and suffering had followed for the little seer.

Deep for a 9-year-old.

Maybe, he thought, that day in the kitchen there had been what he was feeling on the park bench, a feeling that he had finally almost come to terms. The feeling on that day in the kitchen had been gradually covered by a constant stream of well-intentioned lies, and a doping into tranquility, a comforting shield which had recently been stripped.

It's amazing how much we are taught not to think about—how much our mind blocks.

A secretly cynical, sadistic teacher with a red pen and a sharp voice can be quite convincing to a child who is taught to cry. And the child, if weak, will believe that everything that they think is wrong. The stronger child will rebel, get crushed, and go nowhere because of their early strength. A steady balance of strength and weakness is necessary, Sam thought, to create a productive person. A perfect balance is necessary to create the rarest type of powerful person, a leader for good. And this person must realize, again, how wonderful and worth fighting for the youthful world is that they were stolen from. Sometimes, all parts of a formula finally happen and no one knows what the answer will be.

It seemed obvious that if Jesus ever returned he would come bearing God's pistol. When everyone aimed deep inside of their minds and pulled that heavy trigger, division would be gone, and God would smile in death. And the people of the world would live as one.

Sam felt overwhelmed that he knew these things, or at least believed them, and that that leader could be him. It would be so very lonely, and probably deadly.

There was the sound of feet, which in a way shifted the gears of Sam's consciousness. A squirrel was making its way directly toward him, through the green undergrowth. It did not see him. He watched, with a feeling of unexpected joy, the gray, energy-filled thing which seemed to vibrate towards him. It approached to within about three feet, and then stopped on the trail. There it suddenly became aware of him and, shifting gears in a way, made a sudden-squeak noise, then leapt four feet into the air, grasping a low, overhanging branch.

After a short, mad dash, it rested on a limb above Sam, so close that he could hear its light purring, and could see its surprisingly large testicles. He watched it there for a while, tail jumping and settling every few moments. Then, something happened in its head, which prompted the squirrel to bolt. Sam heard it ripping the loose bark from the tree as it scurried up. He watched. It climbed without hesitation, and began chasing what Sam assumed was a female, who had been found, to the top. They spiraled around the tree, leaping from branch to branch in a way that put any human acrobat to shame. The two looked to be having a lot of fun. Sam felt envious. The things seemed so free.

No wonder bitter old men like to shoot them down.

He leaned awkwardly back on the green, wire bench and wondered if the manufacturer purposely made it as uncomfortable as possible. They might have a partnership with a chiropractic clinic.

Sam reached into his bag, sighing as he opened his philosophy book full of little pieces of paper that marked interesting quotes. He began reading on a random page. Subconsciously, he thought while he read, there must be within him a desire for self-punishment. 'Ignorance is bliss' ran through his head, bouncing off the sides again and again.

He had come to realize that words/phrases mean nothing until they are reinforced with experience. Before, they are a vague abstraction. After some experience, they are full of unique, nostalgic meaning. There's no going back.

In the end, it seemed that ignorance is indeed bliss—but that in many cases it's a badge of cowardice. And if he was going to live, he was not going to be a coward.

He resolved to stare the world in the face until it killed him.

As he read, the day became less beautiful as thoughts led to thoughts, to awful thoughts. That old, self-righteous anger at what the world was compared to what it could be was within him. He was tired of it.

Philosophy is madness. Minds can only be expanded so much before they fall apart.

The book went through the air much more gently than when Rob had thrown his gift from Sam against the wall. The affect was similar but much more gratifying. It had been extemporaneous. And it just had to happen. He didn't even think of the fee from the library. All of the bookmarks fell out as the book arched towards the stream, and looked like the fiery trail that follows the explosion of a firework. The book splashed into the stream and the bookmarks fluttered beautifully into it too, one after the other. There had to have been fifty little pieces of paper falling.

The current took everything out of sight.

Sam got up and put on his backpack, feeling much better. He walked down the trail ready for the day, thinking of Clay. The squirrels chattered a hearty applause.

Chapter 8

A man and woman walked through the aisles of a car dealership parking lot. The woman was tall and thin with reddish hair. She had a leather, black purse on her hip and wore blue jeans and a shirt with Winnie the Pooh on it—just the opposite of the clothes that she had to wear for work. The man was a little taller with thick, wavy hair that was a third grey, mostly on the sides, and the rest dark brown. He wore dress pants and shiny, black shoes along with a grey, collared shirt—just the same as he wore at work. They were both forty-six and relatively attractive, despite the years.

It was Saturday. The sun was bright and the cars were shiny. The asphalt was hot and on it tread—prowled—an overweight man in slacks and a white, collared shirt. He spied two people who wanted to exchange some of their time-tokens for something that would seem to justify them. He walked as fast as he could without looking to be a predator in the eyes of his prey.

"How can I help you folks today?"

"Could you suggest anything economical?" asked Sam's father almost just as he decided for sure that they would be leaving the dealership in a brand new Camaro.

He was full of confidence because of his wife's granting to him the full decision in regard to what vehicle would be bought.

Gotta spend the rest of that college-fund money, anyway. And the other kid married a rich girl. A Miami girl...

It didn't take long to migrate towards the car in mind. It was yellow with two black stripes on the hood which itself had a bulge in it above the motor.

Oh, what the guys at work will say...

Her inquisitive look did not deter him. The behemoth grinned like a hyena.

They traded the 4-year-old car that they had driven to the dealership and paid the difference for the brand new Camaro. That difference was quite substantial. The dealer convinced them, though, that he had cut them a great deal. Really, they were saving money—somehow. They were out of Augusta and driving through the forested foothills of the northern Appalachians within an hour, in style.

"So, what do you think?" asked Sam's mother as she looked warmly at her husband's smile.

It didn't really matter that they would not be able to use the 4-wheel drive deficient car very much due to all of the snow which would fall. Owning the car meant something bigger than the driving to him. Which made it O.K. Everyone has their own 'car to buy.'

"In a word, actually six, amazing," he said, turning off of the highway and onto a county road.

His smile became meek. She looked at him and shook her head sadly.

"Oh, Dan. I hope that he is doing O.K."

*

"How's school?"

"In a word, actually six, depressing."

There was no reply for a few moments. It was the first time that they had heard this particular Sam-ism. Both of them counted in their heads the words of the sentence and at about the same time realized that it was a joke which kind of made sense.

They were on opposite sides of the house, both on a phone. Neither had heard from him in the days of the previous week, which was unusual. Generally, he called home at least every other day.

"Needless to say," his father felt a need to say, "you should be enjoying yourself. Last year at college…. these will be the happiest days of your life."

"I'm doomed, then."

He did not sound well. It is most depressing to be in the summer and to not think it sweet, knowing that the weather will only worsen.

"Honey, what's wrong?"

"Oh, I'm not even sure anymore."

"How is Britney?"

"I don't know, haven't talked to her in about a month."

There was silence on the line.

Secretive Sam.

"So, you two aren't together anymore?" asked the mother with alarm.

"Correct," Sam said without emotion.

"When were you going to tell us?" said the deeper voice.

"I hadn't thought about it. But, really, it's probably for the best. She wants to settle down. And I cannot."

"You should tell your father and me these things."

"I know. I'll be alright."

"This isn't because you've been hanging out with that professor so much, is it?"

For the last two weeks—though never when he had been with Brit—he had been regularly screwing Dr. Sanderson. Usually at her house but a few times in her office on campus. But the fun suddenly stopped when she wrote an almost skillful, albeit a bit too transparent poem about their relationship that she read *emphatically* to a room of about seventy-five people, including Sam—who there heard it for the first time. The sabbatical that she was now on had not been planned. Her absence made Sam feel all the more lonely, even though a part of him was glad due to the fact that he had decided that she was almost certainly crazy.

"No, mom. I don't see her anymore either."

"Good. She's up to no good."

"How are things up there?"

The diversion worked. It always did. This time, a story about Rob and Erica was told. They had gotten a cat together, which seemed to enjoy walking on Rob's head when he slept. Supposedly, it was just adorable. They called him 'Whiskers.'

Sam twirled the keys on his lanyard as the conversation winded down as it always did towards a good-bye. They couldn't feel where he was at. And they therefore did not worry like they otherwise would have. Real compassion is only possible if the viewer has experienced what the person in peril is going through, and they are reminded of themselves. Everything is in terms of one's own experiences. It is impossible to feel sorry for another without thinking of one's self.

"Are you about ready for a haircut yet?" his dad asked.

"That just cannot happen."

"Jobs, Sam, *jobs*. Be a poet all you want in your *free* time after you've gotten this writing kick out of your system. But your engineering degree will be where the money is."

"Everything will be fine. Writing is valuable in any field."

"How did that interview go?" he asked sternly.

"Swimmingly for a guy who cannot swim. I accidentally made the guy feel like an idiot. Don't think that I will have the job offered to me."

Sam was wrong about this. The job would be offered. And the job would be turned down, which would be the cause of much consternation.

The mother looked past the hair and interviews.

"Are you sure everything is alright?" she asked.

He was quiet for a while.

In me, they see themselves. In them, I see me. The reflection that I send is not one they recognize, not one that they can understand.

He knew that he did truly know if they could understand, but almost liked to think that they could not. It had always been like a fuel to think that he was alone.

My pain isn't and has never been entirely real to them. I shouldn't even try to explain where I'm at.

"Yeah."

"Alright, take care of yourself. And give us a call every now and then."

"Will do."

"Love you / take it easy." (Mom/Dad, saying the same)

"Love you too."

"Bye."

"Bye."

He slid the phone shut and saw the icon which said that he had gotten a text message during the conversation with his parents. He had heard the beep when his mother was speaking and had immediately wondered who was trying to get in contact with him. Was it Ellen, saying something like, 'want to Frisbee?' Having himself excited, he pushed the appropriate buttons and saw who had messaged him.

It was from Brad, and said, 'hey, did you figure out that econ. hw?'

He slid the phone shut again, and sighed. He had dropped the class weeks before, though Brad apparently didn't, at the moment, remember.

Fuck you, Blind.

Brad and the others in that group—those people whose back that he had always had—were not his friends, he had recently realized. They were nice and pleasant until it was him that needed the help, which must have been obvious even to them. But they did not have his back. It is a terrible to thing to realize that your friends are not really friends, Sam had learned. Someone who calculatingly uses you is not a friend, and it is true—like Kurt Cobain, a mainstay of Sam's iPod, said—that most 'friends are nothing but a known enemy.'

A true friend might be the rarest thing in the world. They are absolutely necessary, though.

He grabbed his laptop from the textbook and paper strewn table, and opened it up. After staring at his screen saver for a few moments—it was a satellite image of the world showing a pale-blue dot in endless space—he clicked on the 'start' icon in the lower left corner and then clicked on 'pictures.' In a few moments he was looking at evidence of warmer days. It was nice, from time to time, to do so. He enlarged the pictures to full screen size and went through all of them. There were pictures of him and Britney, which hurt, pictures of him, Brad, Todd, and Jared, pictures of his dead dog, pictures of the family when they had visited Paris, and more than anything pictures of random things. Looking at those fond memories really did make him feel a little better.

He stopped on a picture that was just of him, close up, about from his chest to his head. He looked young, happy, and had shorter hair—was making a funny face in front of the Eifel Tower. The family trip had been his graduation gift for graduating high school. For a few moments he stared at the picture, at his own eyes. They were full of life and looking forward with complete confidence. They were almost entirely unencumbered and looked so very nice. He clicked the 'x' button to be rid of them.

The portrait of 'yesterday' was replaced by the current one—his reflection on the computer screen. The discrepancy was startling. He looked tired, sad, gaunt and disheveled. It was one of those moments when a person realizes that they hardly recognize themselves, and that they have no idea where they are headed, who they are, what they are. He just looked at himself blankly, seeing a lonely form in an absurd world, a form that could somehow think and somehow feel. Everything was heavy, he could hardly bring himself to do anything.

He was somewhere well past shallow depression.

It had been over a month since had had shaved, and his hair had grown almost to his shoulders—a look which he actually liked. He looked a bit like John Lennon in the later years.

No Yoko, though.

He closed the laptop and placed it on the table, sitting in silence. Tired, he thought, was the best way to describe his look.

The day itself had not even been particularly depressing—just another one. Full of going to classes, listening to an old guy talk for a while, sitting amongst the young-already-old speak of antiquated language, watching the cycle of people pretending, and trying not to do so. But everyone must pretend, as it is.

One of the most painful nuances of it all was that it seemed very obvious that people take comfort in being so busy that they have no time to try anything new—to do anything that was not expected of them. It was as if they wanted the choice of how their time was to be spent to be made for them. No one wanted to think for themselves.

If one is around robots long enough, it makes them feel as if they are a robot too.

There *had* been a particularly frustrating part of the day, though. In the student commons where he usually hung out, two girls and a guy dressed just like them—one of the girls Sam had used to be kind of friends with—kept whispering and looking at him while he tried to read a book. He'd asked them what they wanted, once, and they started to laugh. Their whispers sounded just like knives being pulled from metal sheaths, which was quite appropriate considering that their intention was to stab. He didn't know why the girl didn't like him, but she definitely did not, and for just one bitter talker not to like you is to gain a boatload of disdain from many of those who they talk to. And you just cannot let it sink you. He assumed that at some point she probably had had a crush on him— aptly named, because after it fails to develop, it is exactly what the person who had the crush wants to do to the other person. This girl was extremely arrogant and seemed to like nothing more than to criticize others, which Sam felt that almost everyone, in almost every situation, had no right to do.

Which was why he was not even 'kind of' friends with her anymore. To realize what humans are, one must be humble. Sam tried to associate as little as possible with people who didn't know what they were. It rubs off too easily.

So, he'd gotten up from his seat in the commons and headed towards the door, tossing a 'see ya' later to Todd and Jared, who were laughing very hard about something that was no doubt not very funny. Actually, they hadn't even noticed that he had been sitting near them. They were talking about getting high, finding new drugs to try.

As he went through the door, he passed Brad.

"Hi, man," Sam decided to say for civility's sake.

"What?" Brad said with great alarm, as if he'd been broken from a trance.

He spoke in a very low, jolting voice.

"No…I'm *not* a high man… Been sober for days….Wait, that's not what you meant. That's just sick—calling me a 'hymen'…. I just don't know about you anymore Sammy-boy, with all of your nature-time, *reading*, and… bugs and shit…."

His voice trailed off and Sam left him in the doorway—arguing with himself as Jared and Tom laughed even harder.

Brad's 'bugs and shit' had referenced the entomology class that Sam was taking as a replacement for Dr. Roberts' accounting class. Originally, he had signed up for accounting just to take a class with his friends. He'd dropped the class when he realized that they had never been friends and after he started thinking about Dr. Roberts' speech. Anyways, the fill-in professor had such a heavy accent that he couldn't even tell what she was saying. The entomology class was much more interesting.

He did not miss the stoners—or Brit, who under one of those big stones was consistently pinned.

Essentially the person who says, 'fuck it, just get high,' was the same sort of person, in Sam's opinion, who says, 'just burn the oil,' or 'just believe in that corrupt, ignorant system.' It was like they had already given up, conceded. He tried to stay away from people who got high all of the time. The person who is perpetually stoned is often the sort of person who realizes how beautiful the world could be seen as—are unable to stand how it's seen. It all comes down to who can handle the pain and who cannot when comparing leaders for good and stoners.

There is a reason that we are low, and the feeling is valuable. Artificial switches lie. Without bad feelings, nothing changes. Or, at the very least, these are the conclusions that Sam had drawn.

More than the feeling of dislike, there was the feeling of pity. He assumed it was very bad to be where his old friends were at, whether they knew it or not—and they probably did. That's how he felt about most of those who other people might say they 'hate.'

Such an ugly word...

It was at that moment—when he was leaving behind the muttering, the cackling, and the gossiping—that Sam decided that he would never hang out with them again. It was better to be alone.

From the commons, he'd walked to some random place where he could read in peace while he waited for the last class of the day—an 'introduction to poetry writing' class which he taught as a requirement for his Master's studies. There is something very rewarding about teaching eager students. He tried not to be like the snobby teachers who made themselves feel good by making students feel inferior. There were a great many of them. A failed novelist—who was supposedly a 'poet' because of a piece of paper—might bitchily say to a student that, 'you are laughably misinformed about the publishing business.' Sam hoped that at least one of his students might be together enough to write a novel, fortunate enough to get it published. He would never say to one of them what had been said to him. That is always the best way to decide what not to say to someone else.

It was nice to be out of the commons. Even after divorcing yourself from a group of people, though, their actions are still an observable extension of your own former naivety. It can be painfully embarrassing to see what you were, how foolish. Reading the book helped him to forget.

And for a while he escaped into another world.

Almost before he knew it—considering that he got to the classroom without a minute to spare—the time for teaching arrived.

The class session went well. A student—who reminded Sam of himself—said that a person cannot be taught to be a poet, that poetry classes are a waste of time.

"All that it takes to be a poet is to be naked and write honestly," Sam said with a nod.

He didn't say the rest of his thought: 'And it's people who know that they cannot really be a poet who get a degree in poetry.'

Accidentally, he looked at the Barbie-girl in the class. She had dark hair and a deep tan, long legs, big boobs, and was aggressively chewing a piece of gum. It seemed like she was always looking at him when the others weren't. She would write her phone number on an assignment when Sam became a 'rock star,' but would not be called by him. Though she would look very nice writing naked, he doubted that she could ever really be naked. Most people cannot be. Further, he had had enough with Dr. Sanderson. Sometimes he had the students read their poetry to the class. He could not stand another such recitation. And why sex should be a scandal, he could not understand. But it was. And one must be careful.

He assigned the class to listen to a song by Bob Dylan, Lou Reed, Nick Drake, or Neil Young—hoping to expose them to music which they may not have heard—and to write down some lyrics that meant something to them. And then class was over.

Routines were something that he tried to avoid, but ultimately could not. After the class, he found himself walking back to the apartment by 3:00 PM, like he did almost every day. He walked up the same stairs, walked down the same dirty hallway with the same flickering light, and unlocked the same white door with two black numbers on it. He collapsed on the same couch which he collapsed on almost every day.

Soon, his phone rang, which startled him. And then he had a short conversation with his parents, eventually learning about Whiskers the cat. After looking at the pictures of happier times, and then his reflection on the computer screen, he slid from a sitting position over onto his side.

Lying on the couch, he was experiencing one of those awful times when he was thinking about thinking, which is exhausting, just like it is to think about blinking, or walking, or talking... He laid there thinking about how he could not escape from himself. It had been a very hard realization to come upon for the first time.

From thinking about being unable to escape from himself, his mind went to the things that he had done or not done which elicited the question, 'what was I thinking?' Consciousness can suck if not handled correctly.

Only one thing was sure as he rested on the couch of his room of the apartment of the city of the country of the world of the…something. And that was that most things cannot be escaped from—nothing more than yourself. So he closed his eyes and tried, at least, to fall asleep.

After some unknown amount of time—just the amount that it took to be getting to sleep—the door opened and his roommate, Allen, walked into the apartment. His sweatshirt was dotted with rain drops.

Must be raining outside. Frisbee is out.

The curtains were drawn shut.

Al was a good guy, who generally seemed happy. He was only bothered by the little things, like a window being left open or a light being left on. Then, he seemed to enjoy being angry. Sam just assumed that such fixations on little things were an intentional diversion of attention from bigger things that were not nice to think about. Everyone had their own way.

"How's it going, man?" Sam said without any tone, sitting up on the couch so Al could sit down.

"Hey."

Al took out his earbuds and sat down on the couch next to Sam, who was sitting with his eyes closed and his head resting on the back of the couch. There was a newspaper open on the coffee-table that had something about a band in need of a lead singer highlighted. Al thought about asking about it, but didn't want a cynical or 'funny' answer from Sam.

Sam heard the TV come on. He could tell that the show was Cops. Someone was not happy with their life and screaming about it hysterically. After about three minutes of tantrum the sound went out, and Al mustered the courage to speak.

"So, do you want to go out tonight with Shelby, me, Landon and Ingrid? Going to the bars. Should be a good time."

Sam opened his eyes and lifted his head, looking to see that the television was muted, and then at his friend who had the remote in his right hand.

Shelby was Al's girlfriend, and LandIng seemed like they were just taking off—still all over each other and seemingly with opposite-poled magnets in their hands, even though they had been dating since the first week of freshman year. Sam and Brit had regularly spent time with the two couples. They had had some very good times together. But those times were not nice to think about anymore.

"Fifth wheels are inclined to cause a crash. I think that I'll pass."

Both of them stared blankly at the silent TV for a while. There was a businessman with his shirt off, sitting on the stairs of a deck in front of a nice home. He had a shotgun in one hand, and a framed picture in the other. Police officers were inching their way towards him.

"Are you alright, Sam? You don't seem yourself."

Sam sat there for a few moments, watching the man on TV drop the gun, embrace the frame, and begin to sob. He was cuffed.

"Al, nothing is ever as it seems, it seems. So I guess things must be how they seem."

"Wait, what?"

"I need to get out of this place.

*

"Do you think that we should call him?" she asked as they opened the door and entered their cool, tidy home.

The new keys were placed on the kitchen table in plain sight so as to remind of what was hidden in the garage. During winter, that table would be the keys permanent resting place.

"Not yet. You agreed to his 'emergency calls only' stipulation for the next two months, right?"

He was the sort of person who oftentimes asked questions despite knowing the answer.

"Yeah, but who could go two months without someone to talk to?" she said, full of concern. "I think that we might have been too hard on him in Miami."

Both went back to the moment in the hotel room, as they ate dinner after the last wedding rehearsal, all sprawled on the beds amongst pizzas boxes.

As Sam ate a greasy slice, he had said, dripping sauce on his white shirt, 'Maybe I'll just deliver pizzas for a while. Just about as noble as anything else.'

They had thought it a joke until he had then told them matter-of-factly about the job offer he'd received and turned down the week before. The sauced shirt was instantly forgotten, and a whole ordeal followed, especially when they asked how much the job paid. It got very personal, and things were said that were later regretted. It got very loud too. Grandparents, Rob, Erica, most of her family, friends—even Brit, unfortunately— uncles, aunts, cousins, and nearly everyone from both of the families who were in the hotel ended up in the argument room, drawn by the noise and prospect of entertainment. Really, it was quite a sight to see everyone taking sides, some saying that Sam had the right to do whatever he wanted, others passive-aggressively scolding him, others still out-rightly calling him a fool. The fact that Sam had passed up the job, and a lot of money, strummed all of their different heartstrings to make an awful cacophony which he could not stand for long. Money, a job, a boat—all of the time that they had devoted to the attainment of—it was just incomprehensible to them that Sam had passed up a job which paid six figures.

"You don't know what it's like not to have money," one of the older ones had said, with a shaking, lugubrious head.

From what she read in his journal, the night before, she learned how Sam had assessed the same situation which she had taken as a verbal exchange that was absolutely necessary and would ultimately do him good. He didn't seem to see the necessity or merit of the harangues.

Not surprisingly, his words were convincing, read under the yellow lamp on the desk in his room by a mother who had a faint feeling of guilt for invading his privacy. And reading those words, with some scribbled out and others inserted to conform with grammatical laws, she partially understood why he was doing what he was doing.

"I hate money—blinder of minds." The words were underlined several times, the first words written under the heading, "Florida."

He had gone on to write more about it, seemingly as a qualifier for the bold statement.

"...am grateful for the money had and realize that some simply do not have enough—that to be thrown into this unfortunately money-driven world without access to much money is a very hard thing to deal with. But to live a little less glamorously, and not to have all of the things that you're told that you need, that is to allow the time to be <u>yours,</u> and to not be so dependent on money in the first place. The first step would be discarding the television—or at least demanding that what is presented be educational, practical. But to be rid of a television as we know it, in most American households, would be the closest thing to sacrilege still possible. The media—which could be the most important, veritable source for knowledge and unity if not corrupted—disallows people from deciding for themselves what they need, which is one of the most important decisions to be made."

He had circled: "Be careful. Ask yourself, 'are you programming the television or is the television programming you?'"

Reading the words made her feel like a voyeur. Sammy was writing naked, Frenching a dangerous broad who she did not approve of.

"There is no logical reason to have most of the things that people think that they need. Can't human beings fathom that the world has only a limited amount of resources?   That maybe we should redistribute products that we've already processed to those who *need* it, and stress that a dollar bill cannot be eaten? A global civilization concerned only with profit will starve and be poisoned to death in a sea of cash, dying in a world which no longer is able to support human beings, or most <u>other</u>

animals. With a decrease in the insanely consumptive nature of man, it still might be possible to have <u>some</u> of the Earth's wounds heal. But that is probably just a pipe dream."

For several pages he had rambled in the way that someone who is trying to get rid of pain might do.

"No one else can be controlled but yourself,' I thought, looking at all of the people who think that I'm as strange as an alien from Andromeda—the vindictive ex-girlfriend, the jealous cousin, the businessman uncle, the frazzled aunt... The prospect of spending almost all of *my* life working for someone else, without even the solace of the job being something that I believe will really make a difference, is the biggest sin imaginable—with the exception only, of course, of nihilism (never admit that you are nothing). There were really no words to give the prospective injustice justice, so to them I said nothing but: 'I'm sorry that I've upset you.'"

His words had been so hollow.

Then, he'd gotten up off of the bed, walked through all of the people in the room, and then through the door. She remembered watching him go, feeling only a little bad that she had taken part in the word-ambush. When he was gone, the hushed tones of conversation about him began by people who were nowhere near hushed in his presence. One of her nieces was especially venomous—took every strike that she could at Sam. A mother, or any valuable family member, will always protect. And the girl's words were stopped by a glare.

He'd taken the glass elevator all of the way down, looking: "…at the shimmering buildings without a thought, and went out through the lobby to walk the streets of the neon city, feeling low but still confident in myself. I didn't want to be a distraction from Robbie. And thought that I'd get by, even if it meant selling out in the end, as I passed men whose minds were consumed entirely with business. But I will not sell until I have to…"

He went on to write about an apparently homeless man who was on his hands and knees, observing closely a flower that was somehow growing between the sidewalk and a building. And it was then that he knew that he: "…could never sell out. People stared at the poor guy in rags who saw beauty in the flower, infinity. There is beauty everywhere, to those with open eyes. So many hide from it—in offices, in front of the TV. And that's why people kill themselves, I think. Because they feel like they are alone in seeing. Or worse, they never see the beauty at all. This damn beauty keeps me living. Without it, the decision would be so easy. But it's a double-edged sword."

After what was apparently a long walk through the city, Sam returned to the hotel. The last neatly printed words which she read under the 'Florida' heading—only one of many—were: "And to think, I probably wouldn't have had the courage to embark on this journey were it not for those nasty words before the wedding. 'If you ain't got nothing, you've got nothing to lose'—it's true. Complaining accomplishes nothing. So, I will never complain again. I'll 'be the change that I want to see in the world.' Off to understand what I am. And to find my own words."

The words were heart-wrenching to read. For him to think that he had nothing was painful for her who felt that she had given him everything. And she wasn't a Bob Dylan fan, so she didn't recognize the lyrics. They probably would have cut less if she had known that they weren't Sam's own.

After the wedding, he had slept on the beach, watching the stars, feeling more alone than he ever had before, hoping that his brother would meet him in the morning before he left for the airport as per his request. But none of this was in the journal which he hadn't felt like retrieving from the hotel room. He was glad to be rid of it, felt as though he was freeing himself from everything that he had written about. He assumed that some cleaning lady would throw it away after taking his other things and laughing at his pain. But she had actually been kind enough to seek out Sam's address and immediately send the journal to Maine, unread, along with most of his other things.

The part of her which did not think that Sam was going to get himself killed was proud of him. But that part was only a small fraction of the whole. She knew very well that the ones who think like he did do not live for long. It's easy to keep that heart pumping for a very long time if you don't really live, are without whitened knuckles from holding onto what was given at birth. Which got her thinking about how she used to be, until the thought was interrupted.

"Julie, he should have taken that job. Had no right to turn it down. Would've been good money. *Good* money."

She put down her purse on the same table that supported the keys, shaking her head in disagreement. But Sam had taken a fair amount of their money for school—it was true—which in a way did lessen his rights. If anything is given, there is always something expected. It was too bad the way that sort of thing went. Especially if you did not even ask for what you were given. But that's exactly what life is—getting something that you didn't ask for.

The mother walked down the cold corridor past both of the boys' empty rooms, and then down the three steps into the living room—unable, as usual, to refrain from thinking about the time when Rob had fallen down them.

It was one of the first times that she had left the boys home alone. She had been getting groceries in town. The 5 and 4-year-olds must have had a party, or something. When she opened the front door, she heard sobs and, in a panic, placed the keys to the mini-van and the bags of groceries on the kitchen table. She saw an empty box of bandages on the stone-tiled floor, which made her rush through the kitchen and down the cold corridor expecting a dead child beside a dying one. In the living-room she found both of them on the couch. Sam was hugging his little brother who had bandages all over his face. None of them covered the only blemish on his body, a little patch of rug-burn on his chin.

"Mommy, Robby fell! He forgot the stairs," a wavering little voice said. "He forgot the stairs!"

She had smiled as she hugged them both. The sobs had stopped.

Days gone.

As she stood in the dark living room, her husband walked into the room, turned on the lights, and sat down on the recliner. It always felt good after a long day to sit down. It was what he looked forward to the most each day, sinking into that soft, leather chair after a long day of sitting in a less comfortable chair. He closed his eyes, ready to doze, imagining himself on a beach in Brazil, with a pretty girl, like Rob was. There was also a yellow Camaro in this dream, which had gotten him the girl.

"It's almost been a week. Do you think he'll be coming home soon?"

He opened his eyes and looked at the woman who used to be that pretty girl—who had been gotten with a 1977 'duster.

"Well, we're going to the airport, very early, to pick him up Friday. He had better be there."

"He will. I mean Sam," she said, shaking her head.

"I have absolutely no idea about that one."

He turned on the TV so as to stop the self-generation of his mind. She was out of the room before the blue screen had turned into a moving picture, walking up the thirteen stairs which led to their bedroom. They creaked consistently, rhythmically, as did her knees.

Once in their room, she turned on the light, took out her earrings and looked into the mirror. The face that she saw did not seem like her. It was a little bit sad and much akin to a parent looking at a child who is not like them. The parent and aging mirror-gazer—both of which she happened to be—will ask: 'How did that happen?' However, there is no choice but to accept.

After a few moments, she pulled her eyes away from the old woman and looked at the picture of a young woman and a young man on the wall of the bedroom—her and Dan. There were also pictures of smiling little boys who were no longer little boys.

The answering machine was flashing. She walked over to it and pushed 'play,' thinking that it was probably from Erica—like it usually was.

But it was not.

It took a few moments, and there was the sound of rushing air in the background, but eventually a voice began to speak. It was raspy and seemed to belong to an African American man.

"Hey, uh, this is Will Jackson. I met your son a while back. First of all, he said your secret word is, uh, horse, or maybe rabbit, or something."

She thought of what it seemed like you might get when you crossed the two, 'Donkey.' Strangely enough, she heard old Eeyore bray as Will briefly paused. But it wasn't really that strange, because Eeyore had an attitude, and had not yet been fed for the day.

"Long story short, I'm worried about him—by some of the things that he said. I know that he would be mad if he knew that I was calling you. Seems like a very smart, proud young man. But, uh, hitchhiking doesn't seem like a good idea."

There was only the sound of air rushing in the background for a few moments on the answering machine. She thought that the message was over, and in the relative silence she heard her heart beating rapidly— *hitchhiking?!?* But Will eventually started up again.

"It's just that he reminds me of some other young men who I have known, which worries me. They're just so… I don't know. Guess it's an age of disillusionment that some take too far. He gave me his phone, so you can call it if you'd like. I'd like you to. Oh, and he gave me a note, too. It's actually brilliant, in a way, but it frightens me about Sam's intent. If you would like I'll send it to you. Hope to hear from you. Just thought that I should call—from one parent to another. Take care."

She called him at once.

*

Sam had gotten out of the city in a taxi, heading west until the meter said $20—at which point he told the driver to stop. He paid his fare with a wrinkly bill and got out. He was tired of the city, and it had been taking longer to walk out of it than he thought that it would. He was tired of being near to other people without any real way to escape and did not even try to hitchhike. The thought of some person speeding up and locking the door on him was quite scary, actually. So he had decided to go ahead and flag down a taxi.

There was nowhere to be—which had made telling the driver where he wanted to go difficult. 'Out of the city,' is what he had said. Most taxi drivers are tired of talking to people, and the one who had picked him up and then dropped him off had been no exception. Sam eventually noticed that the driver was doing cryptic circles so he could get a larger payment—which was why he asked to be let out when he did, despite still being in suburbia, and why he gave the wrinkly bill instead of the crisp one.

He decided to walk towards the Pacific Ocean for the day. It was a ways off.

Not long after he had started walking, just beginning to be amongst the fields which were considerably smaller in the northern part of the state than in the southern part, a familiar rusty red truck that was belching exhaust drove by. The drivers of it had stared at him sneeringly at a gas station not far back. He had waved at them. They had started laughing. Sam had walked on as they spit tobacco juice onto the rubble of an old sidewalk.

From the truck, the passenger threw a mostly full Styrofoam cup at Sam. There was a wall of dark liquid glittering through the air before it crashed to the ground.

"Dr. Pibbie for the hippie!" said a loud voice.

He heard them laughing as they drove away. But the man had missed. Only a little bit of the dark brown liquid got on Sam's pants. Even though he was aware that they probably knew no better—just ignorant forms reacting without knowing why—it still did not feel good for such a thing to happen. And he had even felt a bit of anger for a few seconds, which disappointed him.

Never should let people like them anger me.

Many people are incredibly friendly. In the same gas station where he had seen the two men of the rusty truck initially, he had not had enough change to buy a chocolate bar. He had had a dollar and thirty cents, surprised at the counter when told the price. The chocolate bar had cost a dollar and thirty-seven cents. A miserable person, bound by and therefore a stickler for the enforcement of all rules, would have with a shrug said, 'tough luck. Put it back—you candy fiend.' But the young man behind the counter had immediately said, 'no problem, man. I got you.' And it was very obvious that the guy felt really good about helping someone else out. Little acts like that were a reminder of the good that is in most. And dealing with the bad only makes a person value the good.

There really are a lot of people who want to help their fellow creatures through this mess.

So Sam had to smile. And picking up the cup which was intended to soak him—so it could be recycled after he found a bin—he walked on. Thereafter the miles had gone by nicely—despite the heat. He did about two in an hour with his pack.

As he walked, and the sweat ran down his neck, it seemed very ironic that the sun is the only thing which there is any real evidence to worship—given that it supports nearly all life—but throughout history those who actually worshipped it were persecuted and laughed at, converted.

Eventually the sun's heat subsided, and by the time that Sam reached a sign which marked the passage into a new county the sun was just beginning to set. The sky was red with a pattern that few artists' imagination could render. He was surrounded by woodlands and pastures where cows grazed.

There was little to think about other than walking. Less stimuli felt nice—just taking long, steady steps, watching the land pass slowly by. Few cars were passing anymore, and the road was getting less well-kept. Things were beginning to seem more natural. He felt good—even if worn down.

When the light began to fade fast, he left the road, ducked under an electric wire, and encountered the concerned eyes of cows. A few of them let loose their long, mournful 'meeewwwww.' Walking past them, he ran his hand across one of their backbones, and then left the herd to do their thing while he did his own.

His eyes were on trees in the distance. The landscape had a yellowish, golden tint. No houses were around, so he did not worry about getting into trouble for trespassing.

Laws are for the uncivilized.

It felt good to have the soft, crumbling soil beneath his feet as opposed to the gravel.

Without warning, a crazy cow—his favorite sort—ran past him close enough to brush his arm like a playful puppy would. After a few kicks, she went back to the herd. A smile was brought to his face—despite the fact that the exchange almost ended badly for him—as he looked back and saw the other cows looking at the playful one as if it were extremely strange.

It took about ten minutes to reach the cottonwood trees that he had seen from the road. The leaves fluttered in the wind, as if to welcome him. He ducked under the wire again and was in the little woods. When the wind was absent, it was amazingly quiet. There was a wonderful feeling of relief that only a bearer of a great weight can know when he took off his backpack. The straps had been digging into his shoulders, and his lower back had been tormented consistently. He decided to take an unencumbered walk through the little grove that hugged a depression on the edge of the pasture. From his pack, he retrieved and began eating a banana as he walked, drinking from the gallon of water which he was conserving.

He was surprised at how botanically diverse the little island in the pasture sea was. Botany was a favorite pastime of his. There were all sorts of flowers and colors covering the ground—purples, yellows, reds, whites, and little spears of green grass and sedge. To observe this is to see an entirely different level where ants are people equivalents which take much better care of the landscape. On his knees, he closely observed a patch of flowers which were star-shaped and as red as is possible. In the gentle evening air, there was beauty everywhere. With a deep breath—the roses were amazing—Sam took in the fragrance of the flowers, from which one to the other a bumblebee happily buzzed. It was nice to see a fellow pollinator—as Sam himself was a prolific nose-pollinator of flowers.

Life will flourish wherever it is left alone.

Eventually Sam stood and left the patch of Fire Pink, completing a circle in the little patch of life and returned to where he had left his pack. He looked at his meager possessions and felt good at how little it took to sustain himself. It did not look like it was going to rain, and he hoped that it would be how it looked. He unrolled the tarp after unstrapping if from the pack and used a sweatshirt that he had bought at a garage sale as a pillow. After putting a can of soup on his small, lit stove, he lay down and watched the brown liquid until bubbles started to rise. It didn't take much to warm. As he spooned the soup into his head, he relaxed his muscles which were sore from the day of walking. But he laid there, content.

A purple, little butterfly fluttered right over him, heading into the mess of burning orange and yellow wildflowers, which brought a smile to his face. He thought of what Steve had said about butterflies and shook his head. Steve—a very good guy, in fact, despite his claims to the contrary—had laughingly criticized the seemingly directionless way of travel that butterflies utilize.

"Where do they think they are *going*?" he had said as one fluttered by.

Watching this purple butterfly made Sam think how tired he was, and how tired his friend probably was, of tedious and straight paths to nowhere. He smiled at the thought of some person in the future quoting *him*.

"'*As the butterfly flies'…so much more honest in this place than 'as the crow flies'—said first by Sam Steele.'*"

It reminded him of a Peanuts sketch, which he admired, that his entomology professor had used in one of his slideshows.

'Look at those bugs, they don't have the slightest clue what's going on in this world,' Lucy said to Charlie Brown.

'What is going on in this world?' he asked.

'I haven't the slightest idea!' she admitted.

All that it takes is admission. If everyone admitted, this would be a better place.

Though the ground was hard, Sam was comfortable—a bug among bugs. He lay with his head on its side, watching as the last bit of the sun fell beneath the horizon. He was always amazed at how fast it disappeared. Then, even more colors shot up from the horizon. Just another example of something which cannot be described—and should not be missed through the act of trying to get a picture of.

He took it all in like he would have been unable to only a year before. It's strange to see so much beauty where there was only mere commonness.

The faint light showed a couple indentations on a small, smooth stone not far from his head—which he recognized to be ancient tracks from some little creature not that different from him. On them his eyes locked, and from them a candle in his mind was somehow lit which allowed him to look around, see what was in there.

It's amazing how much more we know than we can ever understand.

The little creature which had scampered along on a riverside to make those tracks hundreds of thousands of years before had left a mark which was much longer lasting than any which Sam would likely leave. Western culture only claims to remember a man from a couple thousand years ago—and the other cultures which have not yet been destroyed are much the same. Before that, there's not much as far as people who are remembered.

Now, Sam thought as the colors at the horizon began to gradually fade, it seemed like humans of the world were on the track to be united. Imagine. Indeed. McDonalds, Wal-Mart, Starbucks, the internet, etc. Whereas yesterday man-kind was at the base of the pyramid, it looked as though it was now nearing the point of what the collective mind-set would be. So, he thought, we're all about to be on the same page. The others have been ripped out as irrevocably as the species to which that little dinosaur belonged went extinct.

"That is how it is going to be—a world of greed, destruction, and blindness," Sam said to himself, "unless another page is written, this one ripped out. If not, this place will finally be united. As one, we will be insane. Will be destroyed."

And the world was finally connected, so that things *could* change on a global scale very quickly.

After we sputter out, he thought, and a human equivalent return, future paleontologists will find clues like treeless plains and toxic waste dumps, mountains of automobiles, tanks, and nuclear weaponry. They might then realize that they should put a halt to the path that they will likely be on—will have, thanks to our blunders, the evidence to be listened to. They will end up like we could have ended up—together, peacefully sharing the awe which should be elicited from life. And, at that, the sun will burn out—the book on Earth will be closed.

All this was enough to beg the question, "should I be a part of all of this," which yielded the answer, "you already are—and you must do your best to make things better."

In the body of a sick cancer patient, sometimes the cancerous cells just go away. 'A miracle' is what they call it. There is, Sam thought, a better explanation. He liked to think in such cases that the 'miracle' started with a brave little creature which devoted its life to a stop of the destruction where it dwelt—through intelligence, meditation, love, and bravery. Living on a cell poised to be destroyed by creatures like itself who intend to infect others, a creature which wonders if he/she should remain stops the spread of the cancer which does not know that it is cancer.

Somewhere far above, a doctor tells a mother that her child is cancer-free. And that's not a miracle. It is just pure, rational bravery shown by a little creature, in a little cell, in another little creature, in a little solar system, in a little Universe. The fact that any of it is there to begin with is the miracle—which the child who was cured of cancer may realize. They too just might decide to devote their life to a stop of the destruction of their world, and all of the others.

There was so much beauty. And somehow, he thought—fully aware that he was unable to describe how that thought had happened, how he had felt it, or understood it—he was a part of the beauty. Just a little track wondering what had left it and why.

How unlikely life is. How wonderful. How lucky I am. Why do I deserve this?

Sam could not see the track from the little foot anymore. His candle had burnt out.

Darkness fell very fast. A glance up to the stars was enough for him to know that the battle was worth fighting.

It was the familiar dawn of the dream Universe's day, time for rest. As he began sliding into sleep, words that did not make sense to him ran through his head. *He forgot the stairs, forgot the stairs, Robby, the stairs.*

It felt very nice to know that sleep was near. Sam was gently snoring within two minutes of closing his eyes

Chapter 9

The man stood there shaking terribly. Every muscle in his body seemed to have a mind of its own—all of them restless. His elbows and arms lurched slightly, and he shifted from foot to foot as if he were standing on hot coals. His head went back and forth and his face grimaced over and over. When he was at his steadiest it looked like there was the beat of a song in his head that wouldn't go away. This sort-of reprieve only lasted a few moments before it got worse again.

He was standing alone beside a brick wall outside of the only bar in the one stop light town, looking off into space. A piece of cardboard was beside him, illuminated by the yellow light of a streetlamp. On it was written in black marker: 'Please, any money you can spare. I can't help myself.' It was obvious that he suffered from a neurological disease.

Sam had never seen anything sadder in his entire life.

That could be me.

Sam was covered by dust and utterly exhausted. He had just walked twenty-four miles—most of them in the hot sun—before reaching the little town in the middle of nowhere. It was just after dusk. His feet were numb, his back ached, and the big red '6' that he saw outside of the motel seemed more appealing than anything that he had seen in a long time. He would have camped again if he'd seen a good spot. But his body was not used to operating without a bed. And, therefore, after sleeping on the hard ground in the little patch of woods surrounded by pastureland, not much sounded better than a soft bed. But, nonetheless, he walked away from the bed and towards the person. He felt that he had no choice.

"Hey man, how's it going?" Sam said in as friendly of a tone as he could muster.

"Oh, so, so… sober."

"Let's get a drink and some food. I'll pay."

They went into the bar and got more 'drink' than food. Much more.

*

"So, I can never be quite sure if people believe me when I tell them that I have Parkinson's. Why? Because I'm winking the whole goddamn time."

The man was incredibly high-spirited, and the light had revealed that he was younger than Sam had originally thought. His name was Jake. They were sitting at the bar. Sam smiled and shook his head. It seemed to take a great amount of effort for the man to get his voice started, and once he did the words were slightly slurred—but he communicated effectively. His mind was obviously still strong.

"You see, people look at me and think that I've always been like this. But I haven't."

He took a trembling drink of the half-filled beer that Sam had bought for him. Surprisingly, a Nirvana song was playing and not some twang-twang country song, which was nice. The place was dingy, but homey. Sam's thoughts were quite clear, and he felt as good as possible given the conversation. The alcohol seemed to be working. He listened to Jake.

"I first felt it coming on when I was twenty years old. Twelve years ago. It was like the feeling when a fish is just starting to pull on your line, but the tugging was on my fingers. And then everything else. The awful hooks in my flesh. In my face, in my legs, my toes, my chest. Even in my tongue. Made me feel sorry for all of those fish that I caught when I was little. The feeling of being caught and unable to escape. It's the worst."

He looked blankly ahead and shook his head wistfully.

"I should've started taking chances. Not just with the ladies. I should have done that too. I mean big chances. Like life or death. Russian roulette, almost. Sure, eventually I'd have lost, or won, really. But I didn't. I'd have been forever young, strong—remembered that way at least. And I would have never become this."

The poor man seemed to be shaking more. Sam ran his fingers through his grimy hair, unable to say anything. The man continued.

"We're all given so much life. It's like putty or play dough. Most don't spread it. They just let it sit in a little blob, not making it cover any ground. And then it rots away. I look at them, with my hardening putty that can't spread, and realize what they are wasting. But most of them won't realize what they're wasting until it's too late, if they ever do. I guess that I shouldn't care, but I do."

Sam nodded his head and was able to speak after a few moments. It had been incredibly powerful to hear Jake say these things.

"I feel where you are coming from. I actually have my own little anecdote about *it all*."

He knew that he was at least a little drunk, because he had begun the story without even thinking about it.

"I keep a dream journal—have been doing so for about a year now. I actually have this one really disturbing dream that keeps returning. But that's beside the point. Every night, I record whatever I can remember. So there's a lot of ink about that one. And I've been realizing that I know a lot more, subconsciously, than I thought. It's really interesting, actually."

He took a sip and continued. Jake was a very good listener.

"Anyway, there are those dreams that fool you completely. You either wake up very glad to have escaped or very disappointed to have been taken away. There's another sort. I've been fairly regularly experiencing what's called lucid dreaming. You get to that point in a dream where you realize that you are dreaming, like when you are being chased by a band of sword-bearing rainbow pirates and evil dolphins, and you're like, 'shit, this can't be real.' So you are free to do whatever you want. Free of debilitating thoughts, free of reality, in the dream. It's fucking awesome. Get to that point when you are awake, man, now *that's* got to be the greatest feeling in the whole world."

Jake shook all over, but was smiling—which was an odd combination. He said: "You know, the scary thing about dreams are that your mind has the power to create the whole scene. The rainbow pirates, whack dolphins. All that. Someone says something to you in the dream, but those words are created by your own brain. Now, what if you're mind has the power to create all of this too?"

His shaking hand gestured to the bar scene.

"Maybe I'm trying to hide from something and have created all of this to do so. Are you really next to me, or have I created you? Do I really have a nervous system disorder? A person can never die in a dream. Will I ever be able to die here? Will I suffer forever, from dream to dream? That's scary."

Sam had thought the same.

"Jake, we should all do our best to create something beautiful then. That's the only answer."

After a few moments of silence, Jake broke it like glass.

"Man, look at us. We're a couple of poets, or artists, or something."

"And an artist cannot tolerate reality, or so says my man Fried-rich."

"Yeah, man, fry the rich," Jake said with a big drunk smile on his face. "They are just as poor as us. Listen: In every prison there's 'the *man*.' I told this to the king, who knows nothing of prisons. And that man in the prison, I told the royal prick, forgets that he's a prisoner too. The king laughed at the fool who I had described. I laughed and knew that he had forgotten too."

Both of them felt good, knowing that there was at least one other person thinking like themselves. They weren't *that* crazy. All that it takes is for another to think like you, and you become 'not *that* crazy.' The two sat without any words, everyone once in a while taking a sip of beer, for a long time.

"You know, I still think that I have seen you before," Jake said, eventually.

He had been insisting that he had seen Sam somewhere before and was fairly sure that it had not been in a dream.

"I don't know what to tell you, man."

They both shrugged and continued to drink. It was to the point that the alcohol almost tasted good.

A particularly intense seizure came over Jake, but he was not startled. Sam's wavy mind thought of the cells and things which made up Jake's brain—that a little problem in there had spread from one part to the next until it was evident in the whole of the body. On the television in the corner there was a rocket ship being launched up towards space.

"Jake, there needs to be a revolution in you. Maybe things would be better. There just needs to be a revolution. We should not think the way we do. We should not allow ourselves to leave our cell until we think right. It's not fair to our creature."

Jake's lips quivered, then seemed to be fighting a force which was holding his words back, until finally he could speak.

"I don't know what you're talking about, man. But things should revolve. Just not so much that they get back to here again."

They both laughed sadly.

There were six other people in the bar besides Sam and Jake. The bartender was a man with a ponytail who seemingly had an obsession with polishing glasses that were already clean. Two old bikers were playing pool. They were loud, and quite bad at the game. Balls were routinely leaving the table. A somewhat attractive woman sat three chairs down from Sam. She wore a UPS uniform. Beside her sat a red-faced guy who, slouching and holding a glass which held dark contents and ice, was trying to get with her, futilely.

"I could make *you* a delivery, a nice big package…"

Surprisingly, she did not get up and leave. She must have been enjoying the attention, and obviously liked being hit on. Sam thought of a girl from college, how funny it was to consider the frequency that certain girls are 'hit on' in their opinion. They recount stories of interactions with disgusting men who apparently drool over them, even though it seems to only happen to them when no other witnesses are around. Any friendly action transformed into sexual advances.

"This guy…" said Jake with a nod, and a laugh.

"Has had a bit too much. Verbal reducing valve gone."

Intoxication is a tampering with the chemical balance of the mind. A constant rippling of the water. Happiness is exceedingly difficult in the wake of such regular perturbation. It was a fact which Sam was glad to have learned, made his mind seem considerably clearer than it would have otherwise. Just like a bath in cold hose water which makes the swimming pool seem so much warmer.

The quizzical stares after a declined joint or a shot of whiskey were expected and seemed to say, 'you're happy with where you are at? Really?'

But if in reply to such a look you actually say out loud, 'I'm not necessarily happy where I'm at. Though a balanced mind *is* the key to regular happiness. I'll be ready for the lock once I find it,' the person with some sort of drug in their hand—be it money, cocaine, alcohol, whatever—will give a blank look and walk away shaking their head. Or at least that is what had happened the one time that he had replied in such a fashion to a quizzical look.

Sam did not usually drink and had hardly drunk at all since he had turned twenty-one years old. Before, there had been a vague thrill in doing something illegal—he liked to think of it as 'thr-ill-egal'—even though he drank very little then too, relatively speaking. Drinking was simply not desirable anymore, for the most part. It didn't seem desirable to dull the consciousness that he had worked so hard for, to convolute the mind. It was the same with recreational drugs. They can sharpen a mind, true, but are very likely to eventually break off the sharp point, leaving a broken tool. It seemed logical to get the most out of his mind while he could. There would be plenty of time to be out of his mind. It was actually one of the reasons to go on living—it's such a short time to have to tolerate one's mind. May as well experience it fully until the time to be free of it forever arrives.

Though if one is to the point that they absolutely *need* a break from their mind, intoxication does work well.

For a while, they watched the man beside the UPS woman make a fool of himself. Sam's mind was not yet stopped for the night.

To him, there seemed to be two types of people who drank—those who needed to in order to forget for a while and those who liked to fit in with those who drank, without any other real need. And before long they needed to drink too.

Assuming the role of a clown is comforting. Being oblivious seems OK. Which is why people are obsessed with drinking.

It did not seem right that the society which we have built elicits the need to be intoxicated. Doesn't it seem wrong that we must escape the very world we've arbitrarily created?

And so—because he was not feeling strong enough to resist—Sam took another drink, and then another when he thought about Jake who sat beside him, who was drinking what he did not spill of a shot of undiluted whiskey. That night, Sam drank because there was absolutely no way of understanding why Jake had to be the way he was. Or the way anything was.

'Just the way it is'—answer to any persistent questioner.'

One must realize that there might not be a reason for everything. There also might not be a reason for anything. A universal reason, that is. For those who cannot find their own reason, history has proved, there is always alcohol.

Thoughts won't stop.

He took another drink.

The guy eventually got up and left the UPS girl, when he realized that she was not going to let him fuck her. He staggered across the floor and almost bumped into one of the bikers. Luckily for him, he did not, and made it out of the door without any altercation.

Sam watched her—thinking that she was a great test for his self-imposed abstinence streak. In a petite way, she sipped her beer. And with flashing eyes, she looked at him—as if daring him to approach her.

He saw nothing wrong with not having sex. Really, it was the ultimate rebellion considering that the reproductive act seems to be the only ostensible purpose of anything alive. And to abstain completely from such activities really is the ultimate way to 'stick it to the man.' Some men choose to stick it to other men in order to 'stick it to the man.' Sam was not one of those men—though liked to think that if he had been brewed differently that he would be brave enough to do what he wanted, no matter what anyone else said or thought. To be born gay and to be what you are might be one of the greatest tests that a person can face—is probably one of the most fulfilling tests to pass.

It may have been a wave of alcohol hitting him, but for some reason the UPS woman suddenly looked very good.

"God-dammit," he said quietly to himself.

Sometimes, it is very hard to deny what you are. So, there is no point in even trying. A life spent rebelling against what one is turns out to be a waste in the end.

"Think we should go talk to her?" Sam asked, reluctantly.

"YES!"

She looked over at both of them after Jake's excited outburst which was probably louder than he had intended.

"Let's go."

Sam got up and took the seat that the drunken guy had left. Jake repositioned too, beside him. The woman was older than Sam had thought that she was, probably about thirty-five. He hadn't tried for anyone that old since Dr. Sanderson. And there was something strangely appealing about the prospect of doing so again. He just hoped that the UPS woman was not a 'poet' in disguise.

'Steele in Sand

Sam shook the silence from my breath.

Stroked me so there was nothing left,

gently kissed my left breast,

when gone leaves me feeling bereft....'

It only got worse from there. The words—which were seared into his mind—still made him shudder, because he had been at the poetry reading. In the front row. The worst thing was that most of his students were there for extra credit. And the poem was as absolutely awful as it was transparent. That woman had to have been at least a little crazy— considerably more so than the other mostly old women who read poetry to captive audiences.

UPS had better not stand for United Poet's Society.

He decided that he would take the chance.

"Hey, I'm Sam and this is Jake. We are exciting guys in disguise."

She gave him a surprisingly cold look, seeming to be of the tribe which thought very much of themselves. Her lips were very red, protruding in an attractive way. She would be very nice to be with for a while. The camera might not subtract years, but darkness surely will.

"You wouldn't be talking to me if I wasn't so gorgeous."

Sam was a bit taken aback by the reply but remained cool.

"Yeah, that's probably true. But what's wrong with investigating what I can't see based on what I can?"

She smiled and was just about to say, or at least Sam imagined, 'Clever, I'll save you the trouble. Let's get out of here,' when Jake stopped her and prolonged Sam's streak.

"I've got it!" he almost screamed.

Both Sam and the woman, who was still nameless as far as Sam and Jake knew, jumped due to the sudden outburst. She looked at Sam in a perplexed way, and he shrugged his shoulders to indicate his lack of explanation.

Jake got up and ambled excitedly into the bathroom as the two watched, a bit amused. He ripped a paper off of the wall above the urinal, and returned to the bar a few moments later, placing it emphatically in front of Sam.

"You're missing!"

Jake laughed like someone who was drunk, which made sense.

"I *knew* that I'd seen you before!"

Sam saw a picture taken from his Facebook page—one in which he was making a silly, contorted face. Below the picture there was big, black print which said: 'Missing—Sam Steele. He is special. $50 dollar reward if tip leads to finding.'

Initially, he hoped that he was worth more than that, and could only shake his head. Sam looked at the picture of himself, wondered why in the world his mother had chosen that picture of him, of all those she could have chosen, to use for the missing person posters.

Why haven't I deleted that shit yet?

Of Facebook, he thought, 'shit' because to give a man's car a jump, and then type away about it in order to get 'likes' just makes the initial act insincere. Or so it seemed.

"Missing. You're telling me. Talk about a buzz kill, man."

Sam couldn't help but laugh as he rubbed his face.

"Well, I guess that my mother didn't believe me when I said that I'd be gone for a while, and not to worry."

"Run away from home, darling?"

Her eyes seemed ready to go.

"Ha. Ha. Talk to Jake. He's a great guy. I'm going to make a phone call."

He got up, hoping that the two would hit it off, but doubting it severely. He had known that she was just as shallow as him when he was telling her that he wasn't shallow. He knew by the calculating way that she had looked at him, and by the way that she did not look at Jake.

Shallowness exemplifies the primitive class of animals which we hate to admit that we are a part of.

Sam thought of Ellen. And again, he felt ashamed.

He had seen a payphone when he had walked in, which would have been surprising if the town didn't look so out of touch with modern times. It was just inside the door of the bar. He walked over to it, and put his finger to his nose to test his sobriety, even though he didn't think that that worked. He knew that he wasn't drunk.

Sam put all of the quarters that his pocket held into the coin receptacle. The dime did no good. Then, he dialed a very familiar number. By the fifth ring, he thought that his quarters had gone to waste. But they hadn't.

"Hello?" the tired voice of his mother finally said.

He hesitated a few moments, and then spoke.

"Hey Mom, it's me."

The voice awoke instantly.

"Hitchhiking? Giving away your phone? How irresponsible can you be?"

The voice was angry.

"Uh, that's a lot of questions. I don't know where to start."

"Are you alright?"

"Yeah, I'm doing pretty well. I'm assuming Will called you. He wasn't supposed to. It was merely a precaution. I thought that I was being responsible. I should have called before giving away my phone, I know.

But it was just something that happened in the moment. Can you call off the hunt, please?"

"You're lucky that Will is such a nice man."

"I know."

"Seriously Sammy, this is horseshit. Are you losing your mind?"

Now, when a person starts to get specific about what kind of shit it is—bull, dog, horse, or donkey, for example—you just *know* that it's serious.

"Believe me, I have asked myself that question many times. Definitely not losing it, though. Think about it this way. Losing something happens instantly, doesn't take much, as you and I definitely know based on everything that I manage to lose—wallet, phone, iPod, car keys… that damned hamster. It's the finding part that takes more time and effort. So, I think that if anything it would be more appropriate to say that I'm finding my mind."

She didn't seem amused, or affected at all by his spin on the very common phenomena of 'losing it,' which everyone of a certain mind will experience, or think that they are experiencing.

"Are you alright?" she said.

"You know how you always say that life is a like a marathon? I think that I'm getting to the point where every step is painful, when even the act of breathing is hard."

"Keep on running."

"I will if you do too."

For a while there was silence.

"Sam, where are you?"

"Georgia."

"I figured. Brit told Erica, who told me, that you visited her. I insisted that she put up the flyers down there." It then made sense why that 'special' picture of him had been chosen for the posters. That bitch was vindictive.

"I see. Rest assured—she did. Is it on TV too?"

"No. Not yet."

Sam took a deep, relieved breath and thought about what to say. He spoke as calmly as he could.

"I'm sorry that you were worried—that *I* made you worry. But, I did tell you in Miami that I needed a month or two completely to myself. We talked about phone calls, how I needed a break from them. You seemed alright with it then. And I don't think it's been much more than a week yet."

"You left all of your things at the hotel. They called us. And Rob says that you got naked on the beach."

Sam laughed.

"Well, that's an exaggeration. I didn't quite get naked and didn't quite leave all of my things. Is he back yet?"

"Yeah, they arrived early Friday morning."

"What's today?"

"Saturday. Are you still going to head out west?"

"Maybe. I'm actually headed north right now."

"Headed in the right direction, at least."

"Yeah, I suppose."

The note from Sam that Will had mentioned and agreed to send entirely slipped her mind—because she was so excited to be talking to her son. Which was why she did not ask about it. And Sam—because of the alcohol—did not think to mention it either. Which he should have done in light of the fact that Will was obviously not doing as he had been asked to do.

For a while, there was silence, and then she spoke in a happier tone.

"You'll never guess what we saw just north of Miami."

"A Florida panther," Sam guessed, thinking of the poor creature.

"Yes! The thing was beautiful, just beautiful. Right at the side of the road."

"So cool. It's nice to know that they are out there."

The opaque, lifeless eyes were much harder to forget than the swift, beautiful movement of the animal was to remember. There was a long silence as both of them thought of the panther in much different ways because of only a 1.2 mile difference of position on the highway.

The silence was broken on Sam's end, by a beep in the phone and an automated voice which said that he had a minute left if he didn't have any more quarters.

No Quarter. Zeppelin.

"Well, I'm about out of time. I only had five quarters."

"Sam, just be careful."

"Will do. You be careful too. Watch out for those moose. And try to get some sleep. Please, don't worry about me."

"You know that that's not possible."

"I'll be home again before you know it. And Ma, I don't know when it will happen, but I want you to know that I'll love you dearly until the moment that I die. Because you're the only one who has loved me without a break since before I was born."

"Oh Sam, I love you too. Always will."

The words sounded sincere. And he knew that they were.

"Stay strong."

"O.K. Bye."

"Bye."

He hung up the phone and looked down to see that there was a quarter on the ground, face-down. Looking at it, he thought very intently that his poor mom was not going to get back to sleep easily—imagined her lying awake in bed beside his snoring father. There the quarter was— shiny on the dirty, grimy ground—and he for a long while just looked at it blankly, with his now hazy, sad mind trying to decide if it was all worth it. Finally, he bent down and then put it heads up on the ledge where someone would see it, hoping that their call might cause less pain compared to relief from pain. And it also might improve someone's luck.

Standing in the relative seclusion of the doorway, he listened to the bikers yelling. There was a country song on now, and also there seemed to be the sound of a pool-stick snapping along with a yell. *Geez, country music is bad, but not that bad.*

Sam walked around the corner to see that the UPS woman was gone, which was too bad. She had looked good. He hadn't even noticed her walk by him. Jake sat there alone, with his back turned. His body shook. His head was down. One of the bikers took a swing at the other one, who was holding a broken pool-stick. He missed, unsurprisingly. They looked at each other like two stunned imbeciles, and then burst out laughing. The bartender polished a clean glass, and seemed oblivious to his surroundings. And there Sam stood, watching it all. It was what he had done since he was nine years old.

He closed his eyes, took a deep breath, and went over to sit by Jake for a little while longer

Chapter 10

Rob could almost feel the pain in his own hands as he watched the high school kid on summer break dig into the heavy, rocky soil. The diligent worker reminded Rob of who he was six years before—when he was just beginning the summer job which had turned into a career. The kid was wearing gloves that would likely be torn to shreds by the end of the summer. Blisters were surely already beginning to form at the bases of his inner fingers where the shovel rubbed on them the most. The blisters would soon be callouses—which would be worth it because by the beginning of the next school year they would be on the wheel of an old, but functional automobile.

A two-foot-deep trench led about half way from one pit in the ground to another. There was surely pain in his shoulders, his lower back, and his knees. He would get used to it. Rob assumed that the kid was angry—of that pure, unreasoning adolescent variety—and not fond of the fill-in foreman. He had been digging since 9:00 AM. It was almost five.

"You'll be a monster come start of the season," Rob said as he walked past on the skid steer compacted and printed dirt.

The kid forced a smile.

"God, I'd better be."

Rob walked over to the biggest hole in the ground, and watched the guys who were filling the bottom of it with cement to cover the skeleton of rebar. They were incredibly efficient. He counted the two by fours that were stacked in a large pile not far from the hole. They were all there. All was going according to plan. He made a couple checkmarks on the paper that was on his clipboard, contentedly.

Before long, the men were climbing out of the hole and the kid's shovel was stabbed triumphantly into the dirt, where it would stay until 9:00 AM the next morning. The men with heavy pants joked with the boy who had dirty hands at how he couldn't go to the bars with them. Somewhat angrily, wishing that he was older, the kid got on his bike and pedaled towards a warm meal and home which the cement-men—who wished they were younger—painfully missed.

Rob opened the door of his Ford F-350 Super Duty, which he had bought a year before to replace the old truck that he'd bought after his first summer of work. It had been a good truck—that first one. Throwing his hard-hat into the passenger seat, beside his dirty lunchbox which had in it a flowery note that said 'I love you! – Erica,' he sat on the dusty seat and turned the key. He loved the sound of the diesel engine. After turning the radio dial until he heard country music, he backed out of the construction site and headed home.

It was a beautiful thing—the end of a long, hard, honest day of work.

He cruised down the smooth highway, passing the small high school which brought back so many fond memories. There, he had been 'the man,' even though he had still been a boy. He saw a girl on the tennis courts who reminded him of Kate—his first girlfriend. She lived in Somalia now and was married to a war lord. At least, he imagined this. He did know that she lived in Africa—somewhere. He craned his neck to watch kids in baseball pants run around a ball diamond while a short little dictator in golden shorts—which reached midway down his stubby legs— barked at them. Little men yell the loudest. And it was very apparent, just by listening, that this man was very small. He had always liked Rob, though. The name Rob Steele had lent nicely to his nickname of 'The Thief' because of all of the bases that he had stolen. His knees were still scarred from sliding on the rough dirt. But the sting had been sweet.

Those were the days.

He had no choice but to keep on driving, though.

The road followed a dark river through a deep forest—where the same trees stood that he had played amongst as a child. As his truck rolled over an old, rickety wooden bridge, he remembered when Sam fell in the water all those years ago trying to save their poor old dog that the river had taken away. He had run back to the house, with his little legs—luckily just in time to get help. Sam had been able to clutch onto a root long enough for their dad to arrive. Rob thought about it every day when he went to and from work.

As he drove past the old house he decided—like he did most days—that he didn't want to visit. Because doing so meant seeing his childhood face on the walls, which was just too hard. He did see his father in the driveway, washing his ridiculous new car. Rob honked the horn and waved. After a scrutinizing, squinting look—which resembled the visage of a concerned prairie dog—his father waved and smiled faintly.

His old home marked the fifteen-minute mark from his new home, which was in town. Erica refused to live anywhere but in a town. He was somewhat surprised that she had even agreed to move to Maine and had been ready to move to Florida himself. She was apparently ready for a change, and happily called the little town 'quaint.' He thought that she would probably be ready for a return to normalcy once winter arrived and would have a different adjective to use when describing the town. Probably 'gawd-awful.'

By 5:40 PM he was pulling into his driveway amongst the other houses in the little sub-division. All of the houses looked exactly the same, except that half of them had bricked arching over the doorways and half of them were un-arched.

He parked in the driveway, grabbed his lunch box, and walked happily towards the un-arched doorway that was his own. He noticed that Erica had planted some purple flowers outside of the bedroom window and thought to himself that he must comment on them, or else there would be trouble.

With his dirty boot he tried to brush the potting soil that she had spilled off of the cement, without so much as a closer look at the flowers. He had yet to experience, or really even think about, the law which has frustrated many a husband: after a flower is pollinated, there is no longer any need for the petals—they suddenly drop.

He opened the door which led into the freshly painted mud room and took off his boots. Whiskers the cat immediately jumped off of a chair in the sun and started to rub himself on Rob's leg. He loved the cat, even though it scratched his face sometimes when he slept. After bending down and rubbing its purring throat, he opened the next door, and saw his yet-to-be pollinated flower.

Erica was absolutely beautiful—and absolutely his.

She was sitting at the kitchen table as she always was when he arrived from work and was wearing lipstick. They would try again that night, he knew.

"The flowers look beautiful."

"Oh, why thank you, Mr. Foreman."

"Come on," he said bashfully, "it's only while Rex is away."

She stood up and went over to give him a kiss. He liked the mark it left. After the kiss was given, and he was marked, Rob sat down opposite of where her sections of the newspaper were on the table. She turned on the light for a look into the oven at the meatloaf which was almost done. Leaning her back against the warmth, she looked at her man.

"I talked to your mom today."

"Oh, really? What did she have to say?"

"Well," she said with a white-toothed, red-lipped smile, "we all know that your brother gave away his phone to a druggie and has been hitch-hiking through the state."

Really, almost everyone knew, because Erica loved to gossip. She had just started a job working ten hours a week at the town bank, so drama was her fuel to push through the free time. 'Rob'bery had become an especially popular subject at the bank.

Rapidly, she continued: "But Sam *also* had him send a very disturbing note which has your mother very upset."

"I know. That's why I went over there and stayed so late last night."

"Yeah, I figured. And Brit told me the other day—don't tell your mom—that Sam made her drop him in the Atlanta ghettos a couple of days ago."

Rob shook his head as he noisily opened the sports section that Erica had put out for him. He held the papers in a way that blocked his face from her.

Wonder if all southern girls use that word.

He frowned sincerely about more pressing issues than offensive language as he thought about sitting with his dad at the kitchen table in the old house, the night before, reading the note from his brother which had been sent through express mail by Will—per his mother's request.

After work, Rob had gotten a phone-call from his dad who said, "You'd better get over here," as if he could not understand why his wife was so upset. But the man could understand, even though he wouldn't admit it, and felt much the same.

The note was the one that Sam had written in the truck after seeing the beautiful kid with the red balloons in the rain, intended to be sent only if he did not contact Will within two months. A note which was to be sent based on the assumption that he had somehow died. But the note was sent anyways, due to the trucker's good intentions, just like his choice to make the call to Sam's parents.

"So what has he done this time?" Rob had asked his father when he got to the old house.

There was a considerable pause.

"Well, he may have stopped living. Or might be planning on it."

He'd then handed over the note in an exhausted way that Rob hadn't seen before from his father.

On a piece of paper creased horizontally down the middle and with words written in a hand suggesting the bumpy road that it was written on, the note began with a poem and ended with what seemed to be a farewell.

"<u>Expand and Explode</u>

Think of me as a balloon.

I cut myself loose.

And up I flew.

I've seen the moon,

flown towards it for both me and you.

As I rise, all of the old things look new.

It all turns to a darker hue—darker, darker blue.

And I realize that I cannot come back down,

I've become so full that I cannot remain.

There's regret at having parted the string with the blade.

For that cowardice I am ashamed.

So, I rise—knowing that one of us must.

Aware of the sound I'll make,

hoping that they will hear me burst,

that they might then awaken.

But if not… it was worth that final view.

Just know I didn't die in some clown's room.

Sorry for my poetic antics. But the words just flowed out and seem right. It is a dangerous road to think for yourself, but nothing in this world is more valuable. And I think that I reached the point that I made my own decisions. I have seen some beautiful things. Nothing more than a little boy letting go of his balloon. I am freed.

Stay strong.

S.S."

It's very easy to hate something until you realize that it will not be there to hate anymore. And then you miss it. Rob simply found himself angry at Sam on many occasions because Sam was not like Rob. Hand-me-down clothes might have been part of it too.

After reading the note, Rob sat down at the table with his dad, and they both looked in silence through the window at the black river flowing by. Rob felt like he had as a child, after Sam had fallen through the ice and was in critical condition. He'd been thinking about it a lot of late, not only when driving over the bridge. It was the first really clear memory that Rob had—that day when Sam was almost lost. He could remember the look in that poor dog's eyes, how she kept trying to swim upriver, breaking through the thin ice close to shore with her freezing legs. Daisy was her name. Rob looked at the memorial for her beneath the window which both he and his father looked through. The yellow flowers swayed lightly in the breeze. And the river flowed still.

Rob had thrown the stick that she chased after—which only he and Sam knew about. He still felt guilty about it. They had all loved that dog.

That cold day, after the ice broke and the stick was set in motion, she was whimpering in the water and the two little boys were trying their best to encourage her. But it didn't work, and she started to slowly drift downriver. So Sam had gone out on the ice, despite Rob telling him not to. Slowly, he went to the edge and almost, as she made one last surge, pulled her up by the collar. But there was a big crack and then they both fell in. And Rob had run for help. Sam had ended up a hundred yards downstream, not far from the part of the river that the two were looking at through the window. He was nearly unconscious, but somehow gripping the only exposed root on the bank, when his father had arrived to pull him out. They never found where Daisy ended up.

Rob watched his father—who seemed to be in his own world. He was turning a rusty paperclip in his fingers and looking through the window blankly. The tattered letter rested on the table. It was just as he had been when Sam was in the emergency room, his heart nearly stopped for good by the cold water of the river. And from the table Rob could hear the soft sobs of his mother as she cried in the bathroom—like she had the day that the ice broke, like she had not done since her father had disappeared during one of his routine walks in the forest a few years back.

The note had been enough to make his mother start worrying terribly again, the assuaging phone-call from Sam being almost nullified. She talked about going down to look for him, saying that he must not be in his right mind. Rob and his father were both worried, though tried not to let on, and told her not to go south.

Of course, he just had to give away his phone.

The voicemail messages that Rob had left after returning from Brazil were in vain, which made him mad.

"Typical Sam," he replied to Erica, "never does anything that makes sense.

"Well, he did introduce us to each other. Don't forget that."

Brit and Erica had played on the same tri-state traveling soccer team, which had been the precedent for the introduction. They were supposed to have been very good, but from what Rob had seen of Erica's 'athletic prowess,' he doubted it.

He put the paper down abruptly, and looked to where he thought she was. But she had returned to her sections of the paper, so he had to turn from the oven to the seat that was across the table.

"Only because Brit *made* him I'm sure. And then, of course, he went and let her get away." He shook his head twice. "Read anything interesting?"

"Actually, yes."

She seemed excited.

"You'll never believe it. The same company that owns the resort that we stayed at in Rio was in the paper. A crew that they sent out to break ground on a resort that'll be accessible only by helicopter was attacked by natives!"

The majority of the article was about this 'resort' being a front for an illegal logging operation. This didn't seem like that big of a deal to Erica. What good are trees standing? She skimmed over most of the article, focusing only on the parts that would support a juicy story.

"Oh, it must have been gawd-awful. The tribe had never before been contacted. Out of touch with the world. Imagine."

The song meant nothing to her. She shuttered a little at the thought of not having television.

"They threw spears and blew poison darts at the poor guys who were lucky enough to have AK-47s. They were naked, and awfully vicious it says. The poor workers were forced to shoot them all dead."

*

"I wish that I had something that I'd die for without thinking twice. Because then all of my living would be worth something…"

Sam couldn't see any of his friends' faces clearly—only the darkened forms of their bodies and shadowy countenances in the flashing light of the driftwood-fueled fire.

They'd driven out to the coast after class, through the beautifully colored leaves of yellow, orange, red, and green. It was so nice that going through them almost seemed like a dream. During the drive there had been the liberating feeling of running stoplights that were red for too long, and the solace of movement after another long day of idle monotony. They had gotten to the beach a half an hour before sunset and all walked through the golden eve. It was not cold out. Something had come over Sam and he had started to run once they reached the sand. In running there is a feeling of freedom, no bad thoughts—unless there is a hungry/angry pursuer close behind, which doesn't happen often. So he ran. And looking back, he saw his friends following, sand kicking with laughter. They stopped at the forest's edge, a few hundred yards from the parking lot. It was getting close to Halloween, so they talked about the outrageous costumes that they would wear. Ellen was there, as well a couple of their mutual friends from the Candid Club—Steve and Mary. She'd introduced them to Sam after the second meeting that he attended, and from there it went.

Another dynamic, an additional person, can make all of the difference in the rapport of a group of people—for better, or for worse. In this case, it was for the better. They didn't go to many of the meetings anymore, but rather just spent time amongst themselves. Which in retrospect, to Sam, was probably a mistake. People should do their best not to close themselves off to other perspectives. But they did. And in a way they became a surrogate family during those last months that they were all together—leaning on one another as needed.

Their conversation gradually slowed when the sun became soft enough to look at comfortably and they became silent as it set. The sky was colorful like it consistently was when coldness touched the air. When the striking color of the leaves went to sleep, they sat quietly in the darkness until the fire was lit with Steve's lighter.

Steve, the odd guy who was a sociology major that always wore a tiger-print bandana and dark sunglasses, suggested the 'I wish' game. He immediately wished that he had not spent so much time studying people, saying there was nothing to them, and then called himself a 'passionate misanthrope.' If it were not for people, though, he would have lacked a passion, so it was a double-edged sword situation. Sam had gone second, when no one else would.

"...I mean, we're expected to believe that nothing is sacred by those who study the Hell out of life and told that only one thing is sacred by those who are scared of living. And all of this destruction of beauty—for what? It's almost like we hate life so much that we are systematically destroying the world."

Somewhere not far away an oilrig glowed above the dark ocean waves. And all around people were being born who were programmed to think that they should have a shiny new sports car—when most of them didn't really *go* anywhere at all.

"I feel like I have no roots anymore. Education has torn me down and doesn't allow me to be built back up. After a certain amount of learning, you almost wish that you had taken the oblivious route. Because with an 'education' the less educated will hate you for it. They think you think you're better than them, that you judge them. When you've only learned that no one knows anything, that no one is better than anyone else. Learning and loneliness go hand in hand, though I can never regret either. I used to feel like loneliness was my most loyal friend, which you three have made me question. Thanks for that."

Sam had come to realize that there was nothing as valuable as being amongst real friends once he had finally found some. All of them listened. Too many people are so insecure that they laugh or babble when presented with what should evoke thought, admiration and silence. But not his friends. They all looked towards him, listening carefully.

His phone buzzed in his pocket. Twice.

"Doesn't it seem like with all of these technological 'advances' that we are deeming ourselves even more functionless in this world? With our constant movement towards a virtual world, it seems like we will get to the point that we will no longer exist. Is it all some kind of joke?"

A machine is something that acts and/or thinks without wondering. I was a machine. It's hard being born. Being human. Have you been born yet, Steve? Are you alive?

"Just imagine how amazing it would be not to be how we are. I mean, to really believe in something, to really be able to believe in something."

He pointed up to the darkening sky and lightening moon, where hundreds of stars were visible already, soon to be joined by many more.

"I don't know much, but I do know that we just cannot know. And we probably should not want to know how all this came to be. But the whole literalist religion thing just makes me so damned sad. It's fine to live your life by the Bible, or the Koran—whatever—if that is what you want. Read the scripts like a poem, not like a manual. Religion can be, and sometimes is, beautiful. Some of the most beautiful people who I have met are very religious. But it should be stressed in all churches that when you die, you are almost certainly dead. It's over. You know, it is very possible that there is life after death. But we cannot count on that. Anything else—even many scenarios much more beautiful than life—are just as possible. It should also be taught that all religions are the same. That there should be no feelings of superiority or inferiority between them. No need to convert. It's like putting different prescription glasses on a blind man who is smiling. So much is missed and not really seen in a world where people believe that they will live after death, where they look down on others for not subscribing to 'the truth.' That's the awful thing about religion—it seems that there can be no amendments, even if it is obvious that there should be amendments."

It was one of those times when words were coming out which were not known to be there.

"This could be taken wrongly but think about it this way: if there is the Christian God, then I never want to meet Him. Because He would have to be at least partially a close-minded, narcissistic asshole if we were created in His image—a gullible, cowardly fool. *Indifferent.* Look at most people. I can hardly stand minutes of those traits. Don't think that I could stand eternity. "

There comes a point, Sam knew, after a certain amount of thinking, when a person realizes that they have no choice but to pretend. Because there are many people who don't even know that they themselves are pretending. They are the ones who make the thinkers pretend too. One can rarely tell if they are dealing with a pure pretender, or a thinker who must pretend. Deep down, though, most people feel the same, know exactly what we as humans are, and what we are not.

"Don't get me wrong. Human beings are compassionate, loving, diligent and brave, too. To go on in a place like this, with a brain like ours, we have to be. So, the image isn't all bad. And I love almost every person in this world—past, present, future—which is why I have to talk about that which we have been taught not to talk about. I cannot be indifferent. This place could be so beautiful."

Sam decided to continue saying exactly what he thought—no pretending—and to define himself to his friends, see if they remained friends:

"Heaven, to this ironic fool, is an Earth without God. Because this world is all that we know we've got. Life isn't so bad anymore. We don't have to live to die. *This* place is Heaven. For one speck of time in forever we are alive. We can move, we can think, we can feel, we can love. For a while we are in Heaven. We will always be a part of life—so it is eternal. However, our soul is only alive for a short time—and to be lucky enough to be in Heaven for a short time, but to be tricked into thinking that you have to wait until you are dead to get there, is tragic. Something which only humans could contrive and subscribe to."

Just a single star would have been enough for hope—just a single unknown—but there were an infinite amount above and within. Sam never felt better than when he could see a sky filled with stars. It was so easy to be brave.

"It does not help matters that 'God' is the hardest word in any language to define. How can someone answer the question, do you believe in God? There certainly is a God—something much bigger than us—in some sense. Everyone knows this. But we cannot pretend that we know Him as a single, definable entity. If we just admitted that we don't know, that there are an endless number of wonderful possibilities which could have led to us being here, that there is evidence all around us, then we would not have any excuses. We would have to work together, *love* one another. There would be nothing else. We don't need the Evil Man, the enemy, the Christian vs. the Muslim, the United States vs. China. Yeah, that hate is a fuel, just like oil. But there are better options. I think that we are ready. Be good simply because it's the right thing to do. That's what defines a brave person, a brave new world. It must happen. We are *all* in this together."

Only the waves and the crackling, dying fire made any sound for several moments. Sam was close enough to the fire that his light coat would smell like smoke for weeks, which he thought was a better aroma than any perfume on the market. For a while, he stared into the fire, at those pulsing, red embers glowing in the night. It was one of the few things which could truly transfix his mind. Only elemental things could. After a few moments he spoke again.

"I often find myself thinking, 'the world could be anything, and *this* is what we choose to make it?' A world where people have been taught to believe that there is life after death cannot last, biologically speaking. A world obsessed with consumption is doomed. The extinction rate is now about 10,000 times greater than it was before humans came onto the scene. If we as a species are not a cancer, what are we? It does *not* have to be this way. And it's so damned sad… All of the natural beauty that we have destroyed and will destroy because we do not treat what is really sacred—mysterious, fragile, beautiful, true—as sacred."

In Brazil a bulldozer cracked the last of a people's arrow as it cut into a virgin forest, a tree was toppled on which the last of a certain species of vine grew, on which the last species of an orchid that would have been called the 'Medicine Maiden' clung—which those native people who no longer existed had known of. On that tree—which no longer lived—the last species of a moth with a wingspan the size of a basketball had fed, and would starve, on which the last of a tiny species of insect lived that had mucus lining its digestive tract which dripped into the eyes turned regular vision into sharply contrasting, vibrant colors which allowed it to be seen that leaves breathe—and gasp—too. The rest of the trees would fall and cattle would there graze which would be slaughtered and sent to fast-food chains in the U.S., where people who, because of something engrained deep within their minds—even though many of them had never stepped a foot in a classic, 'this is how it is,' church—went about day to day life without wonder, were not appalled at the destruction of the world, did nothing to stop it.

"I cannot play anyone else's game anymore. So, I've decided that I will not. The waves, this fire, the stars, the heavy air. It's all around us. There should be temples and churches worshiping the mystery rather than temples and churches worshiping certainty. There would be weekly discussions of possibility. And the main tenet of this new religion would go something like: 'Be wary of those who claim to have all of the answers. Protect the beauty. Our duty here is to preserve life—from the smallest plant to the biggest animal. It is also our duty to live while alive—to think, feel, and imagine. Why must this beauty be explained?'"

He looked around at the dark faces of his friends, wondered if he had lost any.

"Wouldn't that be more honest, healthy? We are a part of something infinitely bigger—that's all that we can be certain about. One day, I want to know that I'm completely honest with myself. I want to know that I'm cleansed of what I was born to. I want to know that I've done my best to appreciate this strange gift. That would be 'a good day to die.' And that's my wish—to see that day, be fine with leaving, have something to protect. Because I just can't die yet. Not like this."

Oddly enough, Ellen, Steve, and Mary all knew that it was a Lakota phrase that Sam had referenced with 'a good day to die.' He had spoken at length about his admiration for Crazy Horse, a Lakota warrior who had been content to die—a man who had had the heart to fight to the very end when his people had either been beaten into submission or lulled into forgetting what was, a man who was stabbed in his back by those who he fought for.

There can still be warriors. Must be.

And all of Sam's friends knew that he was done talking.

"Shit just got real," Steve said.

A few moments of silence followed.

Sam reached down into the blue-purple sand which was warm on top and cool below. He scooped the biggest handful that he could, and looked at the hazy figures of his friends. He smiled an invisible smile, and flung the sand in a spreading pattern which hit everyone. Suddenly, sand was flying everywhere. And they were all laughing.

They eventually quieted down, and only plucks of dying laughter remained intermingled with the sound of waves charging the shore and coals wheezing.

"Real just got shit," Sam said.

There were a few laughs again.

Ellen looked up at the stars, feeling very small, and thought about what Sam had said about our Universe looking just like a brain. She knew that it was just another possibility—merely one of an infinite amount—and did not feel that the hypothesis would hold much water if scrutinized by those who were eager to disprove. Nonetheless, she imagined that the streaking comet which goes through the dark, seen sometimes in the night sky, was a bullet that we could watch before it completes the final damage that's already imminent. The trigger of all of our lives already pulled, us just waiting for it to all go away.

Everyone has dark thoughts, I hope.

"I wish that we hadn't waited so long to be friends," she said to the two people who would be graduating in two months and to one who would be graduating in six, along with her.

Sam felt like she was talking specifically to him, and she partly was, which made his chest burn with frustration. She was so very nice, and so very taken. It probably wasn't true, but it did seem like all of the good ones were taken.

There was a murmur of assent, and then a return to silence.

"Alright," Steve said, "I guess that counts. Mary, it's your turn. See if you can top what the rock star said."

There was only the sound of waves gently crashing on the shore for several moments. But she eventually spoke in her meek voice.

"I wish that I could have the courage to speak my mind more often."

She was very moved by what Sam had said but knew that she would say nothing of the feeling to him.

Her sad eyes looked longingly into the dark like they had at the first Candid Club meeting towards Sam's, eyes that did not look back the same way and did not really see hers. It was as if there was always the darkness that was there currently.

"Like whenever I hear someone asking what they should be for Halloween, I'd say what I thought: 'why don't you take off the mask that you wear every day and just be yourself?'"

*

Sam flipped down the mask to the helmet and put all of his weight on the kick-start of the old motorcycle until it finally started again. He liked the way it sounded, and the way that the vibrations felt. The bike was heavy as he gave it a little gas and guided it slightly towards the road. An old man stood with his arms folded in the blue evening. He wore a greasy outfit—the work clothes which he used at an auto-repair shop. There were a lot of rusty, old cars in various states of disrepair on the property. There was also a rusty, old basketball hoop that Sam looked at with sadness as he ran his finger over the gash that was on the helmet.

The man had given Sam a ride to his place in the country based on the promise that he'd gotten via a phone call.

"Just get me there, and I'll buy it if it runs," Sam had said from the bar's phone-booth while Jake was sleeping soundly in the motel room in a bed that Sam had paid for.

It felt awful, but he had just *had* to leave Jake. So, he had quietly left the room early in the morning, with a gently throbbing head-ache from the night before, awake because the floor was so hard and due to Jake's incredibly loud snoring. He left nearly all of the cash that he had in his wallet for his new friend who he would probably never see again—so he could buy medicine.

With what was left of his money, Sam bought a post-card in the lobby on a sentimental whim, thinking sorrowfully of the short phone-call home. Then, he had wandered through the tiny town towards the road that went north and noticed a hand-written advertisement for the motorcycle stapled to a wooden telephone pole. It seemed like a good way to get away. Impulsively, he memorized the number, walked to the bar, and then clinked the two quarters that had been left over from purchasing the postcard into the payphone. After dialing the number, he had a brief conversation with a quiet-seeming man and then made the promise of purchase on the condition of a ride. The seller had said that he would pick up Sam in front of the bowling alley after he got off work in the evening. And rather than going back to the room as he waited for time to pass and the man to pick him up, Sam waited inside the bowling alley.

There was nothing that he could do for Jake. That 'nothing you can do about it' feeling was a much too familiar one which Jake reminded him of, the feeling which more than anything he was desperately trying to escape. So, he hid away until 6:00 PM, shamefully.

The bowling alley was half-full of smoke that smelled dirty blue, coming from the cigarettes of four old men wearing flannel shirts and stiff jeans, who all had raspy voices. They were there the whole time that Sam was—which was for about seven hours. He assumed that they spent every day at the bowling alley, maybe taking holidays off.

In his journal, he wrote lines that he thought should be written on the postcard which would be sent to Maine. It had to be real and had to be a good explanation for his actions. He wouldn't write on the card until he had it all down in his head.

So as not to be a loiterer, he was 'strongly encouraged' to buy both lunch and dinner. And so he did. As he ate a lunch of cheese fries and fried mushrooms, he watched an old guy with odd form who was surprisingly good at knocking down the pins. The man had to have played twenty games, all by himself, was still playing when Sam had cinnamon sticks for supper.

By the time six o'clock rolled around and the guy arrived in an old truck to give Sam a ride, he had a decent idea of what he would write on the postcard. From the bowling alley, they drove past the bar where Jake got his medicine and Sam could not help but look. There Jake stood with his cardboard sign, still waiting. Sam looked sadly through the window at his friend who had probably already spent the money from his wallet and felt like he was seen even though he was not.

It was a long, quiet drive into the Georgia countryside.

They had gotten straight to business once they arrived at the house. The old man nodded his head as Sam sat on the running motorcycle, as if to say, 'told you it runs.' And Sam had smiled the smile that his friends and family loved. The man sold the bike to him for $200. It was actually worth much more than this, about a hundred times more, but neither he nor Sam realized this. The bike had belonged to the old man's old man, who was long dead, and had been what inspired his son to buy a Kawasaki. The kid had always bragged about how fast it went.

"Gently let go of the clutch and give it gas—a little less gently," the old man had said to Sam, with an old and muscled hand on his back.

The bike lurched forward away from the hand, and then stopped after a little resistance. The old man walked over slowly, with a slight smile. He enjoyed seeing improvement, and calmly explained what Sam—who had not let go of the clutch—had done wrong.

If you cannot teach it, you do not understand it.

"It's the link which allows your message to be sent. If you do not release, the message cannot be sent."

As Sam eventually understood the process, and drove around the gravel loop a few times, the old man wished that his son never had.

So, the old man was glad to help Sam strap his pack on the 'bitch-seat,' and gave him the helmet that his son had been wearing when he died in an accident on his Kawasaki, which he mentioned sadly. It had a large gash in it, but apparently was 'still good.' The man insisted that he take it, and Sam finally gave in. It was obvious that the poor guy did not want to throw the helmet away—the same as the bike—though did not want it around either.

Sam shook the man's hand after his pack was loaded, and then went over to the old Indian to start it again. It began to cry harshly in the night. He took another sad look at the basketball hoop and, though he couldn't hear the words, knew that the man said, 'Be careful,' by the way his lips moved.

The pain that the man felt was very obvious—at having lost a loved one. And Sam felt terribly guilty about how close he had come to imposing that feeling on his family. *Terribly.*

Sam waved, and walked the bike off of the loose gravel, giving it a little gas. The yellow headlight went over all of the things that the man liked to mess with. Then the light was on the road which led through darkening fields. And then Sam was gone—which left the old man alone again.

Moths and other insects shot through the light as he accelerated. He'd never driven a motorcycle before but was quickly becoming comfortable. It reminded him of all of the snowmobiling he had done in Maine, the feeling of driving through the cold, open air. The gravel of the road that he drove on was not stable, and his back tire slid back and forth. It was like the purposely induced thrill of sliding on ice and he kind of enjoyed it, as being a little out of control, by design, was the desirable norm. A few times, though, he lost that control—which he did not like.

He did, however, make it to the interstate without falling, to his own surprise. And soon the dashed lines were flying by. The faster he went, the more he forgot his sadness. It felt good to drive something that he owned. He soared over the pavement without even so much as a thought in regard to the deer that were thinking about running out on the road to teach him another lesson about mortality.

It did not take long for him to realize that he was experiencing the illusion of freedom, which also felt very good. Forgetting about oil was easy.

For a moment, he had the feeling which he had dreamed of. There it was in him. And he didn't want it to leave. He remembered the lust for it that had convinced him to undertake the venture upon which he found himself. On the open road, soaring, he left all uncertainty and doubt behind for a while. The night was so cold and dark that he almost felt that he could drink it in. He went faster and drove happily. Thoughts of turning around and going to Mexico were very real, but he realized that he was drunk off of the night and decided to wait until he was sober to make such a decision. He didn't want to stop. There was so much behind him.

Reluctantly, though, he eventually pulled off of the road when he saw a pink, glowing sign that said 'vacancy.' He parked, stopped to look admiringly at what had moved him, and went into the office.

After he had checked in, swiped his debit card, and gotten his room key, he felt good enough to start a mini conversation with the balding guy at the front desk who had cut up lips and a round head.

"How's life been treating you?" he said to the guy with eyes that were full of the reflection of the TV on the wall.

"Not too bad."

Sam smiled to himself. The man looked to him, as if for an explanation.

"The implication of 'not too bad' is not good. It's just some state of bad. Most don't realize what their words mean."

"Oh, I know what they mean."

These words had not been expected.

"I'm sorry."

Looking into the blank, defeated eyes, everything which had been behind him when on the motorcycle caught back up immediately. He returned to the land of the dying. His eyes fell down.

After a few moments of looking quietly at the green counter on which his room-key rested, Sam did as the guy expected him to do by scooping it up and leaving the office. He heard his footsteps on the sticky floor, opened the flimsy door, and walked towards his room through the yellow light of the parking lot where the motorcycle shined lies.

*

In the morning, Sam decided to visit another resting place after he left the motel. If it had a sign, it would have said 'no vacancy.' The place was as full as it could be—a little plot of grass which was alone amongst pastures and oak woodlands, full of gravestones. It was hard to imagine where all of the dead had come from. There were no houses within sight. The cemetery was on another gravel road that he had not been able to resist going down, even though the tires slid without his consent. His bike was parked next to a wire which was attached to two mostly rusty posts that were originally white. There were mangled American flags which had been beaten by the wind tied to other rusty posts. It didn't look like anyone had mowed the grass since it had begun to grow in earnest again.

He stepped over the part of the wire which was sagging the most, and then walked through the stones that stuck out of the ground. Most of them were very old, but there were a few newer ones which seemed to represent the livelier dead.

Sam's mental math skills were always utilized when he visited cemeteries. It was interesting to see how old people were when they died, and to see how many he could find that were near his age, or younger, when it happened. Those were the ones that he thought the most about. The stories that he made up for them were always so much more real than for those who died older.

'William Hooker, 1830-1865.' *Civil War. Shot in head.*

'Gabrielle Baker, September 21-November 4.' *Not even a chance to begin. Hay fever.*

Many of the tombstones where limestone and corroded to the point that he couldn't read them. Commemoration for these people was no longer possible due in large part to acid rain, which in itself was a little saddening.

We even corrupt the rain.

The markers looked like white pieces of soap sticking out of the ground at all angles. A lot of them were even knocked down. Some of the markers were just bricks that looked as if they never even had had a name carved into them. He walked towards the back of the cemetery, eyes cast down, reading each stone. Finally, he found one that he could think about.

'Born in 1782. Mary Smith, 22 years old, two months, and four days.' *Lover's leap.*

There were so many ways that she could have died. But none of them really mattered. All of them meant that she went before her time. He could see the rolling, green mounds of the Appalachians in the distance. He was sure that in them was a cliff that would be tall enough for such a name that had eerily popped into his head. And he felt sure that she had jumped.

Her stone was leaning slightly forward, and isolated in the furthest corner of the cemetery near a large tree that certainly had wrapped its roots around her bones long ago. Her cold gravestone was in the majority which had no pretty flowers to stand beside and attempt to cheer. She had been entirely forgotten, just as the ones that still had flowers beside them would be.

Everyone is forgotten.

There was tall grass that had grown up around her stone. Sam bent down and pulled up the stalks. It seemed OK to kill them, even if for something that was dead.

He found himself wondering if she had ever known love. There were so many varieties—as a parents' child, as a sibling, as an admirer, as a part of something, as a friend, as a parent, as a spouse, as a prisoner. He hoped that she had known as much love as possible in her short life. But for some reason he just could not shake the image of a pale girl wearing a lace necklace and white dress. She had dark, long, wind-blown hair. Her face was very calm. And she was standing on the edge.

"The world, a fucking mirror," he whispered to himself. He shook his head involuntarily as a way to try to be rid of the thought and walked on.

There was a marker that was face down. It was a small stone, which probably meant a meek person. If their ghost could have objected to the thoughtless kid that knocked the stone down, it probably would not have, Sam thought, just like the person probably did not object to anything that was wrong with their life. But Sam knew that he was being cynical. And he also knew that his own stone would probably say nothing of the way he felt, just as the face-down piece of marble likely symbolized nothing accurately for the dead person. And his stone would probably be small if he had one at all.

He made it to the other corner of the cemetery, looking for stories, and then walked towards the road doing the same. He was happy to find one. There was a newer stone with two names on it, which with its red-marble seemed much more cozy and illustrious than the other ones.

'"Old" Dan Samuelson—Margaret "Little Ann" Samuelson.'

They had died within a week of each other, he at 74 years of life and she at 70 years.

Where the red fern grows.

He walked on, thinking of the story that had made him cry as a child. It was strange how something not thought about in a very long time can just come back given the slightest stimulus—there all along. And when dealing with something that was encountered as a child, childlike emotions re-emerge. The story involved a hunting dog that died of a broken heart after its dog-companion died.

Animal suffering is so much worse, for some reason. Probably because they're like naked humans. What they do we hide.

It still made him sad to think about the story—little boy sad. But now he was able to hold back the tears.

By the road there were two little stones that had a square bottom and an arched top. Across the arched tops, one said 'mother' and one said 'father.' There was no mention of names. And there was no question who had buried them. Beside them was a smaller stone of the same form which had no name, dated a few years after they had died, titled 'daughter.' As sad as it was, Sam imagined that she died because her role was dead.

A new role can be very hard to accept.

He took one last look over the cemetery. Strangely, it felt relaxing to be amongst the dead. It was the most level he had felt in a long time. And a part of him wanted to take another walk through, but he knew that it would be less meaningful the second time.

So he stepped again over the wire. The rattling motor broke the silence of the cemetery. And Sam drove towards the eroded mountains which had been dying for a long time. The reason why was not clear. There might have been no reason at all.

Chapter 11

Campus was covered by large-flaked, white, fluffy snow that many of the especially alive people wanted to jump into. And some of them did. There were snowmen all over the place. A few Snow Angels littered the battle fields of the snowball fights. But not many.

There was no wind at all. Really, it was quite beautiful, with the snow glazed on the trees. A white, winter silence was all around. Very few people ran or laughed in the cold. But some did. Students with snow on their coats walked on snow-covered walks between historic, brick buildings. Winter break had just ended, so their minds were still with home or wherever they had chosen to escape to.

Sam sat on a stone bench. He'd mostly cleared it of snow, which revealed a plaque which said that it had been 'generously donated by the class of 1936.' It would have been very interesting to see what campus was like then, what the people were like, how friendly they were, but all that he could do was watch those who shared the current moment with him. And so he did. He took in a deep, cold breath and then watched it come out, vanishing with the time.

Last semester.

Much had changed since the first, and he had learned a lot since then. More than anything, it was easy to learn what not to be. What to be is a much more difficult lesson. There were a lot of things not to be.

He had learned what potheads were. It is always nice to have friends in high places, as most 'elected' officials know, but it is not so nice to have high friends in low places. He had learned what alcoholics were, which made him think a little more about who his idols should be and made him realize why so many rebels drank. Their minds will be beaten one way or the other, so they end up doing the beating themselves. He had learned what a bitch was, which made him careful to not fall for acts. This had been a very important lesson. But, most importantly, he had learned what a friend was, which gave him the strength to keep going.

Two of those friends had just graduated, however, and the other one was still visiting her boyfriend in the northern part of the state. He wondered if Ellen would avoid him now that there would not be the buffer of Steve and Mary.

How easy it would be to leave.

Attending school is to stay in one spot when there's a whole world out there, he had learned, and to have domestic life dangled in front of your nose each day by people who want you to be just like them. It had not taken long for him to realize this. It had taken him a bit longer to realize how easy it would be to just walk away.

But quitting school at the point he was at would be like choosing to amputate a mostly healed finger so as not to have to deal with keeping it dry when taking a shower. Even if inconvenient, school was for the best in the long run. Which was why he was going to finish. Despite the fact that he did not like being told what to read, he actually enjoyed very few things as much as learning—which made school easy.

There was nothing more valuable, more sweet and transcendental, than the attainment of knowledge.

To know *everything* would be terribly depressing, however. The more that is learned is to realize how little is known. It was startling to think how different he was leaving college than he had been when he entered, understanding what it means to know that so little is known. Everything had been so much easier before—when there was no reason to question those in charge.

Really, it seemed like most of his college years, even his life, had been a voyage upon smooth water. His little boat sailed upon an ocean, only occasionally experiencing any turbulence whatsoever. Scrub the decks, patch the sails, smell the salt, sleep, repeat. There was no adventure, no fear. It seemed like both could have happened long ago, but not in the modern age. He sailed in happy, blind seas.

Then, from out of nowhere, everything happened at once. From all directions the waves came, the captain was maniacally screaming things that didn't make sense, water was sloshing over the sides, and the ship was thrown violently from swell to swell. And he nearly sank.

Fear became real. Everything was an impossible adventure.

The compilation of successive detrimental events seemed worse than what even the most twisted author could dream up. Not just the big things—like existential crises—but the little things too, like an unexpected fine, or a nasty rash, or a phone-call that's not returned. They all added up. And that one pervasive thought, the germ of insanity, was placed in his head.

What if the whole Universe really is against just me?

Despite what anyone says, there is absolutely no way to disprove such an utterly frightening theory. It makes as much sense as anything else. The common colloquialism, 'is it just me, or…?' is one of many that, if thought about, could be taken on a literal, terrifying level.

This place really could be Hell.

Eventually, though, Sam was able to be rid of such crippling thoughts. And, in a way, they proved to be useful even though he was glad that they were mostly gone. A taste of madness can be very valuable to the sort of person who can control themselves enough that they eat only a single piece of chocolate out of the heart-shaped box. Otherwise, it's the most debilitating candy in the world.

One thought kept him from unraveling, and even had taken him to the point where he felt stronger than ever before—most of the time.

We are all in this together.

Looking back, it felt good to have gotten through. Having survived what he had, he felt as if he could get through anything. And there was something valuable in that, something that made all of the hardship seem worth it.

His journals showed that he had not written anything great before the dance with death—that storm. It might be impossible to do so. Therefore, he could not regret it.

To be rebuilt, a person must first be torn down. They then pick and choose the parts of themselves to keep, throw the rest out. In the end, it's worth the trouble. But during reconstruction, it is ever so scary. All of the world's madness just might get into your head. If it merely runs through before your roof can be put back on, you'll be stronger for it. Just don't pound in the last nail until what you want gone is out. Because it will never leave.

Sam considered himself a new person. Most of his memories belonged to someone else.

His ship was built—roof to the cabin complete—and everything was beginning to be smooth again, as calm and silent as the cold day full of large flakes falling. He felt surprisingly good. But it just did not feel right anymore scrubbing the deck, patching the sails, and all of that. There was a wheel, he knew. And that wheel is where life is.

It was utterly frightening to think where he would be headed if not for that storm. But it had happened, thankfully.

And he knew that he would be ready for the next one. He would never again allow himself to get to the point where he forgot about waves.

A person who looked like they had to be a freshman—still big-eyed and baby-faced—left some prints on the sidewalk in front of Sam. The tag was still on his boots, but there was no point in trying to tell him. He had earphones on. So Sam watched him walk away, tag fluttering. The kid had no idea. And that kid, not long ago, had been him.

Sam was ready to leave, he knew. Graduation, at the moment, did not scare him. But where he was going to go, he did not know.

A lot of people walked by. One class session had just finished and the next was about to begin. They all seemed to know where they were going. One of them was a girl with wavy blonde hair who was in a sorority. Her affiliation was very obvious because she had a bag with Greek letters on it, dark yoga pants, and hair that seemed important to her. As she walked by, she looked at the reflection of herself in a large window of the building that Sam was closest to. She seemed very pleased, and annoyed at the same time. It was actually very easy to pick out which girls belonged to a sorority, for the most part.

People try to fit in so much that they never know who it is that they are. I suppose it's easier that way…

He had drafted an independent study, which boredom had driven him to conduct one day, for three hours, which showed that forty percent of people that walked by looked at their reflection. He had actually conducted many independent studies. Another one showed that sixty percent of people blocked their surroundings out in one form or another— they had earbuds in, were talking on the phone, were texting, or using their phone to do something else. He had scientifically supported what he already knew: few people are interested in looking at or doing anything that's not reflective. No one wanted to see much.

This particular day, as Sam sat on the cold bench, he didn't even have school-related work to use for passing the time. At the moment, there was nothing left to write about insanity and the class that he had taught was done—the latter of which he actually missed. There was nothing that he wanted to read either, which was generally what he did—just walk around campus, reading whatever book had somehow popped into his head. It seemed like the time to actually *do* the things that he had read about, to experience rather than imagine. And due to the amount of reading that he had done, there was a lot of doing in order.

Watching people was usually vaguely interesting.

Most of the people who walked by were wearing the same sort of clothing, and individual flare was not greatly apparent when everyone was dressed in their warmest rags. There was always that one guy, though, who dressed like it was summer, just to be different. And that guy walked past. He looked to be about six hundred pounds. Other than this, some people wore interesting hats.

But as Sam watched and the snow fell, everyone became the same, not only in attire.

For the first time in his life, he felt to be on the same level as those around him. There had always been an age barrier, or a cool-kid barrier, or a pot-head barrier—always something. But it was very apparent that all were in this together. The old, the young, the dumb, the smart.... Because who can be old when there's no such thing as time and who can be smart when there is no such thing as knowing?

Interacting with others had gotten to the point that it was no longer difficult. For months he had known what he had just realized about all people being the same. He may have thought the words before, but never believed them. He wondered what other epiphanies he was steadily working towards.

Communication was natural, ethical, and necessary, he thought, looking at approximately sixty percent of the surrounding people who had ear-buds in.

A campus inhabited by those who have closed themselves off to their classmates is a lonely, vulnerable one. A society which allows frighteningly insane and antiquated thoughts to live invites them to be put into the minds of the lonely and vulnerable.

People could be thought of as snowflakes in an ice age. Most of the flakes know that there is no fear of melting. Very easily, though, they could come together to create something beautiful and unstoppable—like a glacier erasing all of the old topography. However, the flakes quietly respect the old fear without confronting it. And let it live.

Sam shivered, thinking about burning forever. He thought about fear in people's eyes, silence, non-interaction, boredom, and the explosion which must result from that formula. The human world didn't have to be cold. But it was.

And it hurts to feel one with people who do not feel one with you.

Sam was considering getting up to go thaw somewhere warm when a form of entertainment less difficult than thinking presented itself.

To his right, walking towards him, he saw a girl who had been in the same high school class as him. She wore jeans, 'Ugg' boots and a coat that had a furry-fringed hood. He had seen her many times before but she had not once noticed him. Sam decided to cultivate an interaction with her, even though he hadn't spoken to her in nearly five years. And even then, he had hardly talked to her at all.

He stood and walked casually in her direction. As usually happened, the person he walked towards did not look at him, but rather at some more interesting object which was either to the right, left, up, or down. She took out her phone, and, after looking at her reflection, started to type something into it. It was obvious that she was not even going to acknowledge his presence.

"Anna?" he said in a surprised voice, "is that you?"

She stopped, and looked at him blankly. He looked at her with his hands out, along with a rosy-cheeked smile, and realized how fun this would be to do to someone who did not actually know him, whose name he knew. He had seen the look on her face many times on the faces of those who had not seen him for a while. And, as usual, after about three seconds her eyes lit up.

"Sam! I hardly even recognized you! You're hair, it's so long."

"Yeah, I finally decided to let it do what it's been trying to do all of these years before it gets fed up and jumps ship. And at the very least it symbolizes a certain state of mind that's lasted a while, you know, a strong constitution."

She felt no choice but to laugh, and so did.

"It's been such a long time. You look so different, but *good*. Have you seen Frank?"

"Actually, yeah. I've found Frank Foley's a fat fuck now."

Her eyes once again showed pleasant surprise and a little smile, as the Sam she had known in high school would never have said that about her ex-boyfriend, and his ex-kind-of-friend.

He smiled.

"Pardon me. I've an affinity for alliteration. And I couldn't think of any words that are more fitting."

"Well, it's true. He has gained a little weight. More than a little, I guess."

He looked at her face, which was white and cold in the snow. Her hair was reddish-brown, which contrasted the snow that was speckled on it nicely. Her lips were pink, and her mouth was slightly open. Her eyelashes seemed too long. But all and all, she was very attractive on a physical level. And she was looking at him with eyes that he had never seen in high school. He thought that she must have read about him in the school newspaper but hoped that that wasn't the reason for her eyes. Maybe he'd developed a rugged model look without knowing it? Regardless, he'd soon be in a place where he would not have an article as aid.

The thing about facing rejection is that it usually elicits an emotion which someone who is feeling nothing but a sense of how pointless everything seems will thoroughly enjoy—as a reprieve of sorts. And if he was not rejected, that would elicit a feeling too.

So, his words were delivered in hope that he might feel.

"Want to grab lunch?"

"Yeah."

The word was soft, and elongated.

They began walking side by side towards The Diner, and she began talking about herself.

He encouraged it because he had heard that "yeah" was her default answer to any question and was going to find out.

*

Sam looked at a baby which still had the sweet, milky smell. It was cute, but he was glad that he did not have one of his own.

Oh, so very glad. Not ready yet.

He thought of himself as an artist not yet ready for his Clay. The beginning for the baby would be the end for him, in a way. Or, at least, the end of the life that he knew.

The baby was in its mother's arms, looking over her shoulder. Sam was standing behind her in the line at Burger King. And the baby was looking at him with big, perplexed eyes. He looked back, and quickly made a strange face which made the baby smile. One of the workers behind the counter saw the exchange and gave Sam a wry smile. The mother saw the look that the worker gave Sam and turned around to give a very stern look to him. She mumbled something, looking at him with milky eyes. At the moment, there was a lot of milk in her system. Sam smiled when he saw the worker make a quick face at the child too. When the mother turned around and ordered the baby was smiling again.

He had heard that babies cannot see in color. Or at least that during their first months things become more clear and colorful. Otherwise their little minds would be overloaded with stimuli during the emergence from darkness.

Looking at the baby, Sam thought about how the history of one's life is much like the history of the world, our Universe. The farther back you go, the less clear things become.

Color, black and white, vagueness, nothing.

When it was his turn, he ordered and then limped, only slightly, over to a booth to eat his fries and burger. It was nice being close to the play area, with all of the plastic balls, the slide, the rope-ladder and tubes. He could remember when he was short enough to enter. It had been so much more exciting when there was a toy with each meal. But he was once again recapturing that feeling in regard to most things. Buzz Lightyear didn't do it anymore, though.

It was a beautiful day outside—one of those days when he wished that he had a friend who was as free as he imagined himself being, who was willing to explore. It might even turn out being better than playing in the ball pit and tubes had been. But he wouldn't know.

His elbow hurt whenever he moved it, which he began to do purposely.

Cutters.

He thought of the waitress, remembering that she had a name that he liked, but not what it was—which was annoying—and wondered if her razor had been bloodied since he saw her. And then he thought of poor Jake, and his mother. He moved his elbow again, and it clicked disconcertingly. His skin burnt, but he wasn't thinking about anything besides the physical pain anymore. The sadness was replaced.

Putting his nose to his hands, he took in the smell of oil which he had been unable to wash away. His mind went through the events of the day which had brought him to where he was, dirtied his hands, and pained his body.

He had followed the signs north towards a town called Rome, hoping to see something comparable to the Coliseum. All that he found was a couple guys sucking on the tits of a wolf, which was closer than he had expected. It was actually sort of fun to tear down his missing-person posters around town. It was like a scavenger hunt where he was a $50 prize that didn't want to be found. He'd already taken down four posters. Brit had apparently been spreading them throughout the state of Georgia with a vengeance.

He crinkled the collection of posters into a ball and held it in his hand.

The warm and stagnant air of the dusty town was a deceptive blanket which suggested an unshakable and desired constancy. From point to point most of the creatures walked the same route which they usually did—spinning through town or sitting behind glass or tilting a glass.

As Sam looked for posters, people walked by and he could feel their stares, their suspicions, the stories about him which would be told. Their eyes—those bordered with mascara, those bloodshot and glazed, or those lobotomized, whatever—all seemed to be waiting for him to pull a gun or something. For if just one person in the town were shot, there would be a story for all of them to salivate over.

The busy bees went about their work, buzzing along in a world of boredom which they clung on to despite the fact that almost every one of them secretly wished that the hive next door would be shaken.

Nothing is more exciting than a murder, here—an old-fashioned brain-bashing.

Sam studied his silly face on another poster which was taped on the door of an arcade before he pulled it down. His ball of paper grew larger, and then he shot it into a recycling bin.

A nasally voice frightened him.

"What do you think you are doing, buddy?"

There were the bulging eyes of a slightly plump man with a ridiculously groomed head of hair staring at him from the doorway of the arcade.

"They found that guy on the poster. I'm just taking them down. He was a con-artist, went by several different names actually. Got caught collecting the rewards for his other missing identities."

For a few seconds the man licked his lips—possibly subconsciously. But, he eventually lied: "Wow. I'm glad they got him. Don't want people like that disturbing the peace."

And then he slinked back behind the glass again.

After Sam cleared the town of the missing-person posters, he decided to cruise around on the Indian, and soon found himself on residential streets looking at houses, imagining living in one of them with someone warm—who was not into murders or gossip. It didn't seem so bad.

But his thoughts were forced to immediately change, like they too often did when they happened to land on something good.

The bike took a stop sign far too literally, or at least abruptly. For some reason, it locked up and stopped so suddenly that Sam was thrown over the handle bars. His elbow took the brunt of the impact, and a two inch by five inch chunk of skin was scraped off from the point of his elbow down his forearm. His cheek also touched the pavement, and was bloodied a little bit which, he would later think, was probably what the baby was looking at so intently. The bike seemingly teetered for seconds—like it was deciding whether or not it should fall—and then decided. It fell a few inches from his already twisted ankle. His pack fell off and the hot engine melted his jug of water which resulted in steam, sizzling, and a dying-type noise from the motorcycle. All this caught an old woman's eye from her kitchen window. She left her crocheting material and hurried out, even if with little, hunched steps. She found Sam sitting on the curb, blood on his arm glittering in the sun and dripping down his face.

To him, her sweet face which had a bandaged nose was a reminder of inherent human compassion—the fear for him in her eyes.

"Are you alright?"

He couldn't help but smile, and when he did he tasted his own blood. Strangely, through the numbness it tasted good.

"I'm not much into politics, but I'd like the think I'm closer to all left."

In five minutes he was sitting at the kitchen table in the old woman's house. It was little and well-kept, with a nice, musty smell. There were about eighty brown eggs laying on a bunch of towels on the kitchen counter, for some probably humorous reason. But Sam didn't ask. Everything looked to be from the sixties, or from some other decade that Sam didn't know. From his chair, he saw a large, box-shaped, heavy-looking TV in a shag-carpeted living room turned off, and then heard a man grunting and a recliner squeaking. An old man walked into the kitchen, slowly dropping and raising his slippers on the linoleum.

The place, as well as the two old people who lived in it, was simple. Beautifully simple. They reminded him of his parents in about twenty years.

His elbow already had a brown bandage on it. She dabbed a cotton ball in the antibacterial solution of hydrogen peroxide in a brown container.

"Why weren't you wearing a helmet?" she asked sternly.

"Well, I know that it's an awful excuse, but I like the feel of wind in my hair. I actually have a helmet in my backpack. But at least it doesn't have another gash in it, right?"

Her husband scraped a heavy chair backwards from the table and sat down.

She shook her head, as his answer made her not feel bad in the least about the pain that she was about to inflict. He winced when the cotton ball touched his face. The sting was very strong, which made him wonder if she had some super-potent mixture from the early Cold War days.

Maybe the Soviets' plan was to contaminate antibacterial solutions—death by a thousand cuts.

"What's so funny?" she said in friendly tone as she exposed the sticky part of the bandage that she was about to put on his face.

"My head—I hope."

Her husband looked at Sam skeptically from across the table. His face was droopy, and his shirt collar was ruffled. His shoulders were slumped, and his arms were very veiny on the table. He looked yellow, but brave.

When the old man spoke, his voice was deep and gravelly.

"What do you want to do about that bike?"

"I really don't know."

"My son will have a look at it."

He got up without even the slightest bit of hesitation and walked over to a phone which was wired to the wall.

"Oh, no. Don't bother him," Sam said.

"It's fine. He lives just down the way."

He dialed surprisingly quickly.

Sam watched the poor guy frown as an excuse was given as to why his son couldn't come over.

Sad: In the end a father will seek his busy son's attention like the son did his busy father's in the beginning. And neither gets it like they should.

Gruffly, the old father said to Sam, "I can have a look at it."

He had been fixed up, so Sam followed the old man out the door after thanking the old woman and subtly refusing a couple dozen eggs. He did, though, accept a couple of her milk jugs—for water.

As it turned out, there had been an issue with the chain of the bike which was an easy fix. The old guy told Sam what to do, and the bike was running smoothly after a few minutes. The only trouble was that Sam's hands became greasy, but it was well worth it to get moving again.

"Thanks for the help. I really appreciate it. Want me to pick you up anything from Burger King?"

The old man's eyes were sad and far-off as he shook his head. They were round, dark, and suddenly seemed confused. He put up a wrinkled hand to wave good-bye and took little steps towards his house. Sam wished he knew the address of the old man's son, but he didn't. There was nothing that he could do, again.

So he headed to Burger King, carefully.

After he ate, he decided that he was not in the mood for more travel and thought that it would be a good idea to let some of his cuts that weren't bandaged scab over before subjecting them to the whipping air. He'd seen a sign for a campground at the edge of town that he was going to find—so he could rest and watch the river go by. It would be refreshing to put a nice, new coat of perfume on his clothes, too.

For a while, he listened to a couple of young women—who sounded almost exactly like old women. They were in the booth behind him. It was impossible not to listen, unfortunately. One of them had a scratchy voice, the other a snappy, confrontational one. They both spoke in tones which were embellished by dismay.

Snappy started: "Did you hear about that guy who has just been caught by authorities?"

"No, what did he do?"

"He cut off the faces of his victims to steal their identities and then claimed the reward money for 'finding' missing people who he'd abducted. But here's the sickest part. He claimed the money while *wearing* the faces of other missing people to hide his own identity!"

"OH....MY....GOSH."

There was a headshaking break in conversation.

"People are just *animals*," said Scratchy as she chewed on a piece of flesh.

Just as he was about to leave—unable to stand any more of the ridiculous conversation—out from the play area the mom came with her baby. She gave Sam a worried glance and scurried, half-hurriedly by. Over her orange, vomit-stained shoulder the baby looked. Those big, dark eyes looked just like the old man's. Like they were waiting helplessly for something that they could not control.

That babe has no idea what's in store.

*

My Babe is figuring it out.

The mother was very scared because her son had always refused to be blinded ever since he was a little boy—was always asking questions.

'Why Mommy, but why?'

And she knew that he would not blind himself like she had done to herself, like her parents had done to themselves, like almost everyone does to themselves in one form or another.

Life was a lot like the sun, she'd decided, you just cannot look at it very hard, for very long, without being scathed in some way.

The miles went by quickly, as her mind was full, and soon the headlights of the car lit up a sign which said, 'Welcome to New Hampshire—Live Free or Die.'

She took a deep breath and kept on driving. Sam had seen that very same sign when they were heading to the university for the first time, when he knew how sad she felt about him going away. She was in the passenger seat, and he was in the back. His father was driving, unreadable. He might have been feeling as bad as her. But Sam doubted it, so he had said to her: "Ma, we gotta' live. I know that it's hard. But we weren't given any choice."

She thought about his words every time that she drove into the Granite State. They were very true.

She turned up the radio. A woman with a sickeningly soothing voice was talking about how to be happier. It was 'just that easy.'

Her car was the only one on the road—the older one, only her husband drove the Camaro.

It was two o'clock in the morning. She had tried to go to sleep at 9:00 PM, because she had felt so tired, but could not get to sleep and had gotten a phone call that awoke her mind just as it was about to switch gears. After the call, which had relayed big news, sleep was impossible. The decision to drive down to Georgia had been made when she heard her husband snoring, at 12:30 AM. He had not even so much as stirred when she got up. She left him a note on the front door that said, "I'm going to find Sam—sorry."

She knew that she had almost no shot of finding him.

That stubborn kid could be anywhere.

But when she exited the driveway she felt a little better, like a woman of action. Surprisingly, she had gotten quite a few 'Sam-sighting' calls from people all over the state of Georgia. A few of them actually sounded credible. One of them, who had a very quiet voice, said that Sam had helped her out a lot, inspired her by a note that he left. He had apparently taken the childhood rule 'always leave a note' to heart. They had spoken on the phone for nearly two hours. Her name was Mercedes. She seemed very nice, and said that she had quit smoking, wanted Sam to know that she appreciated the fact that he cared.

"Be a good human being, Julie," Mercedes had said. "With a son like Sam, I'm sure that you are."

She, and most of the other callers, said that Sam was somewhere around Atlanta. A surprising number of them said that they had interacted with him—and all of them commented either about how friendly or how strange he was. Genuine friendliness and strange are exactly the same.

Most of them said that he looked more or less healthy. But she could not put out of her mind the note that he'd written, sent by Will. And so, she felt that she had to look for him.

She did not know what she would to say to Sam if she did find him. Certainly not, 'I know the scary thoughts you have had—I'm a journal snooper.' Or at least not to begin with. She knew that she would bring up his dark thoughts, though. And that damned poem that he had written would be a good way to do so.

The miles melted by in the night. At 3:30 AM the woman on the radio stopped talking, which was nice, and soft music started playing. She knew that she was about through the Granite State. And after a few more miles, she saw those words again on the sign that said thank you for visiting New Hampshire.

Live free or die.

The car only made it a few hundred meters into Massachusetts before she pulled over to the side of the road and put her head against the wheel. She was startled when the horn beeped briefly. She knew that Sam had a right to do what he wanted, that he was only trying to live, even if it was hard on her. The music stopped and the woman on the radio began to talk about how to be happy again. With a sudden scream, she turned the radio all of the way down. After a few moments she turned the car around and saw the reassuring, but heart-wrenching words again.

Several times she found herself nodding off at the wheel, and it was frightening that the prospect of dying in a car wreck was not frightening. It seemed like a good excuse to die. But she stayed awake.

She got back to the house twenty minutes before her husband's alarm would go off. It was 5:40 AM. Quietly, she unlocked the front door and took the note down that she had left. She tore it up and threw it away. Then, she went to sit at the kitchen table. Before long she heard the abrasive beeping of the alarm clock upstairs, and then his feet thudding on the floor, and then creaking steps.

He walked around the corner with squinty, half-asleep eyes, in his underwear. He carried the suit that he would wear at work. His stomach jostled a little with each step.

My, his stomach is not as flat as it used to be.

"You're sure up early, grandma" he mumbled as he passed her and headed towards the shower.

It was going to be another long, exhausting day at a workplace where most of the people could not help but be bitter. It would be especially exhausting since she knew that Rob would be coming over after she got home from work to tell her that he was going to be a father. Erica had been the caller with news just when she was about to fall asleep. She was on Erica's excited call list, and knew that it would be rude to ask to be taken off of it. She'd promised Erica not to tell Rob that she already knew. And she was very proud of Rob, glad that she'd come back so that he could tell her about his baby.

But she was very tired.

Chapter 12

Rob sat on the tailgate of his truck. The vehicle was backed up to and overlooking an abandoned granite quarry. The doors were open so the breeze could come through, and there was a twang-twang country song playing from the speakers. It was nice to hear some classic lyric that he could relate to, like, 'Having a baby, maybe just maybe, he'll grow up to have no fear, sit beside me and drink a nice, cold beer.' There was always something about beer, rarely warm, in the music that he liked.

He did not know why, but there was something impressive about looking at open spaces. In this case the open space was a deep, wide hole with steep, rocky walls—full of very blue, clear rainwater in the middle of an expansive forest.

Damn, wet hole in the middle of a shrubby forest got me into this situation. Not so nice to look at.

After work, he'd driven to the quarry. Just as he'd been doing since news of the baby-to-come had arrived. They'd timed the wedding and all out just right.

There was not a rebellious bone in his body. Everything was set up as it was supposed to be. He'd decided long ago that things were tough all around. Everyone should follow the rules, because there was no point in breaking them. All people should make an effort to dress, speak, and think properly and most importantly to put in one honest, hard day of work after the other until it was time to retire. Just pray to God and let it be. Don't think too much. Let the guys in charge make the decisions. It seemed like they knew what they were doing. There was no reason to complicate things. Look at a pretty girl, forget everything else. There was really no reason to feel badly.

So it was strange that he was not feeling very good, and he did not know why he was feeling the way that he was. He couldn't describe feelings very well and so never tried. If anything, he would say something hackneyed like, 'I need to wake up and smell the coffee.' It sufficed. Overall, he was happy with his life. But it had become so predictable— despite his every effort—that his mom wasn't even surprised when he told her about the baby. And Sam had said that it would be this way, which was the worst thing about it all.

"Robbie, you're going to marry her. Have a couple kids. All of the attention will be on them, one might have something wrong with it— they're very good at finding wrong things these days. And you're never going to leave this town. Never. It's OK if that's what you want. But there's so much out there. *So much*. Once chance, that's all you're given. I hope that you've thought about this."

"Hell no, Sam. Hell no. We won't get married until I'm thirty. I am going to live."

This drunk-discourse had occurred during a night when Sam was back from college on break. As a general rule, anything that Sam said, Rob wanted to prove wrong. Maybe it was just part of being a younger brother—he didn't know. But he was married. Because Erica had made it clear that she would not wait. He was about to have a baby, for the same reason, and would probably not ever leave the town, it seemed. He would still do his best to prove Sam wrong, though, he thought. They would travel—maybe even to Miami, permanently. Erica had been talking like she wanted to. Really, he didn't have any choice but to listen to her, he felt. It was a very frightening thing to be alone.

He kicked a rock and watched it fall. It broke off a few other rocks which fell fast and there were thin shards that fluttered down onto the flat water. He watched the rocks splash through the surface and spiral all of the way to the bottom. It took about ten seconds for them to rest again. Almost everything was deeper than it seemed.

The thought of being a father was frightening. He knew that that was one of the main reasons why he was feeling the way that he was. Erica already had a room half-filled with baby stuff. She, of course, was excited. Having a baby *had* been her idea, of course. Everything that they did was her idea. He had wanted to paint the kid's room burgundy, a neutral color. Out of the question, just *out of the question*, it had been. Neutral colors lead to hermaphroditism, she said. There was a bucket of pink and blue paint in the room, so they were ready either way to paint the room a color which Erica approved of.

There was already a gold crucifix screwed to the door, even though Rob had actually done as Sam wanted. Rob had promised Sam during the drunk-discourse night that he would 'try to raise a child with an open mind.' So, during the evening between commercials of one of their reality TV programs, Rob offered the idea of letting the kid decide for him/her-self what God is from the beginning. That way, there wouldn't be the ripping out later, because there'd be no vines wrapped around the heart, nothing planted in the beginning when anything can grow. But it hadn't taken her long to shoot down that idea too.

"Rob, we won't have heathens for children. Don't you want to see them again in Heaven?"

She had actually sucked his dick that night—so he let the whole God thing slide. The next day she told him that he couldn't buy a boat, because of how expensive kids are. He nodded his head and said that she was probably right. And he still kind of felt like a kid himself. So it was hard to imagine having one.

Despite all of this, probably because of all of this, it was a very nice evening to be at the quarry. The sky was all red and bloody looking. The heat was gone, and everything was so still that it almost seemed surreal. With his calloused, concrete-dusted hands Rob opened up the book that Sam had given him as a wedding gift and started reading from where he had left off.

My Brother Sam is Dead.

He had started reading the book the day after the note arrived that was not supposed to be sent, from Will. That had been a bad evening for everyone. The book seemed appropriate, based on what the note said, and he felt very bad about having thrown it against the wall. The pages were still bent, and always would be at least a little.

There had been a feeling of guilt about having thrown the book once he actually started reading it. As usual, there was thought behind Sam's gift—which was not initially evident.

He'd been surprised to see at the end of the first chapter a note from Sam in blue ink. Just six words: 'I am proud of you. Congrats.' It felt good to read those words, and because Sam was not there he could smile because of them without making a deprecatory or comedic comment to make the words seem to mean less than they did.

Ever since the evening when the note arrived he had been reading a few chapters at the quarry after work. And he had even gotten to the point where he looked forward to it. It was almost relaxing—reading there. The story was OK, but the notes were what he read for. They were always positive, encouraging. It was nice having a little note from Sam to look forward to. The last one that he had read said 'hug mom, for me and for you. Dad too.' So, driving home from work that night he had stopped in to hug her, and said that it was from Sam. Most would say that the arm which he put on his dad's shoulder wasn't a hug, but he thought that it counted. They were both uncomfortable showing affection.

He was on the last chapter, which might have been a contributing factor to the bad feeling that he had. Sam always had had a flare for the dramatic, was generally allusive to some book or something which 'no one else' understood. It seemed likely that he would write words which said something along the lines of, 'you'll never see me again, fool.' So as he neared the end of the story Rob read full of anticipation, salivating for that delicious feeling of indignation, and a little afraid too. He was not sure what had happened in the story. Pages go by without comprehension when something else is on the mind.

When the last words of the story were read, he could do nothing but stare at the writing in blue ink at the bottom of the last page. He read it five times through.

'Robbie,

I'm not dead yet. Not for as long as I'm a brother. Let's not forget all of the fighting that we did together (Our stick-forts still stand in the woods behind the house).

You are a good man—will make a great father, husband. Don't sweat the small stuff, but do see the beauty in it!

I wish that I were even just half as strong as you.

Good Luck! Erica's a great girl.

Love,

S.S.'

Rob sat there on the tailgate and watched the sun go the rest of the way down, stunned by his brother's genuine nature. Erica really was a good person—one who wrote him little notes with hearts dotting the 'i's, who cooked for him, who planted flowers, who listened to him when had had a bad day at work, who was a Whiskers-lover.

And Sam was a good person too.

There was a glowing feeling within Rob as he set the closed book beside him on the tailgate. Everything seemed clear. Everything seemed right.

The horizon was dimly red.

Thinking of Sam, Rob went to the radio and turned it off. He then went back to the edge of the quarry and stood upon the tailgate, cupped his hands, and howled like a wolf. The howl was long and mournful just like his brother had always used to do—and from time to time still did do. And then, to the expanse of darkening green, Rob listened closely.

When Sam was six years old a wolf was shot by a hunter not far from their house, and ever since the kid/guy had been howling. He had actually gotten quite good over the years. But nothing ever howled back. He kept at it, though, saying that he wanted to give hope to whatever lonely wolf might be passing through.

The poor guy has always been looking for something wild. Maybe he'll find it yet.

Rob howled again.

The sound bounced off of the rock walls and floated around, slowing just like a ball that stops bouncing, and settled in the darkness. Rob listened for anything. There was no response. But it didn't matter too much. The wild things would be back soon enough, or so Sam had always said.

There in the hills that he knew so well, amongst all the old memories, Rob felt at home. And that bad feeling which he could not describe was dead.

He got into his truck and pulled away from the quarry, feeling better. In the morning, he would go to work like he did every day at the construction site, knowing that he was helping to build and maintain the stability that he knew and loved for a child not far away. He was going to be a dad. He would be Daddy, Grampy, maybe even Uncle Rob. It was starting all over again, which is what 'it' does. There was nothing to do but accept. The road curved gently towards home.

*

The bike did not sound good at all, but Sam was able to drive out of the campground very early in the morning. Noisy fishermen had awoken him.

When he had arrived there after Burger King, the campground by the river had smelled strongly of dead fish—very dense, sticky, and almost debilitating. An exceptionally good or bad smell must always be investigated. It wasn't hard to find the disheartening source. He saw flies swarming a metal garbage can not far from the river. When he got close, most of the flies scattered—stirring up the awful stench.

He found that someone had thrown five big catfish in there without even cutting off any meat. It had to have been an awful way to go, flopping around like that, suffocating, your panic stricken skin scraping off. Why anyone would ever do that to them, he could not understand. A lot of people just liked to make other things suffer. Plugging his nose, he'd dumped the carcasses into the river, and rolled the can into the weeds. Returning them to where they came from didn't seem wrong to do. The flies swarmed with the current, going out of sight. To change smells, he made a fire and got smoke-soaked, which was good. Sleep was nice.

A good campground is similar to a good library—a beautiful place where people contently go about their way, smiling and soaking in all of the sensations which float about either via words on bookshelves or via gurgling streams and singing birds surrounding. A place like that, around people like that, is enough to encourage a person. It's wonderful to see a young person with a book, trying their best to strengthen their mind, or to see a family or group of friends brave enough to really look at the beauty of nature.

It is always a special surprise to find either place—because both, like anything else, can be easily corrupted.

Beer cans had littered the campground where Sam stayed, as well as an alarming amount of condoms. The two—alcohol and condoms—were almost as inextricably linked as beauty pageant-winning 3-year-olds and insane mothers. Sam had found a bag full of weed under his picnic table—which is especially incriminating in the presence of a long-hair. 'It's not mine,' he would say as some guy with a badge roughly handcuffed him.

Sam dumped the weed in the weeds—which would have been a sin to those who he used to call friends.

The campground's library equivalent would have been one found by a highway which was advertised as 'adults only.'

Overall, he had not really liked Rome, and did not like doing as the locals did—especially the one who had awoken him in the middle of the night with a flashlight, searching the campsite for the bag of marijuana. Luckily, he had given up easily—which wasn't a surprise.

Spartacus Sam, I am.

It felt good leaving the place behind. Going through the crisp, early-morning air on the Indian, he decided to only drive on relatively small roads because of the bike's condition, and so chose a little traveled state road and headed northeast. He wore the helmet now.

The bike stalled twice by the time that had made it deep into the countryside. And after the second time, the Indian would not start. It only took about twenty minutes for a friendly, middle-aged guy wearing a baseball cap, which had an oil logo on it, to stop.

"Ya' nee' hulp?"

Sam said that he did. The guy parked and was out of his truck in a flash.

After only a few seconds of deliberation, the guy took out a can of ether from the tailgate of his truck and bent down so Sam could see the tobacco can in his back pocket. He sprayed in two directions at the same time. It did not smell good Sam's way.

"A little ether fixes anything," he said with a grin when he was done spraying, which made Sam wonder if he was talking about himself too.

Really, the guy didn't seem entirely with it. But that was OK. There was no reason for most people to be.

The bike started up and Sam thanked him over its roar.

The guy seemed very impressed by the bike, and after inspecting it by walking around it three times, he screamed over the engine that it was 'probably worth something pretty.'

Yeah, less than the $200 I paid.

But, of course, Sam was wrong, and did not say what he thought— just 'yeah, probably.' They spoke for a few more minutes, and then both of the unemployed men said that they were late for work. And both of them drove away.

Sam still had no idea where he was going, and drove into and through the winding hills full of cow pastures, rusting cars in peoples' lawns, and forest, enjoying himself. He drove very slow, unable to afford being thrown off again. There was no reason to drive fast, anyways. There was nowhere to be, and he'd seen a dead fawn on the road—spotted with white and red on a tan background—which reminded him that he didn't want to be involved in another road-kill. People hurried all over the place, killing. There was no reason for it.

So he drove on slowly for a while.

In a little valley, there was a small filling station with one red pump outside of a run-down, white building which looked to be a house. There were chickens running around, and lazy cats that dreamed of being saber-tooths. He decided that he should stop, thinking that he probably needed gas—the gauge was dysfunctional—and that someone there might know what was wrong with his bike. He pulled onto the tawny, crunching gravel and stopped at the pump.

There was a nice little strawberry patch in the yard, which reminded Sam of something Mary had said to him when they were alone one evening not long after the night at the beach. She had said it while eating, and closely inspecting, strawberries—which she often did.

"Imagine living inside of a strawberry. There's that nice little air-pocket inside—but you don't know why, or how you got there. Spend your whole life trying to eat your way out, wondering what's on the outside. One day you actually make it out—and the strawberry disappears. But you don't like the bitter truth that you see, disappointed to have ran out of the sweet chewing material. So make life sweet, Sam—whatever it is—and be glad that you can chew. That's how I live my life."

Everyone has their own unique perspective. The produce philosophy, put forth by Mary, was surprisingly deep, and sweet.

Hope Mary's making it.

After filling up his tank, Sam went in to pay, feeling rather good as he creaked the steps which were covered with flaking paint. At the top of them, one of the saber-tooth tigers made a quick move at him, with fur standing, and walked stiffly across the deck through a fleet of children's toys. The place seemed rustic—which he liked.

He walked through the already open door.

There was a normal-looking woman behind the register, reading an old western novelette. She appeared to be about thirty five years-old and had long, sandy hair. She looked up at him from her book with an almost startled look, and then smiled nicely after whatever had startled her wore off.

"Hello, how's the day treating you?"

"Just fine. I took twenty dollars-worth out of pump, well, pump only."

He handed her a twenty dollar bill. The ATM had been steadily dispensing them, which could not last much longer.

"So, how do you like living out here?"

"Oh, I love it."

She actually seemed to be friendly.

"The remoteness of these hills kind of reminds me of home, in Maine."

"Wow. Too cold up there for me."

"Yeah, but my family is there. So it's warm. And the summers are not so bad. Nothing like the open air, the birds singing."

She closed her book, committing to the conversation. It seemed as though she were about to let him in on a secret.

"I used to work in an office building in town. The pay was good, but the work was soul-crushing. But every day I watched this Cardinal right outside of my window. Red body, that little black mask and orange bill. Beautiful bird. It just sat on a bush, whistling purely—always singing for me. My boss was a dick—just loved the little bit of power that he had. And he was especially unbearable one day."

Leaning closer to Sam, across the counter, it seemed as if she was getting to the best part of the story.

"And you know what I did? That day, I went up to him and said, 'If I am going to keep on *being*, then I have to *be* outside.' So I quit, walked outside, and went to the bush. The cardinal flew away, and so did I."

"That has to be the best 'quitting' story that I have ever heard," Sam said admiringly.

"But it looks like I might have to go back to a job like that."

She seemed to be put in a bad mood at the thought of it.

"I'm sorry to hear that."

He really was sorry. And for a while there was silence. But he eventually remembered what he had planned to say.

"Is there anyone around here that could have a look at my motorcycle? I that think it's about to die."

She shook her head very sadly.

"The only person who could have is dead."

There was a picture behind her of a man in a military uniform, and beside it was a cross. Sam assumed that the man had been her husband.

She saw that he was looking at the picture.

"He gave his life for this country. And he knew what he was giving too, a knowledge which is rare."

"Knowing what is out there and still walking tall truly is rare. I'm sorry for your loss. All things considered, this country is a good place—thanks to people like him."

A little girl walked in from another room behind the register, using her small hand to hold onto her mom's dress while looking at Sam. Her hair was just like her mom's, but her eyes seemed bigger.

"Mommy, is that Daddy, all bandaged up from the war?"

Her voice was terribly hopeful, like only a child's can be.

"No, sweetie. Your Daddy is in Heaven. This is just a customer."

The mother looked to Sam.

"You really do look a lot like he did, though."

Sam looked at the picture again, and imagined the guy to be a little younger with longer hair and a less proud stare. He could see the resemblance. It was actually a little startling.

"He was teaching Gracie to play the guitar when he left."

The girl's little lip was curled, and she swayed back and forth. A large tear started to go down her cheek. She had really thought that her dad had come home.

"How do you know," she asked, "how do you even know that Daddy's in Heaven like you say? How do you know that there *is* a Heaven?"

Her mother looked to be about to say something, and then hesitated.

Sam spoke before he thought, as the mom stood there shaking her head. He spoke to her in a tone that he would use with an adult, like he did with all children.

"Gracie. Your Daddy is still alive in you and your mom. I can see it. So that means that you are Heaven. Your mom too. And to me it looks like you both exist. Here, can you hand me that guitar?"

The woman hesitated for a moment, and her waves of sand shifted as she looked from the guitar to Sam. After a few moments she took the six-string from the corner and handed it to him.

"Come here, Gracie."

She did so after getting a reassuring nod from her mom.

Sam walked out on the porch and sat on the stairs. He held the neck of the guitar in his left hand and patted his left knee for the little girl to sit on. Excitedly, she jumped on his one knee and he rested the body of the guitar on the other. She wrapped her arms around the nicely finished red wood, and wiped away the tears.

"I'll press the chords, and you strum."

She nodded happily, and began finger-strumming—very nicely. Her dad had taught her well. Sam tested whether or not his fingers still remembered where to go, and was pleased to find that they did.

The impetus for and process of learning to play the guitar was a pleasant memory. On campus he had sat beneath the shade of an old oak tree and played the beginning to the song 'Pretty Woman' at those he thought qualified. He had gotten a few smiles—but that was all. Learning to play music is a magical thing.

A guitar is an especially good friend for a lonely person.

Sandy was behind them, watching in the doorway with a hand over her mouth.

Gracie's little head was bobbing with the beat, and she was smiling broadly. And before long, there was a nice tune swimming through the forest, which made the day even more beautiful.

With his left hand, Sam ruffled her hair and turned Gracie's head towards his. The nice sound came to a slow stop, and she scrunched her nose and smiled, not looking sad anymore.

"*What?*"

"You see," Sam said loud enough for them both to hear, "in music there is no pain. Just like so many other things, I was crazy to ever try to live without it. I mean, it's just kind of there, in you. I cannot even begin to describe its value. Another example of Heaven, too—something that is in you which cannot be explained. Keep playing your Daddy's song and he will live. Then create your own song."

Gracie nodded her head and grinned. She was pleased, and immediately started creating her own wild song with furious strumming, twisting her head back and forth crazily—which to her at least might have sounded good. That was all that mattered.

After a few more songs, Sam leaned the guitar against a beam which held up the awning and Gracie gave him that disappointed, little girl look.

He whispered to her: "Nothing lasts forever. You'll understand this all too well one day when time speeds up. And never forget to give your mom hugs. How about you give her one now?"

Gracie jumped off of his knee and ran over to her mom. Sam heard her feet on the wooden planks. He stood, picked up the guitar, and then looked at the two. The mom's legs were being hugged, and her eyes had tears in them as she looked at Sam. He felt incredibly moved, and had that feeling below his ribs which he got at very good parts of movies. But this was a lot better. And it went throughout his whole body.

"Well, I'd best get going," he said, leaning the guitar against the house, beside the two.

He ruffled Gracie's hair again, looked at Sandy with a nod, and then walked down the creaking stairs towards his bike, much fuller than when he had pulled in.

"But I'll see daddy again in Heaven, *right*?" Gracie asked loudly enough that it was obviously intended for Sam.

He turned around slowly, and looked at the little girl.

"Yeah, Gracie. You will."

And God's pistol, loaded and primed, realizes that he doesn't have the heart to fire. Just like all of the capable ones before. Bullets clatter on cement.

"Thank you," Sandy said softly. "And I'm sorry that I couldn't help with your bike."

"Oh, that's quite all right. I'll just have it take me as far is it will, and then find another way."

He put on the helmet, nodded, kicked, and drove off slowly. The two waved, and actually did look like Angels.

Chapter 13

The dashed lines in the center of the black, paved road flashed by very quickly, and for a while the motorcycle seemed healthy. This would prove to be like one of those awful diseases where a person seems to be getting better right before they die. But that was a few more miles down the road.

Sam coasted down a hill, hoping that the bike did not decide to lock up again, and came to a bright opening where there were a few scattered trees and a little river, which seemed to shine in the sun. As he approached the bridge, which went over the river, he saw a dusty-haired kid who had his shirt off. Dusty was standing beside another kid with long, dark hair who looked to be a little bit younger. They were both about as skinny as a rail, which did not necessarily mean that they were under-fed, he knew.

Dusty and Dark looked like they were scheming.

Sam slowed down and stopped on the bridge to see what they were up to. Just after the motor stopped, he heard one of them say: "Jimmy, it's a Devil-Angel!"

They looked at each other, certain of what they needed to do, and jumped off of the bridge—the 'Devil-Angel' allowing them to be the dare-devils that they so wished to be.

At first, Sam was startled almost to the point of being petrified. He had good reason to be worried about young kids playing by a river. But at least it wasn't cold and there wasn't a dog involved. After hearing a couple of staggered splashes, he put down the kick-stand right in the middle of the road and hurried over to the guard-rail. He looked down to see the two kids frantically kicking and laughing in the muddy water of the river as they swam towards the shore. There was a girl there, with long golden hair. She was clapping, and acting like a princess who was being rescued.

Sam was beginning to understand why old people got a wistful look in their eye when watching children play. It was not a nice realization. They were just like he and Rob used to be. And they would never be that way again.

He was relieved as the duo left the water and ran across the mud, into the forest. They patted their hands on open mouths and made Indian noises. There would be no dead kids to pull out of the water.

Sam inspected a sign which said 'No Jumping,' close to where their wet footprints were. The sign reminded him of another one. And ultimately their jumping ended up making him think of a memory from school.

In one of the computer labs, there was a door which said 'Not an Exit—Alarm will Sound.' He spent many hours in there as he did work on the computers. Between stints of productiveness, he wondered at that door and the words on it. It led out into the hall, and was glass—which allowed him to watch the people walking outside of the lab. He thought that if it was 'not an exit,' than it must be an entrance, but was never brave enough to go through it because of the off-chance that an alarm actually would sound. There was always a lab assistant who had a scowl on, too, which deterred him further. One day, walking through the hall outside of the lab, he saw a girl in the lab push open the door and walk casually in front of him. It was a complete shock. Hurrying after, he caught up to her just outside of the building. It was spring, and there was that beautiful richness in the air, the dogwoods were flowering white, the redbuds were pink. There were cool breaths from mounds of snow into the warm air, and people were talking and smiling, starting to wear light clothing. Amongst all of this, she turned around—seemingly pleasantly surprised at being spoken to—after he said, 'excuse me.'

It was amazing how memories could come back. Even her face was still in his head, somehow—the face wore dark, thick-rimmed glasses and was attractive, despite slight acne scarring.

He remembered asking, "how did you know that the alarm would not sound?"

This was one of the most spontaneous, exciting single moments of the spring semester of his final year—besides for sitting with random people in restaurants and defending his thesis from a bunch of ghouls.

Could be the girl!

But she had smiled in an instantly deflating way and said modestly, "I saw someone else walk through it."

He was terribly disappointed, though did not show it, and said something like, 'well, now I have too.' He had been hoping that she would say, 'I did not know,' and then wink, or do something to show that she free—whatever that was.

And though this admission of ignorance was exactly how he would *not* have wanted the two boys to answer if asked whether or not they knew that the river was deep where they had jumped, that day at school he had found himself thinking that he wanted to find who the girl had seen for one simple, tortuous reason: he was the sort of person who had to be in love with the unknown, because for the most part he hated the known. And such a person reaches the point where they realize that they simply must have a companion of the same mind if they are to keep on living.

After years and years of being told not to open some door that ends up being opened, a drastic change can occur—he'd found. It takes only the exposal to one lie to be aware of all others. And for Sam, there was something *to* doing an act for the first time, the opening of a door that no one else had before. Because there's so much out there, endless possibilities just waiting to be discovered. And the person who was not afraid to open a door, someone who had the heart to keep on searching, he had decided, was who he wanted to meet.

As he got back on the motorcycle and drove down the road, not feeling so well, he thought again, as he often did, of how he had failed to find that special person in college.

He had been sure that he would, going in. The odds had been so good then, compared to the current moment. But it ended up seeming like he had something deep inside him which acted as a saboteur. Something always kept him from making what later seemed to be the obvious correct choice. There was within him an affinity to trying for something which he knew could not be attained. And what could easily be his with a little effort seemed repugnant. It must be what Poe had described, he thought. When next to a cliff, there is always that little part of you, something way down that is usually suppressed, something that wants to jump just so you know what it feels like to fall. It was the same with failing. And that, Sam had decided, was what constantly caused him to make the wrong choice.

My very own Imp of the Perverse.

Brit had not been the girl for him. He knew this. But he was afraid that someone else might have been—someone who he had passed up, someone who he had made cry. He tried to convince himself that she had not been for him—but could not.

It had not been nice to see her find happiness with another guy when she wanted it with him originally. He had gone out with Brit because she was the unknown to the better girl's known.

Always with the unknown!

But her unknown became known all too quickly. And then he knew that he had made a mistake.

For a person with a certain type of mind, nothing is more important than finding someone who is willing and able to converse in a meaningful fashion. And this type of person will realize how few of such people there are to talk to. It is especially painful to miss out on one.

There wasn't much worse than not getting what you want, when you know that what you want, wanted you too.

*

His eyes ran across the computer screen, over the words that his friend had written. It was a short story, and the first of her writing that she had let him read. He was excited, and even felt more than a little bit honored. It takes a lot of trust to let someone else read what you have written if it comes from the heart. In the bottom left corner of the screen a word-counter said that there were 9,287 words in the document. He had read about half of them. The story was titled: *Mandy's Meteor in Mind*.

Sam was realizing that Ellen was a very good writer. He decided this not by her grammatical prowess, which anyone can learn—almost nothing, he felt, that is learned in English class should be taken primarily into account when deeming a writer 'good' or 'not good'—but by how she was able to translate her soul. Somehow, she could simply write beautifully. Some people still could. There was no question what she was.

Most writers hide behind words—not Ellen.

The two were in a group study room in the library, sitting at a table. One wall was made up of a glass window oriented towards tables that were amongst shelves of books where students studied, slept, or procrastinated. There were also three white, non-transparent walls.

Sam and Ellen both had a gap in their schedule and so had chosen to spend it together. Steve and Mary had already graduated. Her boyfriend had too, a year before, and was beginning a successful career in upstate New York as a lawyer—which was ironic, Sam thought, considering that Ellen had recently told him that she hates most laws, that it's a shame that we haven't reached the point where people no longer need them.

His last semester was a lot like his third had been in that the only person who he spent a considerable amount of time with was Ellen. But it was much different in that while Sam was again lonely she was lonely no longer.

She was reading *On the Road*, which Sam noticed with keen interest. It always felt nice when someone read a book that he had suggested. He remembered mentioning it to her the first time that they had talked since sophomore year, after a Candid Club meeting.

"So you're the one who checked it out," he said, nodding to the book. "Wanted to read it again, can't believe the library only has one copy."

"Thanks for the recommendation, it's *so* good," she said mockingly, resuming reading.

He read on too. It was nice reading something other than his own thesis—a rambling series of poems about a young man who lost one mind and found another. All that was finally completed and done with, a great relief to have finished.

Ellen's story was about a young woman who was kind to everyone that she met. The world was crushing her, but she didn't let on. She helped everyone that she could—and made a point to talk to a homeless guy everyday on her way to work, encouraging him. No one helped her. It didn't seem like she needed it. But she did. She was oftentimes taken advantage of on account of her kindness, and fell for it every time. Her purse was stolen on the subway, a guy she met in a bar used her for a one-night stand when she thought that there might be more, and her careless neighbor's dog ate her parrot. There was too much pain. The story ended with her walking alone in the city with her head down, amongst many others who walked the same way. She walked past the homeless guy without a word, and he sadly watched her walk by. She was done.

"Ellen, I'm really impressed."

He decided to not ask how Raconteur the parrot was doing, fearing the worst. Additionally, he could not help but wonder if he had been part of the inspiration for the woeful tone of the story, specifically considering the whole 'thought there might be more' disappointment of sophomore year. But he didn't mention that either.

She put down the book and smiled bashfully.

"Thanks. I never thought that I'd share my writing with anyone."

"It's a nice feeling, isn't it? Funny how you waited until a week before graduation to share. You thinking you'll never see me again?"

Why does he ask questions like that?

"Oh, no. We'll keep in touch, unless you disappear like you say that you will."

She looked hard at Sam, which was still difficult for her to do sometimes, and he looked away. Though he didn't let on, she knew that he still had the guy in him who had performed at the concert that she'd been surprised to see him perform at. She smiled at the thought, wondering if she was the only one who had noticed his William Blake reference. And that guy who had performed at the concert could not 'just be normal,' could not yet accept what he would probably have to.

He's going to do it.

She had been thinking a lot about how she would probably never see Sam again, even more so after reading the book that he'd suggested. Maybe for a dinner or two after graduation, but she doubted even that. Neither of them had seen Mary or Steve since they had graduated in December. Things just got too busy.

Sam looked at her again.

"Well, anyways, this is probably one of the best short stories that I've read in a while. A lot better than most of the stories I've had to read for class. I like the way you write. It isn't too alive, and is without the dramatic voice of the creative writing joker. And it's not too dead, either. It is real."

"I know that you wouldn't say a bad word about anything I wrote."

"I'm as honest as they come. It's not really for kids, though, is it?"

"No, I've been writing more for myself lately. Feels good to get it all out. What would you say that the moral of the story is?"

Sam leaned back in his chair, and made it obvious that he was thinking for a few moments, and then decided.

"That it's very hard for a good person to imagine another person being anything but good, which is why it is so hard for them to survive."

Ellen nodded her head and smiled her cute little smile, but didn't say anything.

"Only the good die young."

"There's actually a Hemingway quote that I was thinking about when I wrote this, she said. He wrote beautifully, so straight. I can't remember it exactly, but it's not long after the main guy deserts, and thinks that the world kills the good first. Read *A Farewell to Arms* and I'm sure that you'll know which one I'm talking about."

"I've read it. Good writer. Do not like that he enjoyed shooting animals unnecessarily, though. I suppose that I'm savage in some way that I don't realize. It's too bad that he died like your favorite, Woolf."

She was not surprised that he remembered who her favorite author had been. Sam's memory was very good. And he had several times confided to her that he wished it was not so good.

"I know. Seems like most of them did. And Hemingway might be my favorite now. Really, there hasn't been a great American writer since him."

Sam thought of his own favorite author, shook his head and smiled.

"So it goes."

"There has to be another great one, soon, a person who can really see and is not afraid to write honestly, in a skillful, convincing and entertaining way. I think that a great writer has to be willing to starve themselves, and might even *need* to make a series of bad decisions to find all feelings."

"The kid-poet called it a 'derangement of the senses,'" Sam said. "That's what it usually takes to awake."

He thought of his very own Season in Hell.

One evening I took Beauty in my arms—and I thought her bitter—and I insulted her.

Ellen seemed very beautiful, was hard to look at. She spoke so genuinely: "And we need someone awake who is willing to try to entertain many people who are half-asleep, to wake them up. Someone who will say things which must be said because they love those who will hate them for it. And such an author is sort of necessary, for a generation, even if the people will ultimately destroy them."

Now more than ever Sam felt like he could talk to Ellen. He could feel her better, and looking at her, having read what she wrote, he realized how painfully much they had in common. He knew that he had made such a big mistake, not being with her. Even though he was not in favor of such ownership, he thought that she could have been his, and though he was not for being owned, he thought that he could have been hers. It would have been nice. But he had messed it up, sophomore year. Brit had not been worth it. He would try to tell her how he felt, he decided.

"You know, Ellen, I really just don't like most people. Not quite in the way that Steve dislikes people—I don't claim to want to kill them. You just know that we're going to see it in the papers one of these days."

He laughed under his breath and continued.

"I guess it's not really that I don't like them. I just don't want to be around them most of the time. I've given it my best to try, I really have. And I suppose that I love them all. I have found some beautiful souls. But I even had a hard time hanging out with our own little circle of friends sometimes. People keep on hurting each other. The hurt will laugh and smile, and then do something to try and make the person who hurt them hurt. And the person they hurt back will laugh, it'll just keep going."

Silently, all that he could do was laugh.

"I really do like you, though. You're one of the few people who I've really gotten to know who has not made me regret it. And I wish that I had not stopped getting to know you when I did. Because this year has really been nice."

She smiled and shut the book. His words meant something.

"I know what you mean. I'll miss you too. And Sam, the world hasn't killed us yet."

From across the table, she held both of his big hands between her small ones. It felt better, more sincere than when that girl whose calculus homework he had done for a while held his hands, better than when Brit had held them too.

So much better.

Sam was quiet for a few moments, and then looked at Ellen with a very serious look.

"You have to keep on writing, for both of us. Because it will."

*

It was raining outside, which had caused the ceremony to be moved into the auditorium. There were a lot of chairs and a lot of people sitting in them wearing robes. There were also a lot of people not wearing robes who held cameras and had very emotional looks on their faces, wearing far-off gazes.

Commencement ceremonies would be much more valuable if they answered the question that most graduates are asking themselves: 'Commence what?' But they do not, cannot.

The speaker, a somewhat successful and well-known politician who had graduated from the university, finally finished gabbing. He spoke well, though it was the same voice that he always used, so no one could know if he really meant what he said. It probably did not matter. The president of the university had already done his deed. It actually seemed as if he were having bad a day, but he did his best to seem chipper. Watching graduation ceremonies was probably a hard thing to do, year after year.

A guy with a very monotone voice began calling names: "Olivia Alexander"…"Wes Anderson"…

For those who had fought for it, the moment was sacred—walking across the stage and receiving their diploma. But for those who it was given to, the ceremony was a joke.

Sam watched Brad and the others who had last names towards the beginning of the alphabet walk across the stage. They walked with such confidence and contentment towards their office-jobs. After a few minutes, Al walked probably towards a nice family with Shelby. Sam clapped. Then, a few people later, Ellen's little figure walked proudly across the stage, graduating with 'magna cum laude' towards something that would no-doubt be meaningful. She was one of the few who Sam was glad to clap for.

It was a strange feeling to be done with school. The feeling of impending possibilities was daunting. He looked behind him to where his mom, dad, aunt, uncle, a cousin with her baby, three living grandparents, brother, and Erica sat. He hadn't walked at graduation for his Bachelor's degree because he knew that he'd be done with his Master's soon. So the whole college graduation thing was new for his family too. All of them had a different face on.

The love that can be felt from a family is enough to make life seem worth living. In their eyes, proudness can be seen. Dreams had—though never realized—are still alive in a young man or woman for their close relatives. And parents/grandparents, even uncles/aunts, will feel a part of the journey for as long as it goes—because for a while they all helped to nurture the seed which has turned to a flower.

In the face of his brother, Sam saw hidden love, and hoped that it was there. Erica just looked happy to be by Rob's side. In the face of his mother there was unconcealed love, nervousness. There was contentedness in that of his father—as if he were washing his car. The face of his grandfather was proud, and the similar face of the old man's son seemed amused. His aunt was playing with her little grandson from the lap of her daughter—whose eyes seemed to be glass, whose smile was like broken eyes.

He was glad that he could give most of them hope even if he had none at the moment.

There was no choice but to walk up on the stage when his name was called, take his diploma, and be rid of his title of 'student.' And so he did, was. It seemed like there was more noise than before when he walked across the stage towards some unknown destination. He closed his eyes, and shook an old guy's hand, then took a piece of paper.

Rock star, no more.

After the last of the names were finally called caps flew through the air. No one was hit in the eye.

Sam walked through the chaos of hugging people and reached the people who wanted to hug him—his mom and grand-moms. They did.

"You did it, kid, you did it…"

The moment was surreal. His grad-moms and mom were crying. The eyes of his uncle—who had told him as a child, 'knowledge is something that they can never take away from you' were beaming. You can never tell who the wise ones are. And because of this one line, which the man had told him often, Sam thought his uncle to be wiser than most. They shook hands. No words were necessary.

"What did your GPA end up being?" asked his tanned G-pa, who was wearing a flowery shirt bought during one of the winters that he always spent in Hawaii with Sam's grandma.

Sam thought about saying, 'not a snowbird' but was in no mood for telling a joke that only he would understand, and settled for irony.

"About 3.8456."

"I always knew you were smart, ever since you were a little guy. Congratulations."

They shook hands.

"Now you'll get to make a whole bunch of money with your degrees."

Sam half-smiled and nodded at that notion and then the old man started talking to Rob. He hoped that he didn't make too much money.

Erica had walked away to look for Brit. The others were talking amongst themselves, so Sam was sort of alone amongst all of the people.

He looked the opposite way from where Erica walked to see Brit with her family, not looking his way. She had grown very good at doing so. Allen came up with a goofy grin. Sam shook his hand as their parents spoke briefly, and then Al went off to find his other friends. For a while Sam just stood there watching people, feeling hollow.

Ellen came out of the crowd and hugged him unexpectedly. She felt warm, and stayed in his arms for a long time. When she pulled away and looked at him, the corners of her eyes were wet.

"Stay good, Sam."

Her voice was a whisper, and she looked at him lovingly. Sam could think of nothing to say, and just said: "You too."

Ellen walked off holding her boyfriend's hand, beside her mom. Sam felt bad that her dad wasn't there. But that's the way it goes. For a while longer he looked at it all and felt a sudden urge to leave.

As soon as the others were ready, they did.

With his slow-stepping family, Sam walked away from the university through the light rain of the gray day. He looked at his mother and realized that the rain does not disguise tears as much as he had imagined they would. He held her papery hand and walked towards the car. Rob didn't say anything to him at all during the ride—which was not unusual—but Sam could tell that something was going through his brother's head by his quiet demeanor.

He proposed to Erica during dinner for everyone to see. The girl squealed as if she were a child—which really, she was. It was nice to see how happy she was, and Rob looked very happy too. Everyone clapped when she said 'yes.' Even the people at other tables did. The lobster on the plate probably would have clicked its claws too if the life in them had not been boiled out.

Sam felt shocked at it all, watched his brother and future sister-in-law hug, and watched his mom cry again, watched his dad smile.

Rob and Erica soon announced at the table, in a moment of excitement which would cause many hectic ones, that they would be married in three weeks—on the anniversary of when they first met.

Won't be long and I'll be the creepy uncle.

It was like witnessing the last bit of water which seems to go so fast down the drain of an old tub, after being so full that it seemed like it would never be empty. But always it was in the end.

*

Sam's grandpa—the other one had gone on a walk in the woods one day, was never seen again—had wanted to make a night out of it, so paid for everyone's room in a very expensive hotel. He was at the point in his life where he felt like he should be spending his money before it was too late—which was perfectly fine. Sam's cousin, though, was amongst those who were quite concerned about whether or not she would have anything left for an inheritance. Sam loved to see the imbecilic winces she had on her face as the six successive 140-year-old bottles of wine arrived to the room.

The corks flew, the wine frothed over the neck of the bottles, and deep, satisfied laughter filled the hotel rooms. It was a night for celebration. Erica was very beautiful, Rob was very handsome, Sam was very educated. The grandparents were very proud, as were their children.

But Sam felt disconcertingly flat—and, as per usual, did not drink much.

He lay on his bed until he decided that the pool sounded nice. The grandparents had 'hit the hay' at around 8:45 after drinking too much. All of the rooms were connected by doors—only one was closed. Sam's room was between Rob and Erica's and the room that his grandma and grandpa shared—not a good place for a lonely guy with exceptionally good ears considering he had heard stories from his father about what wine yielded when consumed by his grandparents. Sam did not want to listen to that— which he imagined to be like a hormonal pterodactyl stuck in a snare and enjoying it. A vivid imagination is not always a good thing.

So Sam went to see if anyone wanted to go for a swim.

His parents were in a room with his mother's mom on the other side of Rob's room. So Sam walked through the room which did not have funky music coming from it and went to sit on the bed where his parents were. There was a Court TV episode on.

"Sam," his father said after being asked if he wanted to go for a swim, "this is a very important decision. A woman had the gall to bash in the headlights of her man's truck just because he hit her stinkin' cat on the road."

"Cat-astrophe, eh?"

"Yeah. Have you seen this one?"

Sam saw that his mother and grandmother were misty-eyed and sipping old wine.

His aunt and uncle were trying to make his cousin's baby stop crying. He didn't know where his cousin was—and took note of that. If there was one person in the family who would murder him it was her. So, being sure to check behind doors, Sam walked back into Rob's room—who was alone. Erica was out on the balcony, talking on the phone. She was excitedly phoning nearly everyone that she knew to tell them about the engagement.

"Want to go for a swim, Robbie?"

Begrudgingly, Rob agreed. He really did not like being alone. There was no telling how long his fiancé would be yakking.

So, after getting dressed in the appropriate attire, the two of them walked side by side down the carpeted stairs in their swimming trunks, towards the pool—just as they had many times before on family vacations. They were ready to burn their eyes in the water-diluted chlorine. Even that can be sweet if associated with a pleasant memory.

They walked in silence, both thinking of old times. Walking through the lobby, it felt good to be shirtless in a public place. Their father would not have liked so being because, 'his stomach was not like it used to be,' as their mother so often said. This was actually the reason why he had not gone to the pool with them. He had seen 'cat-astrophe' before and knew that the man was sentenced to buy the woman—who was actually a man—a new pussy.

Sam dove headfirst into the cool swimming pool, and Rob went straight for the hot-tub. Before long, Sam eased himself into the hot-tub too and was glad that it was actually hot, so much so that it seemed to bite. He had been in many lukewarm 'hot' tubs before.

Sam and Rob were the only ones around.

"Big day, big day," Sam said, going down to his chin in the bubbly water.

Rob nodded his head in agreement. There were a few minutes of only sloshing suds and silence before Sam spoke again.

"What made you choose my graduation day?"

"I don't know. It just seemed right."

This response was very frustrating.

Sam knew that he probably would not get an answer—he rarely did—but asked the question that he had been thinking about all day.

"Rob, have you ever thought that something, even most things, were shameful and insane, but something happened and you realized that justice and sanity have many different faces, and that the one you had embraced was ugly, that you just need to run?"

"No."

Sam felt especially awful, boiling all too knowingly in a stew of confusion and all too unknowingly in the piss of a 4-year-old girl, a 22-year-old man, and an 89-year-old woman, as well as several other bodily fluids. As he spoke the decision was made.

"I'll stick around until your wedding, but then I'm gone."

Chapter 14

The old Indian motorcycle made it into the area much as most of the Indians of old had gone out, Sam thought—proud but sad.

Trail of Tears.

In this case, the tears were viscous, black oil droplets steadily sobbing out of the bike. He imagined that the dark, billowing smoke was probably comparable to a soul leaving the body. Soul made the eyes water, he noted. Anyways, it was not looking good for the soulful bike.

The way it ran had only gotten worse in the hills after he'd filled it up. He thought that the gas from Sandy's pump had probably been bad, was likely a big part of the problem. But he didn't really mind. It had been worth a stop, regardless.

It had not been long after seeing the boys jump off of the bridge that the bike had begun to die very rapidly. He took the hills very slow, so as not to be thrown off again. The thing eventually began stalling like it had before—which made Sam wish that he had some ether. The bike had then proceeded to develop an awful vibration all of the way through it, which made handling very dangerous. And then the smoke began to pour onto his face. Not long after that came a shrill war cry—long and uninterrupted whenever he gave it any gas. The Indian was not going quietly. There was no good reason to.

After several miles of lurching and terror, he spotted a brown sign with an arrow on it and did not even read the words. Brown meant park.

And park probably meant facilities and a phone, even though he didn't really need the facilities that a park would have or know who he would call. It seemed better to be off of the road than on, though.

So he was glad to pull off of the winding road and onto the gradually curving driveway of the state park.

The bike's motor sputtered to a stop in the parking lot in front of the nature center and he took off the helmet, placing it on the seat. Sam doubted that it would start again. The thick smoke eventually dispersed, so he was able take in his surroundings. Strangely, there were quite a few cars in the lot even though there were not many people around. The day seemed like a Tuesday—but he wasn't sure. He shouldered his pack and walked towards the brown building which was surrounded by forest.

He was surprised to see what he saw.

Tied to a post in front of the building was a black dog on a long leash with a darker face and pointy ears. It looked like a small wolf. He had always liked wolves—anything wild, really. The dog wagged his bushy tail as Sam approached, but otherwise sat there very calmly, looking up with his strikingly blue eyes. Sam ran his hand across the sleek head. It was the most dignified creature that he had had the pleasure of meeting in a very long time. The dog enjoyed very much having his chin scratched. He closed his eyes and seemed to smile. But all scratches must end.

Sam hoped that someone had not left the dog there without the intention of returning, but the thing was so nice and well-behaved that he was fairly sure that its human companion loved him and was probably in the nature center. He would ask.

"I'll be back."

The dog nodded.

Sam watched his reflection as he approached the glass door, seeing a haggard, bandana adorning, grimy, tie-dye wearing, bandaged person with hair down to his shoulders and incontiguous scruff on his face. He hadn't shaved since Miami. If he did not know his own story, the guy he saw in the glass would look like someone to stay away from. But he knew better. And he had no choice. He opened the door and went inside. The glass watched him as he walked into the building. If the glass was capable of volition, it probably would have cracked with laughter because of the hole in his jeans which revealed a bluebird, on his yellow boxers, seeming to fly out of the tear.

More than likely, the glass was immature, Sam thought. The constantly reflective generally were, it seemed.

What a strange mind I've.

It was nice and cool inside of the building. He had no idea what he was going to do in regard to travel, but it looked like hitchhiking was going to be the most likely option. He didn't want to call a shuttle because it would be very expensive. Regardless of his situation, there was always a comfort in visiting such quiet, natural places for a while. And he was in no hurry to raise his thumb. So he relaxed as best he could. Maybe he would go for a hike, he thought.

He saw four people.

There was a tall, young man with a full beard and a large, backcountry back pack beside a young woman with short hair and a big pack on her back too. It looked especially large because she was small. They were walking around quietly, looking at displays. A young guy with curly brown hair wearing green and brown park clothes who was exceptionally thin and pale sat behind a desk looking at a computer screen. Solitaire was his game. There was also a woman in the same brown and green clothes behind the counter. Other than them, Sam was the only one in the building. He was sure that the man and the woman with packs on were friends of the dog.

The nature center was quite nice. There was a split-rail fence, behind which was positioned a little natural scene. Amongst flowers and ferns there was a bear, a woodpecker soaring with the aid of transparent string, a cross-eyed fox, a bobcat eating a quail, and a fawn hiding—waiting for its mother. The wall beside the forest creatures had on it a painting of a waterfall, after which the park was named—'Amicalola Falls.'

Sam read about the natural history of the animals, of the region in general, and looked at some snakes and other little animals which were caged for people to look at.

Caged in a cage in a cage…

The animals reminded him of the dog on the leash. He walked to a map on the wall beside the taxidermy animals where the couple had stopped, and stood beside them, thinking of that proud dog.

For a while he absent-mindedly looked at the map, trying to think of something clever to say about the dog. But the map stopped his mind once he realized what it showed.

When what he was looking at registered in his mind, an unusually good feeling came over him. It felt almost like he was supposed to be where he was at—which had become the rarest feeling that he experienced. A big smile crept across his face. He was looking at a map of the eastern United States, specifically at a red line which snaked from Georgia to Maine. He couldn't hold in his glowing feeling, so he spoke.

"You know, this trail leads to my home. I live in Maine. I just happened to stumble upon this place—by chance I stumble upon the *beginning* of a path that leads home. My bike threw me off and then stopped running right. Took me here."

The two were the sort of people who one could tell were kind just by looking at them. The woman had a nice face and cute brown hair. She had looked up sweetly when Sam spoke, smiling. The man was a few inches taller than Sam, more strongly built, and had a prominent nose. His dark, bushy eyebrows arched as he prepared to speak in a smooth, friendly voice very much like Sam's.

"God, that sounds like quite a coincidence."

Sam looked at the man for a few moments, thought about the words just said.

"Yeah, it does. But actually I'm not a religious man. And I don't believe in coincidence either."

After a few moments of looking at Sam and thinking about the words just said, the man smiled through his beard, and looked to the woman. To Sam, they seemed to be like a younger version of the couple who searched for the Ivory-billed Woodpecker—possessing the same loving, wordless rapport.

"Sounds like a formula for freedom," she said in a warm voice.

They all stood there for a few moments before Sam spoke again, remembering his reason for approaching them.

"Is that dog outside yours?"

"Yeah, he's alright, right?" the man said with a bit of worry in his voice, looking through the glass.

"He's fine, just making sure that there's someone around to claim him. Beautiful dog. Have a name?"

"His name's Restlessness," she said proudly, "the adorable, cold-nosed, warm-heart and soul of our journey. Always been by my side since he was a pup. He's finally warming up to Johnny here, after three years. Always at the end of the leash, wanting to go somewhere, but not sure where. Just like us. We call him Russ, for short."

They made a beautiful trio.

"I love it," Sam said with a smile, letting the words she had said soak in, trying not to fall in love with the witty woman. "Being the restless soul that I am, I envy the fact that you two were able to find each other. And that spirit animal of yours, he's special. I haven't given up hope yet, though. It has to happen sooner or later for me."

"Hope. That's one thing that you can never give up," she said seriously. "Because when you do, you are done."

Johnny was tracing the trail with his finger, seeming to be attempting to roughly measure the distance that they would travel.

"So, how far are you going?" Sam asked.

"We have friends who agreed to pick us up about sixty miles from here in the Smokies," he said. "We might go further, though, if these two can hold up."

He gestured to his girlfriend's stomach.

"Wow," Sam said, noticing a little, barely-bump. "You two seem so warm. You'll be great parents. That kid is going to stand a chance."

They smiled again, both a little surprised at the conversation with the strangely candid man who wore bandages on his face and elbows, smelled like soul—smoke—and had tears—oil—all over his shoes.

"So, where are you headed?" she asked warmly.

He stopped to think for a few moments.

"Well, I'd like to think that I'm headed towards home."

"You'd better get going."

They exchanged good-luck wishes and then Sam watched them head out of the building. Through the glass, he watched Russ greet them with a coy stretch, and then the three were off, Restlessness leading the way.

Sam was exhilarated by the unexpected, and felt like immediately walking through the door and onto the trail. But he decided to slow down and think about what he had and what he might need for the journey. His pack already had water and some food in it that he'd bought the day that he met Will. The minimalist route was always one that he had admired, but he decided to grab a handful of energy bars and a first-aid kit—to be on the safe side. So he did. Then, he went over to a little room of souvenir-type items, looking for something which might augment a message. After looking for a few minutes, he saw a sticker which said what he sought. It was green, with white print, and said, 'no rain, no pain, no Maine!' beneath a big 'AT' and the words 'Appalachian Trail.'

He went to the desk with his things. As the kid was checking him out, Sam thought to ask: "Is there a place around where I can send a postcard?"

"Yeah, at the Lodge."

The kid handed him a map of the park. The Lodge was north of the nature center, not far from the falls.

"After I start the trail, how long before I reach the first town or major road?"

"Almost thirty miles from here."

The kid's face turned inquisitive suddenly.

"How long have you been planning to walk the trail?"

"About four minutes."

The kid shook his head. He was terribly serious.

"I hate to break it to you, but the AT is *not* something to do on a whim."

Sam did not feel like explaining that he had a fair amount of camping and hiking experience in the Adirondacks which may have made the whim more reasonable in the kid's eyes.

"Don't worry, man. I have been walking almost all of my life and am in the best shape that I'll ever be in. I probably walked two thousand miles from my apartment to campus over the four years that I spent at school. And I've got time."

The last sentence felt good to say.

Time.

"You'll need a permit for your vehicle if you want it back."

"Well, it doesn't seem to want me anymore. I don't want what doesn't want me."

The kid shrugged, Sam paid, grabbed his things and walked through the door. He went over to his bike and without a second thought put the keys to the motorcycle in the ignition. Under the helmet, he pinned/penned a note which said 'It's yours, yes you, but be careful! It will scalp you.'

He walked around the nature center and came to a stone arch with a sign beside it which said that there were 2,108.5 miles between him and Mount Katahdin, Maine. He took a deep breath.

Just when he was about to start walking, the door to the nature center opened behind him. The woman wearing the same green and brown clothes as the boy walked out. She looked to be Native American and had long, black hair which had streaks of grey in it, with little wrinkles around her eyes.

"Do you know how many stairs there are to the top of the falls," Sam asked.

"604 one-way, honey. Are you really going to walk all of the way home, to Maine?"

"I am."

"Good luck," she said with a kind smile

"Thank you."

She watched him walk through the arch.

A human being will usually leave home. Then they will be without. They will be hungry, they will search, and they will come to appreciate what they had. And eventually they usually try to head back to where they came from, in some form or another. It's a lonesome journey that makes home so sweet. So nothing at all seemed more appropriate, to Sam, than taking the long walk towards home, through the mountains, beside the rivers, past the moonshine-crazed hill-people, through the storms, towards shelter. He'd always been a sucker for symbolism. And, from his experience, a nice long walk was the best way to think anything through. Duly, there was a lot to think about, over two thousand miles worth of walking to do.

He felt good, thoroughly, full of something almost like contentedness, as he began walking on the relatively short trail which led to a very long trail. It also led to the falls, first. The forest was green and dense, full of that sweet, early in the day, summer smell. The birds were singing beautifully, at the peak of their morning show. There were a few species of trees and shrubs that he was happy not to know the names of. The trail crossed the road and went through a dense thicket of rhododendron beside the stream which had already fallen. He felt like he could be a thousand miles from anything, though knew that he was not.

A very big, black woodpecker soared overhead, breast-stroking through the air. It had a red crest on its head and white flashed beneath its wings. Sam wondered if it was the species that the birder who he had met searched for. He didn't get a good look at the diagnostic bill. Very few people did.

He walked past a large pool of water fed by the stream, bricked in by people who like form and inconsiderate of those who did not. Up he walked, beside the white water which gradually traveled from little pool to pool through rocks and logs. The grade became steeper. Before long, he heard the gentle roar of the big falls—and soon he saw them through a gap in the trees, steadily shimmering down through steep and rugged rock. The cascading falls were the tallest east of the Mississippi. There was something special about the fall of water that had an almost hypnotizing, magnetic quality about it. His pace quickened.

He jumped up to the fourth step once he reached the stairs, knowing there were only 600 left. There always seemed to be a lot of steps for anything worthwhile. He traversed them the only way that he knew how—by running up them. When he reached an observation platform a very light mist from the falls rained over him. It felt nice in the early morning air, and there he rested for several minutes.

But he had to keep going. So he continued to run up the steps—which is hard to do while wearing a forty pound backpack. It felt like childhood, though. A bridge crossed the falls again, and the mist was stronger. The stairs spiraled towards the top.

He was panting by the time that he reached the summit but felt good despite being a little disappointed to see the development that was there— a road and a large parking lot, benches and paved trails. It was not as he had imagined. The little stream was hugged by trees until it went under the bridge atop the falls, and then went over the edge to create the beauty.

Upon that bridge Sam stood. The water made soothing sounds as it headed calmly towards the falls. There were no people around, at least. And it was easy to imagine the top being a dark forest, warm light coming through the break in the trees where the water fell.

The view was amazing, but his mind had not settled enough to see it yet.

Sam jumped down from the bridge onto grass. He did not enjoy feeling like a tourist. So he walked down to the rocky stream where he could forget the trodden path. He took off his wet bandana and put it in his pocket. Traces of fog hovered above the stream. The day was just beginning to turn bright blue. And the fall of the water brought up wet air which felt like being breathed into.

He unstrapped his pack, and it fell to the ground. The freedom from the weight felt wonderful.

There on the gravelly edge—at the spot where pebbles of a certain kind had held on while those of another kind had been washed away—a nice breeze touched his face. He could see as far as a person can see across the green, hilly, tree-covered countryside—consisting of a mix of evergreen trees on the hill-tops and maples and oaks everywhere else. The horizon looked like a wavy line drawn in a classroom on the sheet of a bored child's paper.

It is a great feeling to finally reach the top after a long trek and to look down to the low spots where you have been. The importance of the low spots is never more evident, as having been through them gives meaning to the view from high ground.

For a while, he just took it all in.

Eventually, he found himself grappling with that part of himself which wanted to know what it would feel like to drop freely through the air. And as he looked at the falls, Sam suddenly could not help but think of his own falls. There were a lot of them to think about. He watched the water fall, slide glitteringly, and fall again, falling until they reached a steady pool. There they were calm again for a while, but would soon have to keep moving. After any fall, the most important thing is to keep moving if at all possible. From the moment that a person stands, the only certainty is that they will fall. Thoughts became clear there at the top.

There are some things that when in mind one must write down, because they never last for long. And so from the pack he took out the postcard that he had bought earlier which had yielded change for the call to the old man who he had bought the motorcycle from, which had ultimately led him to where he was now.

Everything's led to now.

The thought was a bit daunting. One cannot be where they are at without having been where they were. So, if you are happy with where you are at, you should have no regrets about where you've been. Sam realized this above the falls.

He backed away from the edge and sat, leaning his back on the mossy base of an oak tree, and took in another deep breath. From his pack he took out a stubby pencil and his journal in order to look at the notes that he'd compiled for the card which he was going to send home. After thumbing through the pages of his journal—returning from the places that he had been when he wrote the words—Sam closed the journal, ready. He put the AT sticker carefully, diagonally across the front of the card which depicted some flower-filled place that was nothing like Jake's town from where it had been bought. He began writing in a very small, neat style to ensure that he could say everything that he wanted to.

It was very important.

'Dad, Mom, Rob,

I have this dream. Over and over again. It all has to do with a thing that I went through, that I got through. I wake up on this rocky ledge, half-way down a deep gorge in the desert. It's almost like the Grand Canyon—that deep. My head is always throbbing. And there is blood in my eyes. I can't move. I look up at the wall of rock. It's always the same. You guys are looking down at me. Your tears fall on my face. They are warm. I see all of the way that I fell, and all of the way that I could have fallen. I also see a bunch of loose stone, tumbling down from your feet, but can't bring myself to remember what had happened. The sun is hot. I know that I am dying. I think of my whole life. And there is only one question that I can ask myself. Slipping almost seems OK. I have always had the tendency of getting closer to the edge than anyone else—which I know that you all hate. It would mean that I died alive—to slip. But to jump would mean to throw away the only gift that's guaranteed. I hope that I didn't. But I fear that I did.

And even when I'm awake, looking at where I'm at, I sometimes ask the same question. I realize now, though, that I was hanging on the edge my whole life, but was blinded to it. I wasn't brave enough to climb, or even see. Luckily, I fell. And that awful fall, which really only I can fully understand, woke me up. Then I had to climb, which wasn't easy. I've only just made it up over that edge where you guys stand in the dream. And it's so frightening now—to walk, think, and suddenly be alive, being aware of many things for the first time, seeing those who are how I used to be, knowing what they don't see. It's like my shell of armor has been stripped. I can finally wander the scorching plateau. That mournful howl that I hear means something now, and I can actually see the beautiful mountain-peaks in the distance. Sometimes I go back and look down to where I was at, on the edge, and on darker days the ledge, but not often and never for long. Whenever I think of those mountains, standing like they do despite it all, I get a feeling of hope that makes the awful dream and everything that followed worth it. I cannot act on any decision that's not my own anymore. There's so much to learn, to feel, to experience. Which is why I'm taking the long way home. I hope that you can understand.

Love (which only just recently I've learned the meaning of),'

It was done—besides for his signature—and he was proud. He felt good to have finally gotten it out.

There was a sudden urge within him to stand, and so he did. He wanted to get in the water, experience that great feeling of getting hot, cramped feet wet. So, he put the postcard and journal in his pocket, placed the stubby pencil behind his right ear. He nudged off his shoes and socks, felt the moss on his feet as he walked from the base of the tree towards the falls. He made his way down the steep, forested hill to the second ledge of the falls—where there were rocks which made walking a bit painful.

He eased into the water which was wonderfully cool—about up to his calf—and carefully walked on the smooth stones towards where the water fell the furthest. The current was swift but not strong enough to knock him down. It was beautiful to look ahead and see the water curve down and away, gently disappearing. He followed the flow until he was at the point where he could actually look down and watch the water fall.

It was not a good time for some dam upstream to break.

There was a nice, flat rock which arose just above the water level very near to the edge—only about a foot away. Sloshing towards it, and after making sure that the stone was not too slippery by sliding his hand across the surface, he stepped upon it. It was a long way down, with water rushing all around, and the rock was close to being too slippery. But he was glad to be standing on it. His feet felt incredibly cool on the slick surface.

He thought that the 22-year-old girl from the cemetery might have stood on the same rock, with more than likely smaller feet, but probably a view much the same—almost exactly the same, except for the single sliver of road with yellow lines, the bricked in pool at the base of the falls, the lack of towering American chestnut trees, and the single house in the distance.

How *easy* it would be to step off the edge.

Death was just a step or stumble away, which was slightly dizzying but exhilarating. It was very clear there at the top that he who measures the success of life in accordance with how many times death is near does not live very long—or lives unhappily.

And thinking of that which humans are obsessed with, on the familiar edge above where a stream sheened, feeling that all too common sense of déjà vu that couldn't be placed, he had to ask himself: "Did I die that night?"

He closed his eyes and just allowed himself to feel for a while, and to not think—which is the only remedy for thoughts like the one that had just floated through his head. The sounds which surrounded were very nice, he thought, mists of a moment that may have never ended. It was very hard not to think.

Sam felt a familiar twitching and looked down, watching the index finger on his right hand tug persistently for several seconds before finally resting like the others—which sometimes too twitched, along with seemingly all of the other muscles in his body. The twitching happened a lot, though less recently. To not be able to control a part of yourself is disconcerting. Losing control of a part is the first step in losing control of the whole. Which is terrifying.

He figured that the twitches were probably caused by stress, but knew that they might not be. There was never complete certainty in regard to what something might be. He thought of Jake.

Hooks in flesh.

And the last shred of doubt dissolved. There was simply no room for doubt anymore. So much evil could be. But despite it all, while able to do so, one must live and somehow focus on all of the beauty that could be.

"For some reason, I *am* alive. There is reason for my life," he whispered, "which I must choose."

He experienced a flowering of warmth and fuzziness that was almost overwhelming and never before felt within him.

And fueled by this emotion, into the almost surreal, painting-like landscape seen from its peak, he screamed in a confident, strong way that even in solitude would have been impossible a year before: "Alive!"

The word settled—was accepted.

Sam took the card from his pocket and re-read the words—very proud of them, still. As words age, it is always important to see if you are able to remain proud of them. And these words passed the test with flying colors, which is a special, almost magical thing.

His conviction only strengthened as he watched the water rush to fall.

He would not do what he had feared he would do when walking up the steps. The card would not flutter down through the air and into the water, unsent. There would be no sorrowful walk back down all of those stairs, through the mist at the bridge, and back to the nature center, no desperate hopes that the motorcycle was still there. He would not try to sell the old Indian. The Native American woman in the nature center would, and her daughter would go to college because of it. He would not go back to Maine beaten, and he would deal no more for a while with all of that which saddened him and could not really be understood or changed.

And a terrible lot could not be understood or changed.

There were too many little, and big, girls with dead parents wondering why, and others hurt so bad that they had to hurt everyone else along with themselves, and too many eyes not seen that wanted to be, and too many diseases that keep you alive so that all you can do is suffer, and too much worry about it all, and too many words unsaid, and too much opposition in a place tailored for coalescing, and too much faith in what there should be no faith in, and just *too much*.

He needed a break from that world for a while now that he had taken a long, hard look at it. There always had to be a last look.

So he would go to the Lodge and send the postcard. And then he would start to walk the long trail, experiencing the natural world which should not have been so quickly transformed into civilized madness. He would walk aware of life's end but focus on each step, towards the only people who were so much a part of him that he could not think of abandoning. He would look at all of the beautiful things on the way, trying to appreciate the gift of seeing them—that gift which might be the most squandered as far as humans go. He would leave the stale, certainly dressed wilderness that he was born to in favor of the fresh, honestly naked wilderness that might reassure him of what he was. Because a long stretch of solitude—where it is just you and the world—is what allows a person to become themself.

And the thing about a long walk like that is, you—not some tragic imitation of everyone else, but *you*—never know what sort of wonderful person you might meet along the way, who has chosen to walk the same path. Even only a shred of hope for the making of that special acquaintance makes every step a step in the right direction.

Sam decided all of this in an instant, which is all that is ever needed to set, change, or end a path. There was no great reason for his decision— never is and never can be. Only a simple feeling, exactly the same one which causes a young Florida panther to cross a dangerous road in search of something better, something unknown. Sam knew that he probably was sentenced to a long, painful—though wonderful—path ahead whether or not he went anywhere, the same as anything born into this world. But there *just had* to be something worth walking towards, he thought. Exactly like there *just had* to be an Ivory-billed Woodpecker to be found for some.

If there was one thing he had learned, it was that it simply does not matter what is really there and what is not there. All that matters is what is believed. In order to keep going in this absurd world and to fit in, currently, it all just comes down to finding ways to fool yourself. And the biggest fool might be the person who does not allow themselves to be fooled. But if that poor fool, that obstinate, brave person who might be best described as a 'saint' can somehow survive, stay true, and find a way to be listened to, then what the majority of people believe and how they live *can* be changed immensely for the better. There were two problems: people fight change to the bitter end, and saints do not survive for long.

Sam was a man who knew that he could be a saint without anyone else's religion, and for a moment everything made as much sense as it could.

Go forth boldly, react unhesitatingly to all of the things which seem to have no purpose, cannot be understood by human beings. I will not miss the path of any day, will not for an instant close my sails or cower in the wind for fear of where it seems to want to take me.

A nice, strong breeze came from the valley and pushed Sam's hair—the easiest flag to display—back and away from his steady eyes. Nothing blocked his vision. It would be much easier not to see, he knew, but self-blinding was intolerable. There was no greater crime than the closing of eyes merely for the sake of convenience when there was something that needed to be seen. He felt that he had no choice but to look at the beauty all around, as endless and out of favor as it was.

To look the same way as everyone else might be to miss what is really worth seeing.

It is incredibly alleviating, in a way, to contentedly decide what your life will be. He knew that his two most valuable tools were in between his ears. From behind his right one, he took the pencil from its place and studied it closely—his eraser-less mind thinking how much change could be caused by the one yellow stub of an eraser-less pencil.

He signed his name on the card.

There was one place in the sky that he could not look, which was reason enough for him to want to look there. Closing his eyes, though, made it possible to do so for a few moments. Up towards the sun he looked—and the red network of veins and cells in the skin of his closed eyes looked uncannily like what our Universe is thought to—past which there was darkness for unimaginable distances. He looked towards where there was then light again for a tiny bit, and then darkness for a much longer distance, and probably eventually towards something that was looking right back towards him, experiencing similar mixed-emotions, wondering about it all—if there was reason to go on living.

The situation that all living things find themselves together in was astounding to Sam—all the more so that such a large percentage of them never even stop to think about it.

It was very comforting knowing that everyone is in this—whatever 'this' is—together. From blind men driving trucks full of optical supplies, to women who are tired of thinking and serve food which must be had to think, to new fathers who build houses so that a home might be had, to dogs which run with their friends, to young men who stock shelves at stores during the day and read novels at night, to trees still standing, to people who preach the same story to everyone so that the hopeless might have hope, to young children who ask 'why, mommy, why?' to old women who sit in libraries to help facilitate the spread of knowledge as their minds lose the capacity to hold onto it, to professors who teach what they believe, to those who spend their time wandering, imagining, to the young poet who decides that his dream must be shared.

Everyone, everything, are a part of this mystery—together.

Sometimes a person feels like they can save the world—even though it is not the world that needs saving—and sometimes they feel like they cannot even save themselves. The mind flickers with each instant. And one instant is always replaced by another, the good ones far too often by the bad.

There are only two things, he thought, which cannot stop creating, and both are inventions of the other. A living mind will create time, and time will create a living mind. All for one moment, one decision—from which life begins or ends.

Sam only had two choices during his moment on the edge. He opened his eyes.

After a deep breath, maybe even the beginning of a beautiful Universe, he took that one last look and decided that he was ready to leave. So, he pocketed the card, put the pencil behind his ear, and took a big step away from the falls.